THE LAST GIRL

•

Penelope Evans

St. Martin's Paperbacks

First published in Great Britain by Black Swan.

THE LAST GIRL

Copyright © 1995 by Penelope Evans.

All rights reserved. No part of this book may be used or reproduced in any manner whatsoever without written permission except in the case of brief quotations embodied in critical articles or reviews. For information address St. Martin's Press, 175 Fifth Avenue, New York, N.Y. 10010.

Library of Congress Catalog Card Number: 95-41986

ISBN: 0-312-96315-7

Printed in the United States of America

St. Martin's Press hardcover edition/January 1996
St. Martin's Paperbacks edition/October 1997

St. Martin's Paperbacks are published by St. Martin's Press, 175 Fifth Avenue, New York, NY 10010.

10 9 8 7 6 5 4 3 2 1

THE
LAST
GIRL

Chapter One

They've found a new girl for the second floor.

All I can say is – what took them so long? I mean, two weeks since the last one left; Ethel has never gone that long without taking rent in her entire life. You've got to look at this way – she is a professional, a land-lady in the same way that some women are matrons or prison officers, right down to the uniform, which in her case is the statutory flowered pinny the sort your granny used to wear. Your money goes into the pocket in the bib, along with all the peppermints and shopping lists, so that you tell yourself she's bound to lose it one of these days. Which only shows how much you know. That pocket runs straight down into the lining and the money you've just handed over has as much chance of being lost as the pattern coming off your plate.

Anyway, back to the new girl. I heard them moving about downstairs, her and Ethel, and reckoned it was about time to put in an appearance and, more to the point, see what was new. Not that I was expecting anything different. Always the same these girls are. You'd think Ethel had a mould turning them out. But there, you live in hope.

It's twelve steps to the middle landing, not counting the turn in between, but I haven't come down more than two of them before Ethel, sharp as ever, pipes up with: 'Ah, here's the gentleman I've been telling you about.' Followed by: 'Come on down, Mr Mann, so we can see who we're talking to.'

Two things to notice straightaway: first, 'Mr Mann' she calls me. Not Larry, or Lawrence even, but Mr Mann. Forty-three years we've known each other and we're still not on first-name terms. The same goes for Gilbert, or the Living Skeleton as we used to call him, eighty if he's a day, and nailed to his chair by the gas fire these last ten years. I doubt if he even makes it to the toilet by himself any more. Anyhow, that's as maybe. Ethel and Gilbert they are to me, and always have been, even if it's never to their faces. They may own this house, but we were here long before them, Doreen and me, the only reason they could afford to buy the place at all. Naturally she did everything she could to get rid of us – especially after June came along – but she never did succeed, and here we all stayed. Now there's just me, all on my ownsome up here, a sitting tenant, and there's not a thing she can do about it.

Second thing to notice: seeing that that's the case, Ethel is driven to getting her own back in all sorts of other, nasty little ways. Like now, when it's plain as a pikestaff that I was coming down anyway, she deliberately calls up for me to do it all the same. What she wants is to make it look that she only has to say the word, and I'll jump to it like I was born to obey. Small things, but the sort another man might allow to get to him. Me, I don't even notice them.

Meanwhile, Ethel is repeating word for word what she told the last girl and the girl before that. 'Now, you and Mr Mann will be sharing the little-girls' room and the bathroom, but I don't think you'll find that a problem. Mr Mann is a gentleman of very regular habits. Is that not right Mr Mann?'

'Right as rain, Mrs Duck.'

Mutt and Jeff they should call us really. What she's saying is, in a house where the habits are regular, there's no reason why the paths of anyone should ever

8

meet – except on rent day when we all beat the same path to Ethel's kitchen door. So there's nothing new in what Ethel is saying. However, something is afoot. Hard to say what exactly, only that for some reason the woman is looking as pleased as Punch about something, and take it from one who knows, that is quite definitely not like her. Mind you, it could always be a trick of the light – what there is of it. We're all standing here in the gloom – me, Ethel and the, so far, invisible new girl, with only a forty-watt bulb to throw any light on the subject.

Suddenly Ethel Duck herself drops a clue. 'Why don't you come a bit closer, Mr Mann? You can't expect Miss Tyson to see anything of you over there.'

It's there, in that 'Miss Tyson'. Two words to make me prick up my ears and wonder what on earth has got into Ethel. 'Miss Tyson' is what she said, not Miss Gupta or Miss Patel, or whatever. It's been five years since Ethel discovered that Indian girls make the best tenants, being quieter, more respectful, and generally easier to boss around. So it's been one Indian after another ever since. Don't ask me how she finds them. The name of Duck must be famous in New Delhi or wherever it is they all come from. Except that the supply must have dried up suddenly because after the last one left, nothing. Two weeks with an empty floor, and now this – a girl with a name you can actually pronounce.

Naturally, Ethel knows when she's sparked my interest, which is why the moment she tells me to come a little closer, she manoeuvres herself right into the middle of the landing to make sure that without a periscope being handy, Miss Tyson stays as invisible as ever. Still, Ethel remains a talking-point just in herself. The thing you can't help but notice each time she's opened her mouth is that she's using the voice normally kept in reserve for the doctor, or taxmen

9

knocking on the door wanting to know what she does with all that rent money.

'You'll find Mr Mann a very handy gentleman to have around. He'll do anything if you ask him nicely. Isn't that right, Mr Mann?'

I can't answer. I'm too busy marvelling. There's enough cut glass here to decant a sherry keg. Not even the Queen could talk like that and breathe at the same time.

'The other girls have always found him wonderfully obliging. You see, dear, he's one of those lucky folk who, unlike many of us, has got a world of time on his hands.'

And with that she lets out a sigh, the sort that goes on to speak volumes and is supposed to remind you that she for one hasn't had a moment to herself for the last ten years, what with Gilbert needing his special feeds, medication round the clock, not to mention visits to the toilet, all to keep the old bugger alive against the odds. Doubtless Miss Tyson will have got to know of this within two minutes of walking through the door.

Yet even Ethel couldn't have expected what happened next. The answer she gets comes, not from me, but from the other side of her, where it's still dark, and there's only Ethel's word that there's anyone there at all. From out of the gloom, there comes a noise to take us both by storm. In actual fact, it's absolutely tiny — more a suggestion than real, less than a squeak, but more than a sigh. Yet the effect is deafening. Because it was the sound of someone being sympathetic. Here, in this house.

And even Ethel is silenced by it. Ten whole seconds must have passed before finally she picks up again and says, doubtless to give herself more time, 'Well really, Mr Mann. Are you going to stand there all day and never say a word to anyone? Miss Tyson is going to wonder what sort of unfriendly house she's come to.'

And, at long last, she steps aside.

A girl is standing there, small, barely high enough to reach my shoulder, and I'm hardly what you could describe as over-tall. Victorian shoulders, by which I suppose I mean drooping, underneath her mac, and above, dark hair, lots of it, dead straight falling right across her face. The temptation is to call it untidy – I mean you would in anyone else – but for the moment it makes you think of a curtain you want to lift aside, politely, so as to discover what's going on behind. And, more importantly, find out just what sort of person it was who made that surprising, sympathetic noise half a minute ago. Only you can't go pulling the hair of perfect strangers, so for a few seconds all I can do is stare, until suddenly, as if to oblige me specially, she lifts up a hand and pushes it aside. And that's when I see her face.

And for a moment, I'm almost disappointed. I mean, it's a very pleasant face. It's just not what you could ever term pretty. Although I will say that it only wants a few rollers and maybe a touch of colour and she wouldn't look any worse than some of the other women you see on the street. And her eyes are nice, big and brown, looking straight at you with a really lovely expression in them. The sort you'd expect in someone who could make that sort of Noise. It's just that she's so pale; you can't help but notice it, even in this light, and way too thin, like she wants feeding up. All in all then, absolutely nothing special looks-wise.

Only who's interested in looks? People used to tell me Doreen was attractive, and see where that got me. And what's wrong with Pale if it comes to that? Pale can suit some people. Pale even stands out better on dark landings when normal colour simply leaches into the background. There's nothing wrong with Pale.

This is what's going through my head when out of the blue comes the most surprising thing of all. A voice reaching out of the dark, no more than a whisper, yet clear as a bell: 'Lighten our Darkness, oh Lord.'

Surprised is hardly the word for it. Especially when it's obvious from the faces of the two opposite that neither of them have heard a thing. Trouble is, there's no time to think about it, not with Miss Tyson smiling at me, and Ethel already getting restless. A moment later, they're both squeezing past me on the way to the bedroom and there's only space for another quick, dare I say, shy smile from Miss T. And they're gone. What was more, in all that time, I'd never heard so much as a pip from her – apart from that first little noise. That's what happens when you have a woman like Ethel making all the running. Yet if I'd only had my wits about me, I could have winked, let her know there'd be plenty of time for a chat later. But what with words floating in from nowhere and Ethel doing her worst, I never had the chance.

Funny thing is, I'm not a bit downhearted. Don't ask me why, but suddenly I feel as if there's gong to be a change in this house. And all thanks to this girl. There's something about her that's different – not just from the Indian girls, but all of them, by which I mean Doreen, June, Ethel and anyone else you care to mention who belongs to the female tendency. She's not like the others.

Now Larry's not a man to get carried away, but you know what? I'm shaking.

I thought about waiting for them till they came out of the bedroom, then worried that it might look a bit odd, me loitering with intent as it were. Besides, as I told myself on the way back upstairs, there's going to be all the time in the world. The girl is here to stay. She's only got to look at the place to know it's a one-off. You simply can't find anywhere in London nowadays with a whole floor to yourself for twenty-odd pounds a week. Of course, she'll discover the drawbacks later, when she's all settled in, and realizes she can feed the meter to bursting to keep her gas fire going but nothing's going to stop the draughts, or the noises in the walls (Ethel will look at her straight in the eye and swear it's just the pipes), and that nothing happens in this house that Ethel doesn't know about in the end. Those are just the small things; there are others, but really it will be too late. By the time she finds out about those she'll have got used to paying half the rent of everybody else and won't have the heart to move. The odd thing is, the Indian girls never did seem to mind, not about anything. Not even when you tried to draw them out – maybe by suggesting that they'd fit in better if they left off filling the house with the smell of curry and made do with a boiled egg like an English person would. They would just smile and carry on – or curry on. I was only trying to be friendly, but they were all – how can I put it – offish. You'd never get more than a good morning out of them, if that. Yet I could have done them any number of favours. I know where to find all the cheap electrical goods this side of Finsbury Park. They'd have found that useful when it came to loading up to go back to the Subcontinent. They only had to be a bit more friendly.

But it's not going to be like that with this one.

All the same, there's no harm in getting the ball rolling. Know what I'm going to do? I'm going off to Harry's stall right this minute. I'm going to buy her a whole load of fruit – apples, oranges, all kinds, and give them to her straightaway, with my compliments. A little moving-in present. That would be worth ten good mornings on the stairs if you ask me.

See, the more I think about it, the more I reckon we're going to be the best of friends, me and Miss T. You mark my words.

*   *   *

13

As we used to say in the army, however – the best-laid plans and all that. I'd swear I wasn't out more than half an hour, and that's even with Harry never content simply to pass the time of day. Then it was straight up those stairs to the middle landing. And I didn't mess around, gave her lounge door a good hard knock, reckoning that even if she was in the bedroom which is next door she'd hear me. No answer. So back I went to the top of the hall stairs, to her kitchen. Knocked there. Still no answer. Well I was disappointed of course, but hardly surprised. I just thought she must have gone out to buy a few essentials like tea and sugar. I only wished I'd managed to see her before so as to tell her I had more than enough upstairs to tide her over. As it was, I just nipped inside to put the fruit down on her kitchen table along with a note on the back of an envelope saying 'Welcome to Colditz!!!' That was my little joke. I tell it to all the girls, even if I have to end up explaining it. The trouble with the Indians is that they haven't seen half the TV that we have.

So I was quite happy to leave it at that for the time being, until out on the landing again, it occurred to me – what if she smokes? I'd have given my right arm to have known there and then. Remember the old days? All sorts of things used to happen once you'd offered a stranger one of your cigs. Naturally, I'm talking more about the films than real life, but the hope was always there that one day it would work for you – that you would bowl someone over with the way you handed them a smoke. Not that I was looking to bowl anyone over here – perish the thought. But something to break the ice would be nice, set the scene so to speak. Anyway, the upshot is, no sooner has the thought popped into my head but I'm turning to go back the way I came, meaning to hotfoot it to the newsagent at the end of the road to get something a bit more suitable than my Old Holborn.

Only, you might have guessed, who should be waiting for me at the bottom but Ethel. Obviously been keeping an ear out from the moment I got in.

'Off out again, Mr Mann?'

To hear her with that little tiny voice you'd think butter wouldn't melt, or to look at her either with her old lady's curls and hankies stuffed up her sleeves. But don't be fooled. For one thing, she's hardly what you would call old, not at seventy-two – my age exactly – which anyone would tell you is nothing nowadays. For another, it's all part of the act, and what's more an act that should be the envy of senior citizens the world over. You should see what that little tiny voice can do for her – free eggs at the market, the last seats on the buses. Shopkeepers rounding off the price of every mortal thing to save her scrabbling for change. She must have made a small fortune just from that. Some folk don't come into their own until they're old, and Ethel Duck is one of the breed. But what I'm saying is: I know the sound of the real Ethel – well I could hardly help it, not after the times I've stood outside her kitchen door listening to her barking on at Gilbert like a regular sergeant major. Poor old Gilbert – you could almost sympathize. You never would have found him in khaki doing his bit for his country. No, he stayed at home, nursing a weak chest. Yet who's the one who's ended up under orders? The Old Skiver, that's who.

Best to answer quickly, for the sake of peace.

'You know how it is, Mrs D. No rest for the wicked.' (So how come Doreen used to fall asleep the second her head hit the pillow?)

And that, you would think, would be the end of it. No more to be said. But not today, not when Ethel is still hanging on to the banister, making no sign of moving, which can mean only one thing. She wants something. Which in turn means I can forget about the cigarettes until she's told me. Always did have first call

15

on me, did Ethel. Doreen was forever saying it, and for once she was right about something. The trouble was Gilbert: he never did know how to change a fuse, not even in the days when he could still have made it up a ladder. That left Ethel with two choices – either she got someone in and paid him, or she turned to yours truly who would do it for free, and not have so much as a penny cut off the rent at the end of the day. Which naturally begs the question of why ever do I do it. I'll tell you why. Because every time she has to ask, she's having to admit that the one and only reason this house is still standing is in the person of Larry Mann. And she hates it. Wonderful, isn't it?

Except that today, there doesn't seem to be any list of orders. Ethel is hanging around because, as sometimes happens – like once in a blue moon – she just wants to talk.

'You know what, Mr Mann, I can't help but worry. If Mr Duck doesn't have an extra specially good rest today, I wouldn't like to be held answerable for the consequences.'

Sometimes Ethel lowers her voice – usually when speaking about Gilbert. She wants you to think the one thing keeping him alive is an optimistic front. When her voice sinks to a whisper – as now – it's only to let you know how bad it really is. As if that same whisper wasn't loud enough to be heard from halfway across the Albert Hall. Mind you, maybe she has a point because it's just at this moment that Gilbert can be heard coughing up what sounds like his heart and soul. And I'll be the first to admit it sounds nasty. Only watch Ethel, she doesn't turn a hair. And says:

'It's the new girl, you see. She's got him that excited.'

Has she indeed. As a matter of fact, I can feel my own ears pricking up a bit. But it's no use saying anything, not if it's information you want. You show the teeniest bit of interest, and she'll drag it out for ever. Mind you she can talk about Gilbert being all of a fluster, but it's herself she really means. I could have sworn I heard a touch of the old West Country there, what she brought up with her from the sticks all those years ago. And look at her – she's like a dollop of jelly underneath that apron. In fact, I'd almost bet it wouldn't matter what I said; it's going to come out anyway. So I risk it.

'Oh yes, Mrs D. And why's that then?'

She lets go of the banister, pushes herself up against me. You'd think it was nothing less than a state secret she was about to drop. 'Well it's her parents, Mr Mann. Hong Kong.'

'Hong Kong?'

'That's where they live – just like Hubby years ago, when he was still with the Merchant Fleet. He swears it's where he caught his chest. Anyway, it's hearing that that's got him all in a tizz. He still talks about it as if it was yesterday – when he's got the strength, poor soul. Now suddenly, he's going to have someone else to talk to, someone who knows all about it.'

Well, maybe. Though it seems to me that a girl like her is hardly going to want to waste time with an old codger like him. Hong Kong. My eye. He might have spent a year or two there, way back in the olden days, but I happen to know he spent a good deal more time as a filing clerk in an office below the White Cliffs of Dover. I bet he doesn't tell her about that.

There must be more to it than that, then. And there is. Ethel is moving closer still. I'll be dusting the rouge off my cardigan after this. She's coming to the meat of the matter. Between clenched teeth, the words reach me, the real reason for the excitement:

'Out there still, of course. Father. Doctor. Brain surgeon.'

That's it. That's what excitement has done to Ethel. Turned her into a talking telegram. But the message is there, loud and clear, and it explains everything. Such as why after years and years she's reverted to having a person on the middle floor who actually speaks the language. Who's one of us.

Except that she isn't one of us, not her, this Miss Tyson. The fact is, this house hasn't seen the like, not in seventy years, not since the days when it and all the other big houses belonged to just one family apiece, with a room for every man woman and child, and then some left over for the servants. It might even have belonged to a doctor. Now what should have walked back through the door but the actual daughter of one. To Ethel's way of thinking, that's the next best thing to having the doctor here himself.

Not one of us then, not in the normal way. But I'll say this. She's the same colour, and that goes for something, surely?

Still, it doesn't do to go on letting Ethel believe herself to be the fount of all knowledge. It's high time to break it to her that Larry Mann knows a thing or two himself.

'That's as maybe, Mrs D. But you didn't need to tell me all of that in a whisper. She's not going to hear, no matter what you say. She's gone out. In fact, I reckon she must have been hard on my heels.'

Now there's a thought. Like she was coming after me.

As for Ethel, that stops her. It's a law of nature in this house that not a soul goes in or out without her knowing about it – and the reason to boot. Only somehow or other, this time, little Miss Tyson has caught her off guard. But then, you try getting Ethel to admit she's wrong.

'I'm sure not, Mr Mann. In fact, I can assure you, the young lady has done no such thing. And what's more, I'll show you how I know. Just take a look at that.' So saying, Ethel plucks a duster from the front of her pinny and shakes it in my face. When I've done coughing, she takes up the argument again. 'Half an hour I must have spent doing the hall. From the moment you stepped out of the front door to the second you came back. And you can take it from me, there's not a soul been in or out in all that time.'

What could I say? Knowing Ethel, every word would be true. Set one foot outside this house and Ethel will be there, like the waves rushing in, filling up the space you've just left empty, till the moment you get back. I believe she was in the hall the second after me, then. That's how she is.

Yet talk about confused. There's Ethel ready to swear on the Bible that Miss Tyson is just where she left her, but less than two minutes ago I was knocking hard enough to wake the dead. And while I consider this, there's Ethel herself, getting more triumphant by the second, chalking up the points. I never knew a woman more small-minded. The only option left to me is to get away with as much dignity as the scene allowed. But I should have watched where I was going . . .

'Silly me,' Ethel's voice floats after me. 'There was I thinking you were on your way out. And yet here you are, halfway up the stairs again.'

And it's true. Because entirely thanks to Ethel, I'd forgotten what I'd come down for in the first place. Now there was nothing for it but to turn full circle to head back towards the front door, while Ethel watches, enjoying every second.

Once I'd bought the cigarettes though, I felt a whole lot better. In the time it took to get to the newsagents and back again I'd worked it all out. Quite simply, I hadn't knocked as hard as I should have. I might have *thought* I had – but that was my mistake. This is the sort of house where you do everything quietly. Not wanting everyone to know your own business, not wanting to cause offence – it all becomes second nature really. The result is, even when you think you're making a great racket, you're not doing any such thing. That knock of mine – you'd laugh if you thought about it – it probably wasn't any more than a tap. As for her, Miss Tyson, she was probably asleep. I mean, I could tell she was tired when I saw her, just from the way she was standing. Poor girl could probably do with a good rest. And if that was the case, the most important thing now was not to wake her on my way back upstairs. I didn't hurry though. I was still half hoping that she'd come out of her bedroom at the very moment I was passing, covering up a yawn maybe, mouth all dry after her kip. What better time could there be in that case to ask her up for a refreshing cup of tea?

No luck though. It must have taken me a good two minutes to get from one end of the landing to the other, but nothing stirred. The poor kid must have been dead to the world. What's more, I didn't hear a peep out of her all afternoon, and believe me I couldn't have missed her.

Then at last, just at the very moment I'd put kettle on to boil, there was the sound I'd been waiting for all that time – namely the click of the bedroom door, followed by the faint pitapat of feet on the landing. I was still holding my breath when I heard the flush of the loo, more footsteps, and at long last the noise of the kitchen door. This was it, you see, the moment of truth, when she walked in and saw all that fruit waiting for her, not to mention my little note.

Funny thing though, now that it had come to the crunch, I suddenly started to feel ever so nervous. You could put it down to us not being properly introduced. I mean, what hope have two people of getting acquainted when there's Ethel smirking away between them? Luckily there's a mirror above the sink, kept there for shaving purposes, and I only had to take one quick peek to see there was nothing to worry about there, at least not in the looks department. Larry Mann was the soul of respectability – and a bit more besides. Being the modest sort, I'd be the last one to boast, but the fact is I'm not half bad for my age: nice and trim, good colour in my cheeks. And smart – it's not every man who'd take the trouble to wear his hairpiece night and day, but Larry does. Today I've got it combed forward in a light fringe, not too formal you see. And then there's the old moustache below, not the same colour admittedly – it would have to be brown for that – but there's nothing wrong with good old salt and pepper. There are plenty of military men who've got the same. Anyway, the upshot is, I don't have to run around at the last minute to make myself look decent. Larry Mann is that already. Which meant I could breathe more easily, calm down and remember to throw another bag in the pot.

After that, all we had to do was wait.

Chapter Two

Even then it seemed like an age, though to be honest it couldn't have been more than five minutes. It's just that I thought she'd be up sooner than she was. I mean, all she had to do was see the fruit, read the note and then put two and two together. Then suddenly there comes this little knock on the wall at the bottom of my stairs. Even then it made me jump because I'd expected to hear her come along the landing. Still I must have remembered to say something, because the next thing I know, she's standing in my kitchen door, large as life and twice as natural.

But just that little bit different from what I remembered. She was wearing a woolly jumper, way too big for her, that could only have looked right on a man, plus a pair of those trousers that are one step up from pyjama bottoms. And I don't know if it was simply my imagination but, tucked behind Ethel, she had seemed smaller than this. Now she seemed to be taller. For a second I thought she might have popped on a pair of heels just to come up and see Larry, but when I looked at her feet I was a bit taken aback to discover she wasn't wearing shoes at all. She just had on a pair of socks, black, the sort that men wear. That's why I hadn't heard her. Now don't ask me why, but in anyone else I'd see that as a warning. I mean, you've got to wear shoes when you go visiting, and maybe be a touch smarter in your dress. But again, it was like with her hair. You simply didn't think any the worse of her because of it. You see, her saving grace was her face.

This really was just as I remembered it – although I'll admit I might have overdone the part about her being so pale. But she had had a sleep, after all. The important thing was, her expression was just the same. Something shy, bordering on the anxious even. What I suppose I'm saying is, she looked like the serious type, a far cry from the young hussies you meet everywhere who'd laugh as soon as look at you. The good thing about a face like that is, it puts you at your ease. I mean, it's the over-confident types who throw you off your stride, isn't it? The know-alls and the clever dicks. In other words, the Doreens of this world. But you only had to look at her to see she was different. That's what made it so easy for me to smile and say cheerily as if she was an old friend, 'Hello stranger. Had a nice sleep then?'

To which she answered: 'Sorry?'

Isn't it wonderful? Some people you can feel you know from the very start. If anyone had asked me what I thought her first words might have been, I'd bet you almost anything I would have said: an apology. Not knowing what she was apologizing about was neither here nor there. Maybe it was for sleeping all that time when there were folk just waiting to be neighbourly.

'Sleep,' I said. 'It works wonders. One minute you're feeling like an old rag, then you have a little snooze and you're on top of the world again.'

'Oh,' she said. 'But I haven't been asleep.'

Well, that put an end to that. I waited for her to tell me what she had been doing all this time, but she didn't. In fact, she didn't say another word. Another few seconds passed while she looked at her toes and the danger was that things were getting a bit awkward. Then just in time she stepped in with:

'Mr Mann, there's an awful lot of fruit sitting on my kitchen table.'

'Oh yes?' I said, all innocence, but in actual fact

breathing a big sigh of relief. This was the bit I'd been waiting for, you might even say, been rehearsing for, all the time she'd been keeping herself to herself. Also I was enjoying just listening to her. No wonder the snob in Ethel got so excited. Beautifully spoken she was, but not in the way that makes you feel put down. She had the accent for it all right, but her voice was too quiet for that, and so high that if you heard her on the phone you'd think you were speaking to a kid of about twelve. It said a lot for her, that voice, showed you that here was a girl who had been nicely brought up, yet wasn't trying to be superior. What her actual words were hardly mattered.

Trouble was, now she was frowning because I'd made it sound as if I didn't know anything about any fruit. But that was only meant to be part of the joke. There was my note as well, and that should have given the game away. Otherwise who else did she think could have left that stuff? The Ducks? Surely not. See what I mean about her being the serious type?

I'll come clean and admit it. I panicked then. Jettisoned all ideas I'd had about being coy and stringing her along in friendly fashion. There was too much at stake. You just couldn't tell how she might react. She might have been the sort who wouldn't wait to hear the end of a sentence because she was that eager to rush off and thank the Ducks for their kind gift.

'Don't look so worried,' I said. 'Of course I know about the fruit. It was me that put it there. It's just my way of saying hello. I try to get on with all the new girls. Specially when they seem as nice as you.'

Well there you are. I don't think anyone could have put it more pleasantly than that. Not clever, not pushy, just kind. But would you believe it, even that didn't seem to wipe the frown off her face. I'd be starting to think she was born with it soon.

'Mr Mann . . .' she begins. And that's when I decide to be firm.

'Now, look here, love,' I said. 'There's only one way you can upset me, and that's by calling me Mr Mann. That's strictly for the Ducks. My name is Larry. Got that? Anything else just isn't friendly.' And since even that didn't seem to cheer her up – she was biting her lip like she was trying to chew it right off – there was nothing for it but to give her a little push towards the lounge. Otherwise she might have stood there all day, at the top of the stairs as if we were a couple of perfect strangers, and where would that have got us?

Mind you, it's as we're stepping into the lounge that I could see why it might seem a bit much to take all in at once. There wasn't a lot for her to notice in the kitchen, what with us crowding each other out, but here in the lounge it's a different picture. Standing here, she wouldn't have been human if she hadn't taken one look and wondered if we were living in the same house, the same street even. Judging by what she's got downstairs, she could hardly have been expecting – this.

But she is human. You can see the effect on her straightaway. She takes that one look, then stops. Clams up completely, doesn't say a word. It's the surprise you see, it gets some folk like that. They see the state of the rest of the house, and then they set eyes on this. It's the reason that I don't even hold it against her that there's half a barrowload of fruit sitting on her kitchen table, but there are still two little words that have yet to be spoken.

All the same, it's nice to have a bit of feedback, and you never know, opinions might vary, so I press her, just a little.

'Well then, what do you think? Bit different from what Ethel's charging you for, don't you think?'

'Oh,' she says, and you have to hand it to her, those

25

lovely brown eyes of hers are nearly falling out of her head. 'It's . . . it's very nice.'

Well, that was fine as far as it went. But when it was clear that that was all she was going to say, I couldn't help thinking she could have done a little better. Brought up the way she was, and probably educated to boot, you'd have thought she could have managed something more than just plain old 'nice'. You might as well call Buckingham Palace 'nice'. Not that I'm suggesting for one minute that this could compare to what HM is used to. Only you wouldn't be doing it justice if you didn't admit this room is a bit of an achievement.

To start with, everything's got it place; nothing jars. Not even the TV. There's a twenty-six-inch beauty behind those mahogany doors, but you'd never know it, not unless it was on. And cosy. You should see me in winter. You don't have to worry about draughts up here. I sealed up the windows years ago. The gas fire pumps out the heat and not a scrap of it escapes. You can still feel the warmth, trapped in the flock of the wallpaper, the next morning when you get up. Lovely. But most importantly, it's me that put it all there.

You probably think I'm leaving something out, claiming all the credit like this, that somewhere along the line there's been a wife putting her oar in, making sure that what she says goes. Not here. She left, didn't she, and good riddance. Except then it turns out that leaving isn't enough, not when every mortal thing she's left behind has her stamp on it. It's like having the woman here herself, looking over your shoulder, never letting you know a moment's peace. A man doesn't need that sort of thing, not after what Larry's been through.

So I threw it out, all of it. Every last stick of furniture, ornaments and all. Got rid of every mortal thing she ever touched. The best way of course would have been a blooming great bonfire – with her sitting on the top – but there's regulations against that sort of behaviour. So I did the next best thing. I started again, only this time with no expense spared. Always wanted wall-to-wall carpet she did, and that's what I've got. Pile. Shag. And a three-piece suite with matching pouffe and magazine stand. Not to mention the cocktail cabinet with drinks dispenser and feature lighting, display shelving, and the two wall niches installed by none other than yours truly. All in the best possible taste. My taste. There's not a thing here that's not me. What's more, I've been adding to it over the years, a novelty ashtray here, a statuette there. And one day, just to cap it all, I'm going to have one of those Royal Doultons – maybe a young girl with billowing skirts holding on to her hat. I'll be a happy man then.

Meanwhile there's enough here to impress. Only more importantly than that, you'd never know that a woman called Doreen had ever been born, let alone lived up here for thirty-five years. A triumph, that's what this room is. A veritable triumph. No wonder I feel so much at home.

Of course, I don't go into the reason for the place with Miss Tyson, not now. For the moment it's enough just to see her face – even if all she can think of to say is 'very nice'. Yet to be perfectly honest, even that doesn't matter. Because if you were to ask me why it was I'd suddenly gone all quiet, I'd say it wasn't just a case of standing here with a new acquaintance. It was as if I was looking at the future, a future where two people get together in the spirit of friendship, in a room that fits around them like a glove.

Which only made it all the more important to break the ice, properly, before she got the wrong impression. Because if I stood there much longer thinking about the shape of things to come, she'd decide that Larry Mann was not the sociable type. As it happened, though, she was staring straight at my pride and joy, what you might call the jewel in the crown.

'Yamaha,' I said, half thinking that she might know that already. 'Top of the range. Got everything, it has – violins, percussion, brass. You name it, and I can put my finger on it.'

'Oh,' she says, in that way I'm already beginning to recognize. 'You mean it's an *organ*?'

Well, I have to tell you that just for a second she had me wondering if, nice as she is, she might not be just that little bit stupid. Then I looked again, the way she would have done, and realized that, with the lid down and the antimacassar on top, and the family of woodland animals on top of that, there was always the chance you might mistake it for something different. The room is too small for it really. If I'd known ten years ago that I was going to become a musical type, I might have thought twice about the feature bookcase. Then again, who can ever say what the future holds? The fact is, I wouldn't be without the Yamaha now, not for anything. Two fingers, that's all you need for the Liberace touch. The organ does the rest. There's even a book that shows you how.

And once again – it seemed to be happening all the time since meeting Miss T – I had a picture of the future, this time with me sitting at the organ barrelling out all the old favourites, and her on the settee, listening to every note. The gas fire would be glowing, the TV shimmering in the corner, and on the table a little glass of something for us both.

Which reminded me.

'Right then. What's it to be – port or sherry?'

You know, it was getting to be comical. Everything I'd said to her so far seemed to bewilder her. Right now she was staring at me as if she wasn't quite sure she had heard me right. Still, patience is my middle name, and so I said again, slowly, 'I was wondering what it was you would care to drink. I've got port and I've got sherry. So you've got to tell old Larry, which is it to be, Miss . . . ?'

I let that hang in the air deliberately, bearing in mind that I'd been telling her to call me Larry all this time, yet quite obviously she had forgotten to return the compliment. For once though, the penny dropped straightaway, and she smiled and said, 'Amanda. My name is Amanda.' Then the smile disappeared. 'As for that drink though, it's terribly kind of you to offer, but I really don't think . . .'

Quite what it was she thought I never did hear, because by then it was too late and I'd already plonked a schooner of sherry in her hand. The fact is, you only had to look at her to know she wasn't the port and lemon type.

'Oh,' she said. Then remembering her manners just as you'd expect in a girl like her, added, 'Thank you very much.'

Now then, if someone had told me yesterday that I'd be sitting here in my own lounge with a young person of the female tendency, sipping Old England and chatting away like old friends, I'd have told him to pull the other one. Yet there she was, looking for all the world as if she belonged there. It was enough to make a man feel quite disorientated really, and I hadn't even touched a drop yet. So I raised my glass and said, 'Here's to you, Mandy love, and many happy days ahead.'

And you should have seen the way she smiled. Lovely teeth she has.

'So where is it you hail from?' I asked, expecting her to tell me Hong Kong. It would have been nice to have a few words on the subject before Old Gilbert got his oar in. Only the answer she gives falls a bit short of that.

'Scotland,' she says. 'Edinburgh, to be exact.'

29

'Yes, but is that where you call home?' I said, giving her another crack at the answer. Only still she doesn't come up with what you'd expect.

'It's where my friends are. I don't know a soul down here. I hope it changes.' Then she gives me this wonderful smile, wide, but a bit shaky round the edges. 'I'm really not very good at making friends.'

'Never you mind,' I said quick as a flash. 'You know me now. Anything you need, Larry will be here.'

Now then, if there was any friendlier way of putting it than that, I'd like to know. Because what happens next is just about beyond belief. I was all set to come straight out and ask where Hong Kong came in, when she puts down her glass and stands up. 'I'm sorry, Mr Mann, I'm going to have to go. I've hardly done any unpacking, you know. Oh, and by the way, thank you so much for all the fruit. You really shouldn't have. Good night.'

And that, as they say, was that. She had hardly touched her sherry. Yet there wasn't even time to point this out to her. She was already gone. Leaving me with half a glass of the stuff in my hand which presumably I now had to drink by myself, and that's not to mention a packet of cigarettes sitting there, unopened.

What was that she said about being no good at friends? All of a sudden you can begin to see why.

Not to put too fine a point on it then, I was disappointed. To put it mildly. What sort of person is it who gets the sort of welcome I'd given her, then hardly stops long enough to say thank you? I mean, that was bad enough, mentioning the fruit as if it had been the last thing on her mind, but what about what she called me? I thought I had made it quite clear: call me Larry, I'd said. So what does she do? Goes straight ahead and calls me Mr Mann again. That's what hurts. You do your best to be friendly, and then someone goes and treats you no better than a stranger.

After that, there was only one way to think. Namely, it was business as usual on the middle landing. Half the world has forgotten how to behave. I poured the sherry back into the bottle and tried to get on with the evening, turned up the fire and switched on the TV. In short, I decided not to dwell. But you know, I couldn't help it. If it had been one of the other girls, I wouldn't have minded, but what you couldn't get away from was – she's one of us. You'd expect her to behave a bit different.

Gradually though, I started to see sense. You mustn't be too quick to judge a person – even when it is a woman. Of course you would have expected her to stay and chat, but you've got to look at it from her point of view. We are talking about a girl who's been nicely brought up. Maybe she thought she had no business to be sitting at night in a man's room, talking and drinking. What if I'd been someone quite different, and something had happened? You would have said then that she'd had it coming.

You know what? The old kid just needs to get to know me better. She'd soon see there's nothing funny about Larry. She could be Sophia Loren, and he still wouldn't be interested. Doreen saw to that.

If it carries on though, I'm going to have to tell her. We can't have her getting the wrong idea of Larry, and what's worse, letting it come between us. It's the sort of thing that can ruin a friendship before it's even started. A short history of Larry, then, and his experiences with the female species might be entirely in order. What's more, she might be just the sort of person you'd want to tell. Remember that noise on the landing? What we might be talking about here is a thing that goes against the grain of all creation. A woman with a sympathetic ear.

Am I jumping the gun? Am I expecting too much? I

don't think so. When you've seen as much as Larry, you get so that you can judge. That girl is different.

So there you have it. I say there's every reason for giving Amanda the benefit of the doubt. Forget this afternoon. As someone wisely said: tomorrow is another day.

Chapter Three

Do you know those days when you can tell from the moment you wake up that everything's going to turn out right? Today was one of those days. I lay down and slept like a baby – and woke up like a lion, ready for anything. Not that you could ever call me the gloomy sort. But the way I felt first thing today made me hum while I got dressed, whistle when I picked up the milk, and actually sing as I got everything going for breakfast. What's more I found myself throwing in an extra rasher on top of the rest and never even gave it a second thought.

In a nutshell, I'd woken up in a good mood, and that's not like me. Being a stable sort of chap I'd always have said I wasn't one for moods of any kind, good or bad. I'm just the same, all the year round. Only not today.

Mind you, I wasn't quite such a happy boy when it's nine o'clock already and there's me, in urgent need of my constitutional, yet no sign of movement down below. You'd have thought anyone with a normal job would have been up and out long before now, but not, it seemed, with our Mandy. It was only now that she was getting up. The long and the short of it, it was causing me no end of distress having to wait for her to do what she had to do and go. In all the years I've lived here, I've never once gone to the loo for *that* reason while there's been anyone at home downstairs. Not in the week anyway. My insides seem to know when it's a weekend and hang fire till the Monday. But in the week, when there's not supposed to be anyone down there, that's asking too much. They have a mind of their own, and that mind is as regular as clockwork. But what could I do? *The bedroom is right next door to the lav.*

In the end, just when I thought maybe she was taking the day off, I heard her feet on the stairs to the hall, and the slam of the front door. And just as well. If she'd left it any longer, I reckon I would have needed hospitalizing.

Blessed relief then you would have thought would be the order of the day. And indeed, no-one could have got down those stairs faster than me, thundering along the passageway deaf to everything else. I'd almost made it too, when what should happen but Mandy's kitchen door opens. Not Mandy though, but Ethel. And the girl not gone more than two minutes.

There was nothing for it then. Since wild horses would not have persuaded me to carry on into the smallest room and get on with matters while she was outside, all I could do was stop and say, as casually as was possible in the circumstances, 'Good morning, Mrs D.'

And that's when I saw the look on her face.

Catching Ethel in one of her moods is like getting too close to the bonfire on Guy Fawkes night, with a wind blowing in from all directions. Stand anywhere for long and you end up showered in sparks. In a little while you come to understand what the guy must feel. And it's no good telling yourself you haven't done a thing wrong. When Ethel's got you in your sights you just have to get used to the fact that you're guilty.

The only way of dealing with it is to stay as cheery as can be. Resolute under fire.

'Mr Mann. I understand you've had words with Miss Tyson.'

'Indeed I have, Mrs Duck. And a lovely quiet girl she seems to be. Ever so friendly.'

34

'She can be as friendly as she likes, Mr Mann. But that doesn't excuse a thing.'

So it wasn't me, but Mandy. You would scarcely have thought there could have been enough time. But done something she has. Already Ethel is marching back towards the kitchen, and naturally I'm right behind her. She throws open the kitchen door, then stands aside for me to have a look. But even that is not enough. As I poke my head inside, a vicious little jab between the shoulder blades pushes me halfway across the floor.

'Now you tell me,' hisses Ethel. 'Just what do you think of that?'

It's a mess, that's what I think, though I don't actually say so. There are a couple of plates in the sink, unwashed, as well as cutlery, a table covered with breadcrumbs, and in the middle a lone tea cup, with a spill of coffee where the saucer should be. The table is Formica, so it's hardly going to come to any harm. But that's not the point of course, that's not the point at all.

Ethel pipes up behind me, 'I need hardly tell you that this is not what I expected of her, Mr Mann. Oh no. What sort of place does she think this is? If I'd have thought for one second she'd be the kind who . . .'

'Mrs D,' I said. Seeing where this was heading I'd butted in before I'd thought what I was going to say. But I carried on anyway. 'I'll have a word with her tonight, save you the trouble. How's that? If you ask me, all she wants is to find her feet a bit. This time next week you'll have forgotten it ever happened.'

'Mr Mann, she hasn't made her bed either.'

Oh, this was bad. Ethel wasn't going to stand for that. Down here the walls may be peeling and the ceiling coming down in flakes, but Ethel doesn't see it like that. All she can see is the mess that people cause.

'It's no good, Mr Mann. I should have stuck to my

usual sort of girl. They may not be like you or me, but they never gave me one ounce of trouble. They knew how to keep a place tidy. But this one, well I ask you. What would her mother say?'

Up to that point I'd been thinking all was lost, but mention of Mandy's mum gives me an inspiration. 'Her mother wouldn't like it, I'm sure, Mrs Duck. But she wouldn't make too much fuss about it, not the first time. See, I reckon she'd understand. Out there where Mandy comes from, they must have got servants for all this kind of thing. Poor girl's probably never known anything else.' I don't mention Edinburgh. 'Leaves her with a terrible disadvantage really. I bet she's not used to looking after herself. But she's a lovely girl. She'll learn. You mark my words.'

I said I was inspired, and I was right. The effect on Ethel is a little miracle in itself. The thought of having a tenant whose mother keeps servants brings about a transformation. You could feel the tone of the whole house rising even as we talked.

So why did I nearly have to spoil it all by adding, 'All the same, these young girls. All they want is a guiding hand. Remember our June as a youngster . . . ?'

Luckily for me, I saw the look on Ethel's face almost before it appeared. She never could stand having a kid knocking around the house. Doreen used to go on about her being jealous because it never happened for her and Gilbert. As if. The truth is, the thought of Ethel with maternal feelings is hardly what you could call a likely proposition. Anyway, what was wrong with me? Comparing Mandy with June is like comparing chalk with cheese. June might have been all right when she was very little, only she grew up, didn't she, and with every year that passed she grew more to be her mother's daughter. The saddest thing was just having to watch it.

The main thing is, I managed to stop in time,

finishing by mumbling something like, 'hark at me wittering on,' and hurrying back upstairs. Funnily enough, whereas five minutes before I'd been in a state of mortal distress, coming face to face with Ethel had somehow put paid to that. Good thing too, at the time, only just let's hope that between the two of them they haven't thrown me right out of kilter for the duration. There's a lot to be said for being regular.

Anyway, it hardly mattered. I had enough to keep me occupied for all today, namely, to think of a way of putting it nicely to Mandy that she would have to tidy up a bit if she wanted to stay on here. I was hard pushed to find the time to go out, and even that was only to check on what Harry had on his stall. As usual it was a struggle to get away, but I'm glad I went. He had some lovely peaches today. Luscious is the word, and suffice to say, two of them ended up on a certain young lady's table. I noticed Ethel had cleared up the mess.

In the end I had it all worked out — knew exactly what I was going to say and everything. Come half-past five, all Larry had to do was sit down and wait for her.

I should have guessed she would be late, though, after the start she had. That way, I could have saved myself the bother of popping out to the top of the stairs every five minutes just to check she hadn't arrived, and I hadn't gone and missed that little knock of hers. Yet as it happened, that was the last thing I needed to worry about. Not only did I hear her on the landing loud and clear, two minutes later there came a banging on the wall down below. Definitely not what I'd expected after that timid little tap of yesterday.

Then everything seemed to happen at once. There was no time to tell her to come up because half a second later, there she was in the kitchen door. She must have bounded up those steps three at a time. That's youth for you. Well, youth and something else.

37

It couldn't just have been the exercise that had got her all flushed. Two bright spots of red on either side of her face. *Peaches*, I thought. *She must really love peaches.*

'Mandy, love,' is what I said aloud. 'Come in.'

But do you know, she was already in.

'Mr Mann,' she said, 'Mr Mann.' And stopped. She seemed to be having difficulty getting the words out. But I didn't hurry her. I just looked forward to what she had to say.

Only once again it's not what you'd expect.

'Mr Mann.' *No mention of Larry.* 'Someone's been in my rooms. Been all through my belongings. I can hardly believe it. Nothing is where I left it. Everything has been tampered with, moved around. My books, my clothes, you name it. I'd say I'd been robbed, yet nothing is gone. I don't understand it. So I'm asking you – do you know anything about it?'

Stunned. That's the only word to describe it. There I was expecting something on the lines of: 'Good evening Larry. Thank you so Much for the Peaches however did you Know they were my Favourite.' And instead, I get this. It's only a wonder I remembered to wipe the smile off my face.

'Well, do you?' She was glaring at me, and if it hadn't been clear before, it was now. She was barking mad about something.

'I don't know what you're talking about, Mandy love. Didn't you lock the doors to those rooms before you went out?'

'No of course not. I don't even have keys. Mrs Duck offered me them, and I told her I didn't need them. Not when there must be fifty locks on the front door anyway. How could anyone have got in?'

Well, you should have seen my face then. Never mind that the old kid was shouting at the top of her voice – and only the good Lord knows what had happened to those lovely manners – what she had done was taken my breath away. Ethel had offered her keys, like she does to all the girls. And unlike them, she'd turned them down. It didn't matter that Ethel has her own set – she wasn't to know that. The fact remains, it's like having her come straight up to you and say she trusts you. Makes your heart miss a beat just thinking about it.

'Anyway, I told you, nothing's missing. All that's happened is that someone has been through my rooms, getting into everything. It's as if all they wanted to do was meddle.'

Well, it's at this point that light begins to dawn. But what could I say? I didn't want to be the one to break the bad news.

Still, say something I had to. In another second she'd be taking all this silence for guilt, and thinking it was me. And it wasn't. It was Ethel, who else. And what was more, it was only to be expected. It's just that usually she doesn't go this far. Getting her own back for the mess, I suppose.

Remember this morning? Mandy hadn't been gone two minutes when I met up with Ethel. Yet already she'd managed to visit every room on the floor. But you might also have noticed that I wasn't in the least bit surprised to see her. That was quite simply because she was only doing what she's done every morning from the first day she started letting out the rooms. It's like this: the moment she hears that front door go, she'll be up those stairs faster than you can say Jack Robinson. After that, you can sit up here and listen to the patter of Ethel on the move, flitting from room to room, taking her time, touching things, shifting them – probably no more than an inch to the right or the left – swapping round the cushions or the ornaments, just what you might do yourself if you were the occupier here, the sort of thing you do to leave your mark. It's called treating the place as your own. Except that in this case, it's Ethel who's doing just that.

Only Mandy doesn't know that yet. How could she? She's never come up against a woman like Ethel. When she runs up here, talking about 'her' lounge, 'her' kitchen, 'her' bedroom, she should think again. All she's doing is paying for the use of them. Meanwhile, Ethel will keep visiting regardless, because in Ethel's mind these rooms have never belonged to anyone but her. She's the true Lady of the House.

If Mandy can live with that, she'll be all right.

But if she can't? You can see the problem. Right at this minute, it was my guess that Mandy wasn't prepared to live with any such thing. The old kid's blood was up. If I gave the answer she was looking for, there and then, all unprepared, I reckoned it was a fifty-fifty chance that she'd turn straight around and pack her bags. And it would be no good telling her that she'd regret it, the moment she started looking for somewhere else to live. She wasn't in a mood to listen. No, one word out of place now, and it would be a case of goodbye Mandy.

Something else was needed. Something to take the heat out of the situation. What though?

'Hold on a bit,' I said.

I turned, reached up into the cupboard above the sink. 'Here,' I said. 'Have one of these.' And so saying, I flipped open the packet of Silk Cut and offered them, all in one movement, smooth as anything you ever saw in the films. You'd have sworn I'd been practising all my life.

I wish I could describe the effect. She takes one look, turns a brighter shade of red even than before – and stretches out a hand. And that first puff – you could watch as it visibly hit the spot. Took all the fight out of her, it did. Calmed her right down. She's a smoker all right, just like Larry. Another thing we've got in common.

After that, all I had to do was steer her towards the lounge and the settee, not forgetting the cigarettes. They went straight down on the coffee table in front of her, within easy reach. No arguments, no nonsense about having to be somewhere else. She sits down, starts hugging her knees, and goes on taking drag after drag.

Finally, she looks up, and you can see at once she's back to normal, got back her lovely pale colour. 'It's Ethel, isn't it, Larry? Doing all those things?'

'I'm afraid so, Mandy love.'

'Does she do it all the time?'

'I'm afraid so, Mandy love.' I push the packet a little closer.

'Would it make any difference if I asked for the keys again?' She's asked the question, but you can see she already knows the answer. She's learning, is our Mandy. One shake of the head, and that's the last we hear of Ethel. Half a minute later, she breathes one last whoosh of smoke and stubs out the cigarette.

'I shouldn't have smoked that, really, you know.'

'Oh get away with you,' I tell her. 'A little bit of what you fancy does you good.'

'It's not my health I'm worried about. I'd smoke myself silly if I could afford it. But they kept on getting more and more expensive, so I gave up, quite a long time ago actually. Now it's a case of trying not to go round smoking other people's. You know what they think of you otherwise.'

In other words, what she was telling me was, she actually cared what I thought of her. Tell that to the likes of Doreen.

'Now you look here, Mandy love,' I said, all serious-ness. 'There's always a cigarette or several for you up here. Any time you want one. You just remember that. Quick visit, that's all it will take. And remember, Larry isn't counting.'

'Oh dear, Larry.' She was sighing, Lord knows why, and shaking her head again. All the same, I noticed she was trying not to look at the packet that was there level with her knees.

What's more, it was interesting, finding out that not only was she so hard-up she would put up with Ethel and her funny little ways, but she couldn't even afford to treat herself to a pack of twenty every now and then. You'd have thought with a brain surgeon for a dad, she would never be that badly off. I was about to ask her about it when all of a sudden it was too late.

'Larry, you've been so terribly kind. I haven't thanked you properly at all. Believe me though, I'm so grateful . . .'

Well, if that wasn't music to my ears. No wonder I forgot what it was I was going to ask her. Anyway, I didn't want to butt in, not if she hadn't finished. So I didn't utter a word, just waited for her to say something else, about peaches perhaps. Only that was no use, because all it left was a silence between us, but by then I was beginning not to mind. It just showed I had been right about Mandy. She really is that rare creature – a girl of few words.

'You know what, Mand?' I said, not just to fill the gap, but because I genuinely wanted her to know. 'It's going to be a real treat having someone like you coming here to live. You won't believe this, being so nice yourself, but there have been folk staying here who wild horses couldn't have made sociable.'

I stopped there, to see if she was listening. And she was. She didn't have to say a word. Her not speaking was just a way of telling me to go on.

'They never think of the old folk, the ones who would give their right arms for a bit of company now and then. You know the sort of folk I'm talking about, don't you, Mandy love?'

And that's where I stopped. Not because I was

42

expecting an answer, at least not in so many words. But I was waiting for something, a particular kind of something, and all of a sudden, there it is: the exact sound I'd been waiting for. Not a word, not even a sigh, but that one tiny unmistakable little sound I'd heard before. Some people might not even have noticed it, it was that quiet, but I heard it all right, and I knew straightaway what it was. The sound of sympathy.

There, what did I tell you? She's a girl in a million. And that noise, that squeak, that cough, call it what you like – it was an invitiation, and a promise. It was letting me know that she is the sort of girl who will understand, the sort of girl you could trust with your whole life's story. In other words, or rather in no words at all, that little tiny sound was a signal, and Larry has received it, loud and clear.

Well I couldn't let the conversation lapse, not after that. It would have been an insult. 'Of course,' I said, 'it was different before I retired. I used to meet all sorts then. Too many for comfort really. Locker attendant I was, up at Camden baths. What's more, I can't say that I miss most of the people I was working with either, not the way they used to talk, telling folk they were lifeguards when most of them couldn't swim a stroke. No, locker attendants we all were, in charge of towels and general hygiene. Still, they were company, even if half of them don't so much as pass the time of day when you go up there now. They take a bloke like me for granted, knowing I'll be there regular as clockwork every Thursday for my own bath . . .'

You can tell how nicely I'd got into the swim of things from the way I nearly didn't hear her interrupt. Had to beg her pardon and request that she repeat what she had said. Which, fair play, she did, without complaint.

'I said, there's a bath here, Larry. Why ever do you go out for one?'

'Habit,' I told her. 'Though I should say that none of the other girls ever fancied using the bath that Ethel's got here. They couldn't seem to get on with the boiler. It scared the living daylights out of them. I suppose what it is, you turn on the tap and nothing happens, then WHOOMF the whole thing goes up in flames. Nothing wrong with it after that, mind. So long as you remember to keep the window open for the fumes. The water's beautifully hot.'

She must like her baths an awful lot because all of a sudden she was looking gloomy again. I was just about to try and cheer her up by offering to turn on the TV when she put paid to that by getting to her feet.

'What's this?' I said. 'You're never leaving already?'

Well, I couldn't help it if I sounded a bit hurt, could I? After all I'd said and done to help, as well as the bit about the old folk, you'd have thought she'd have had a little more time to spare. And she noticed. You should have seen the way she blushed. When I saw it, I was sure she was going to sit down again, but she didn't.

'Oh Larry, I'm sorry. But you can see it's getting late. I haven't even had my supper yet, and after that I've got to get down to work.'

'What?' I said, scarcely able to believe my ears. I took a quick look at the clock on top of the fire. Five to nine it said. 'You can't be going off to work at this time of night. What sort of job have you got, Mandy love? Night watchman or something?'

She didn't have to laugh quite so loud at that, as if it was me that was funny and not the joke. 'No of course not. Didn't Ethel say? I'm at college. Which means I have to study. You know – book work.'

'Oh, I'm with you,' I said. But I wasn't, not really. Of all the surprising things to have happened in the last couple of days, this just about took the biscuit. I mean, Ethel, letting a student within a mile of her house. It

44

beggared belief. I notice now she didn't say anything about that when she found the kitchen in the state it was. And I can't even say I blamed her. It would have looked too much as if she was only getting what was coming to her. And that's not all. If I put my hand on my heart, I'd have to say I was none too keen on the idea myself. If nothing else, it made you look at Mandy in a new light, when you think what most of them are like with their banners and their foul language, drugs and who knows what else besides. It was an unexpected blow, that's all I can say. And it explained her clothes.

Finally I came up with a reply, one last attempt to look on the bright side. 'You sure you're not having me on, Mandy girl? I mean, don't get me wrong, I'm not saying you're old, far from it, it's just I wouldn't have put you down as an eighteen-year-old. That's the age they go, isn't it, these student types. It's only their beards that make them look older.'

And there she was, laughing again. 'I know what you mean. But it's my second time around. I did start a couple of years ago, up in Edinburgh. Then I had to stop, you see. So now I'm starting again, down here. Hardly any grant though, that's the problem.'

And she looks at me, as if that explains everything.

'Well go on then,' I said, when I realized she wasn't saying any more. 'Don't stop there, Mandy love. Aren't you going to tell your old Larry why?'

'Why what?' For some reason, a funny, guarded little look creeps all over her face.

'Why you left your last college. I mean, you must have passed all sorts of exams to get there. So, natural question – why did you stop?'

Well, you wouldn't believe her face then. It's as if I'd asked her what she was doing on the night of the fourteenth. What did she get up to in Edinburgh – rob a bank?

'Larry, I don't . . .' Then her voice just peters out.

Well, you can imagine. You ask a simple question and suddenly it's like you're not talking to the same girl. One moment the old kid is laughing when by rights she shouldn't, and the next she's twitching like a nervous rabbit. There's no logic in it. It's what makes me say, 'Oh come on, Mandy love, don't leave your old pal in suspense. Once and for all, why did you stop?'

And that seems to do the trick because she tosses back some of that hair of hers and says, all in a rush: 'If you must know, something happened. I had a sort of breakdown. A little one. Not even a breakdown. More like a blip. It happens to lots of people. All the time. They get a bit depressed and then they get better. Does that answer your question?'

Well yes, I suppose it did. But the thing that leaps out at you is the way that she went about it. I may not know her all that well, but I can tell you now it was completely unMandy-like. Defiant, as if she expected to be told off about something. And hardly what you'd call friendly.

Needless to say, I kept my hair on, and was careful to stay pleasant. 'All right Mandy love, only asking. And if you're still upset with me, just remember this – the first fifty years are the worst.'

Now Lord knows why anyone should think that was funny, but suddenly the girl is laughing like a drain again. Talk about changeable, you hardly knew where you were with her tonight. 'Yes, Larry,' she says. 'I expect you're right.'

Which was all very well, but there was still no call for speaking the way she did. And I was on the verge of saying just that, then suddenly everything's all right again. She's almost out the door, when she turns around for the last time.

'I really am sorry about having to go, Larry. Especially when you've been so kind. I was in such a state when I came in. I don't know what I would have done if you hadn't been there. Thank you again.'

'Wait on a sec,' I said. 'There was something I meant to tell you.' But it was too late. She was gone, and blow me if I could remember what that something was.

But her words were still there. Blooming well imprinted on the wall they were. *Didn't know what she would have done without her old Larry.* What nicer thing could there be to say to a chap? And you can tell me again it was a student that said them, Larry doesn't care.

But seeing she was a student, and she had all that work to do, nothing was more important now than she should be able to get on with it. So I switched the TV back on, but so low only a lip reader could have heard it. Tiptoed to the kettle and back again. But I didn't mind, not for a second, because all the time I was thinking of her words, and what a lot they said for the person who spoke them.

Only what, I ask you, is a blip when it's at home?

Chapter Four

What a way to wake up though. I was dreaming happily that I was having a bath. It's one I have quite often – don't ask me why. There I'll be, up to my neck in water, no need for soap or anything, just lying there soaking, then the next thing you know is an awful great knocking at the door. It's Doreen of course, up to her old tricks, ruining everything. At one time I thought I had stopped that knocking for good, but she keeps on rearing her ugly head. After that, there's nothing for it but to wake up, unless you want to go on and dream about bad language.

It's always a warning, though, that dream. It means that you've got to start looking out for something Doreen-like, i.e. unpleasant, cropping up in the day. So that's how I knew, the moment I woke up – something was wrong.

Then it hit me. Dishes not washed, crumbs all over the table. Mess. That's what I should have been telling her about.

'Oh Lord.' I actually shouted this aloud. And jumped out of bed. All that chat with Mandy, all those careful words to make her want to stay, forgetting that Ethel was on the warpath. If Ethel found the place in the same state today, Mandy would be out on her ear anyway.

I must have stood a full five minutes, rooted to the spot, before I remembered. All was not lost. Mandy's a late riser. The thing to do was catch her before she went out. Then I could tell her what she needed to hear and even help her tidy up a bit. Simple. As if on cue, there came the sound of her kitchen door.

I was down those stairs faster than a fireman on his pole.

'Mandy,' I said, scrabbling at the glass, and peering through the frost. 'Mandy love, open up. I've got something to tell you. It's ever so important.'

Through the blur I saw a shape hurrying towards me, and that was a relief in itself. You never know, she might not have wanted to open up to anyone this early on. Then the door was flung open.

'Mrs Duck!' It's more than a shout than anything. Because there, where Mandy should have been, was Ethel, and, so far as I could see without actually shouldering my way past her, not another soul in the room.

'Why Mr Mann,' she says. 'Whatever is the matter?'

The answer was – everything. I could see Mandy's little life flashing before my eyes. Yet all I could do now was try not to let on.

'Nothing,' I said. 'Why should anything be the matter? I just thought it would be nice to have a small chat with Mandy.'

At this point, Ethel, catching me trying to look over her shoulder, yanks the door closer behind her, and prepares to come out with her worst.

'But you're too late, Mr Mann. She's been gone this long time.'

'What? Oh, Mrs D. When?'

For an answer, she gives me one of her looks, and says, 'Like I said, a long time.' Then, because she's Ethel, and can't resist rubbing it in, 'Actually I did tell her I was sure she didn't have to leave right that minute. She could have stopped a bit longer.'

But of course the poor kid would want to leave. After what Ethel would have put her through. Oh Mandy.

'. . . But she would insist. Said it was absolutely vital

to be there early. And what's more, that she'd be there till late and all. I never knew those youngsters had to work so hard, I was just saying to Mr Duck . . .'

This was all going a bit fast for me. 'Wait there, Mrs D.' I said. 'Where did she have to be? I don't understand.'

'Well, college, Mr Mann. Where else? And not coming back till late.'

'Coming back, Mrs Duck.' To hear me, you wouldn't have thought it was my voice. It was more like a croak than anything. 'Did you just say she was coming back?'

'Well, of course I did. What else should she be doing?' Ethel for her part sounds just as always – a bag of nails falling to the floor, clink after silvery clink. 'Really, Mr Mann, I don't know what's got into you this morning.' What happens next is pure Ethel. Not taking her eyes off me, she *sniffs* the air between us.

As if.

But that didn't stop my cheeks tingling. It was a whole combination of things – distress, relief and Ethel not letting you know what to think. There's not many folk would have been able to find the words then, but I did, and you've got to give me credit for that. 'Mrs Duck,' I said. 'You can't deny you were having second thoughts about her. You told me so yourself. You made me look at the state of her kitchen, remember?'

She remembered all right. And what's more she couldn't take it back. Which is why she was so vicious pulling the door shut and pushing past me, just to make clear that that was yesterday. If that was the score, then, I never would discover what had changed her mind – if changed her mind she had.

'Mrs Duck.' It was terrible to have to hear myself beg. 'Mrs Duck, are you really not going to tell me what happened? Are you keeping her on or not?'

Thank the Lord, she turned. Give the woman the slightest bit of knowledge and she simply can't resist

50

the chance to show off. 'If you must know, Amanda and I have had a little chat about keeping the place as it should be. The young lady in question was perfectly understanding.'

'But Mrs D.' I had to interrupt. I couldn't stop myself. 'That was going to be my job . . .'

'Mr Mann, if you please.' Ethel snaps. 'There never was the slightest need for anybody else's help. Again, if you must know, she came down to see us herself.'

'What? When?' I cried. By now I was getting to be what you could almost describe as reckless. It was just that I couldn't think when the old kid would have found the time.

Ethel narrows her eyes, gives me another of her looks. But all the same, she answers. 'Just before nine last night. Took us quite by surprise. As it turned out though, I don't know when I've enjoyed an hour more. As for Mr Duck, in his element he was, with all that talk about the Chinese and their funny little ways . . .'

The rest of what she had to say floated right past me into oblivion, while I fixed on that one important fact: just before nine, she said. Less than five minutes after Mandy had left me, claiming she had to work, that she really couldn't stay. That was what she said – that and about needing her tea.

And there was me, tiptoeing around my own home so as not to disturb someone who wasn't even within earshot.

After that there didn't seem to be much else to say. Except to ask, 'So how *is* the kitchen this morning?' Not that I was really interested.

Which must have been the only reason Ethel answers me. 'The kitchen is lovely, Mr Mann. Just as I expected.'

What can I say? I spent the rest of the morning in a daze, as would anyone else, having been told one thing, and found out another. I'm not even sure that 'daze' is the proper name for it. What do you call a seeping disappointment that won't let up for a minute? Hardly surprising that it wasn't until nearly dinner time that I began to think straight again.

Mandy was doing exactly the right thing, which is to say, rubbing up the Ducks the right way. I would have suggested the self-same course if I'd only got the chance. When it's a question of keeping the roof over your head, you do what you must, even when that means wasting precious hours chewing the fat with the likes of them downstairs. Anything less and it's my guess she would have found herself out of here by now.

No, the truth is, that girl is finding her feet like a good one, and with a little more help from me, she'll keep on finding them. She might even end up thinking that this place suits her like nowhere else, and decide she never wants to leave. Because with Larry up above her for friendship and those below nicely under control, she might see she's got everything she needs. All she wants in the meantime is someone to lend a guiding hand.

And it was with that in mind I laid my plans.

When she came home tonight, I was ready for her – relaxed and waiting. First you know about it are her little footsteps on the landing, no louder than a mouse. You know, it's the small things about the girl that count – like the way she comes in as if she's doing her best not to be heard. The old kid would die rather than disturb, I reckon.

Just for the fun of it, I tried to imagine what was going through her head. Probably asking herself what little treat would be waiting for her today. Answer – forty cigarettes. Four Oh. There on her kitchen table. And one thing she could be sure of – it was never Ethel who put them there. So it was only a question of time. And I was right.

You could tell we were back to normal just from the way she knocked, a timid little tap, like the first night. And to prove it, there was her face when she arrived at the top – paler than pale and with that serious look of hers back again. When we're even better friends than we are already, I'm going to warn her about arriving places looking like the weight of the world was on her shoulders. But for now, all I do is smile and let her know what a treat it is to see her.

'Ahoy there,' I said. 'And how's my Mandy tonight?'

Ask a question like that – just as a way of saying hello – and most people would answer, 'Fine thank you and how's yourself?' But you've guessed it, not with our Mandy.

Sure enough, that forehead of hers folds up into one great mass of wrinkles – the very thing I'd want to warn her against – and that serious look of hers turns into something even worse. 'Larry,' is all she says, and brings the packets of cigs out from behind her back, puts them on the draining board beside her. Apparently no other words are necessary.

'What's all this?' I said. 'Why do you want to go bringing those back up here? They're for you, love. Or don't you like them?'

'Larry,' she says again in a voice hardly worthy of the name, it's that low-pitched. 'You're very kind, but I just wish you wouldn't. Every time I come home, there's been something ... And now these. It's too much, Larry.'

I was beginning to see what the problem was. The poor girl was just trying to be polite. That's why she was bringing back the cigarettes and looking so miserable while she was about it. In which case, all she wanted was some common or garden cheering-up, even if it meant being firm.

'None of your nonsense,' I told her. 'There's no need for all this with old Larry. Those cigarettes are just a friendly gesture. You take them and enjoy them. And after that, don't give them another thought.'

'Larry, I . . .'

'Larry, nothing,' I said. I was beginning to realize that you could get no end of fun making friends with someone who's too polite to breathe. Meanwhile she's standing there, rubbing her hands together as if she was cold.

'Come on through into the lounge,' I said. 'It's lovely and warm. The gas fire hasn't been off all day.'

Immediately she takes a step backwards, says in that quick, shy voice of hers, "Oh Larry, I can't. You know how much I'd like to stay. But as I told you the other night – I've got to work, and have something to eat, so . . .' And she takes another step back again. If she wasn't careful, she'd be falling down those stairs in a minute. But that wasn't going to happen. Because when she says, 'You do understand, don't you Larry?' I reply, like a flash:

'Of course I do, Mandy love. That's why I've made you – this!'

And open the fridge.

You see, I was ready for her. It was all there, laid out on a plate in a way that would have made Fanny Craddock proud: cold ham, cold tongue, hard-boiled eggs, lashings of lettuce and cucumber and tomato. A proper feast for the eyes if I say so myself. However, while she's looking at it I say, 'I would have cooked you something hot, really I would, but I know how you young girls like to watch your figures. Point is, it's all here, ready and waiting. Mandy love, you don't have to go anywhere.'

You should have seen her face. I only wish I'd had a camera. She'd go down a storm on one of those game shows, the ones where they like you to look as if you've been hit by a bus when the screen moves away and there's your long-lost brother from New Zealand. Some of those folk look as if they don't know whether they want to laugh or cry. Anyway, that's Mandy for you – thunderstruck. As for words – they don't come into it. The poor girl is completely at a loss. But it doesn't matter an ounce. Larry can do all the talking necessary. 'Maybe you could do with some potatoes though, bulk it out a bit and blow the diet. I've got some all cooked. Cold of course, but fine with salad cream.'

No prizes for what comes next.

'Larry, please. I don't think I can . . .'

The thing to do then is pretend to go a bit deaf. Otherwise we'd be standing here all night. It's the only way with Mandy. Rather than argue, I just pushed the plate into her hand and gave her a little nudge towards the lounge. It was all waiting for her – knife, fork, serviette, salt and pepper, even a glass of squash to wash it down. And for that little extra touch, a couple of carnations off the stall next to Harry's, in a vase. The old kid takes one look, and sits down like she was in a dream, plate on the place mat, ready for the off.

Only trouble was, she wasn't eating.

'Wake up, Mandy girl,' I said to her. 'It's not just for looking at. It's your tea, not a work of art.'

'But Larry, I can't,' comes the faint reply.

'What's the matter? Don't tell me you're waiting for me. Larry had his ages ago, with the six o'clock news like he always does. So dig in, love. Don't stand on ceremony.'

'No Larry, I really can't eat this.' At last I noticed there was a funny note in her voice, and to tell the truth, she did look a touch green.

'Oh Mandy, love,' I said. 'What's wrong? You're not ill are you?'

'No, I mean yes. I mean I don't know. Perhaps that's

why. All I know is, I can't eat this. I'm sorry. I can see it looks lovely, but you going to so much trouble, well . . . I just can't go along with it.'

And as if that little explanation said it all, she stood up. Just like that. Without so much as lifting a knife and fork. Any second now, judging by the look on her face, she would be saying to me that I did understand didn't I, as if it all made sense.

In which case my only answer would have to be no – it didn't make sense. To tell the truth, I couldn't quite believe it was happening, that I could do all this for someone only to see them turn it down. I looked at her and looked at the plate, then up at her again. 'You saying you don't want it then?' was all I could come up with, finally.

Even that didn't get a straight yes or no out of her. She just started mumbling on again about me going to too much trouble. As if somehow that made all the difference.

I know what you're saying. I should have let it go at that. The girl just wasn't worth the effort. I could have taken the plate away and said nothing more about it. That way we could have another couple of minutes chat for politeness' sake, then she would have tripped off downstairs again, telling herself she was in nobody's debt, and didn't have to worry about a thing. Especially not about how there was someone upstairs, all on his ownsome, night after night without a soul to keep him company. I could have done that, let her off the hook.

Except that *she would have regretted it in the end.* Not now maybe, but in later years, looking back. It would have been on her conscience, the way she turned around and acted tonight. It would be there all right, nagging her in the daytime and not letting her sleep at night. Because it was only then she would have come to know what ingratitude does to a person, the damage it can do. By then, it would have happened to her.

All this went through my mind as I looked at her, and thought about the sort of girl she was, and half of me was saying, let her go, as the other half was whispering, give her another chance.

Here's what I did: I addressed her, quietly, but with dignity. 'I know it's not much, love. And probably not what you're used to, not with your background. I expect it's more a case of smoked salmon and champagne where you come from. But what you've got to understand is, it was the best I could manage. OAPs aren't millionaires, you know.'

'Larry . . .'

'No, no, love. Don't say a word. You're right. There's no use in forcing it down. You leave it. I daresay it won't go to waste. With a bit of luck it'll keep for dinner tomorrow. I'll put it back in the fridge.'

But I didn't. I stopped right there where I was. The plate stayed and so did Mandy. A few seconds later she sat down again, and a few seconds after that she picked up her knife and fork. One more tiny pause, and then she started to eat. Like a little bird she was, to see her, picking at this, picking at that, but she got through it, every scrap – well, nearly. She would keep on taking sips from her glass between every bite and I reckon it was that that stopped her having room for the rest. But I didn't say anything. She'd eaten enough – what you could call an elegant sufficiency.

Afterwards, when I was sure she was finished, and didn't fancy a scoop of icecream or anything, I turned up the TV and we settled down to watch a programme on Wildlife in Africa which I'd starred in the *TV Times*. When the adverts came on, though, I did what I should have done before, and told her a few things she didn't know about Ethel Duck. How the first and most important thing was not to be taken in. And just to illustrate the point I told her about the time I accidentally let it drop that one of the girls – this was before the Indians came along – had entertained a man here the night before. Next thing, the poor girl comes home to find that Ethel has packed and hauled every one of her suitcases out into the front garden and left them there. Ethel, who looks as if she couldn't lift a telephone directory without help. And she could still do it, I reckon.

And Mandy? The old kid just listened. Never said a word. If you ask me, it must have been the shock. Learning the truth about Ethel would be enough to shut anybody up. Still, she needed to hear it, if only to make things easier for her in the long run. I could have told her a lot more besides, but before I knew it the little clock on the mantelpiece had pealed out eleven and she was getting up to go. I was sorry to see it, but I could hardly complain.

'Good night then, love,' I said to her.

'Yes Larry,' she said, doubtless meaning, 'and good night to you'. But short and sweet, that's the essence of Mandy. I'm beginning to know her now, and you'll not find me grumbling because she doesn't fall over herself with talk like most women. Then off she went, back to those cold rooms of hers downstairs.

But what matter? The old kid is here to stay.

Chapter Five

Believe it or not, she was actually back early this evening, long before I'd thought about listening out for her. Not that I was complaining. The sooner she came home, I thought, the sooner we'd be seeing her. Which shows how much I knew. The minutes rolled by, and where was Madam? Not up here, that was for sure. After last night you'd have expected the first thing she'd want to do was bound up those stairs to see her old pal. But did she? Don't ask.

Round about seven I started to catch the smell of toast burning, and that was almost like the final blow. You see, never mind that I'd told her I always eat my tea with the six o'clock news, I had actually begun to wonder if the reason she hadn't been up was because she was busy cooking a meal for us both – to return the favour, so to speak. Well, unless she planned on serving up charcoal, you could forget that.

Then I told myself not to fret. I'd see her soon enough. After all, it doesn't take two minutes to polish off a couple of rounds of toast.

Only then, another hour went by.

I even started to worry a bit. Especially as, try as I might, I couldn't hear a sound from downstairs. If there had been anything I would have heard it. Yet it was that quiet, I couldn't even tell which room she was in. Then finally, I heard a door open.

I was in the kitchen at the time, ideally placed for calling down to her in friendly fashion. But I didn't. I wanted to see if she would do the decent thing and come up all by herelf. So what I did was cough, only the once, but loudly, just in case she thought there was no-one else at home.

Worked like magic, it did. That one cough and you could have heard a pin drop. It was as if that same little sound had caught hold and kept her from taking another step. Result – you could almost see us both, like a pair of statues, me up here and she down there, and everything so still we could practically hear each other breathing.

Then at last, it came. Her knock. Like I knew it would.

'Evening stranger,' I say, just to make a point.

Which she surely gets because at once that pale face of hers colours ever so slightly and she says, 'Oh Larry, I'm sorry not to have been up. And I can't even stay now, I'm so tired.'

Lucky for her then that Larry's got the answer to everything. Not to mention the cure. 'Oh yes, love?' I said. 'If it's that bad, you'd better sit down before you fall down.' A kindly little push towards the lounge, and what can she say? Hardly that it's not relaxing here, not with deep plush to take the weight off her legs, and everything she could wish for there for the asking.

Anyway, it just so happens that I was feeling a bit peaky myself – before I set eyes on her, that is. But it's as anyone could have told her: there's nothing like a chat with an old pal to put the life back into you.

The truth is, I'd been looking forward to this moment all day.

I'd been thinking, you see. There are things that up to now I haven't told a single person – one, because it's none of their business, and two, because you were only bound to be disappointed by their reaction. But Mandy is different. We might not have known each other more than a few days, but believe me when I say, you could tell that girl anything. Not only will she listen, but most important of all, she'll understand. You can see it in her eyes, you can hear it in her voice. That's the sort of girl she is. If you didn't have a trouble in the world you'd want to make one up, like Ethel, just to have her listen and look at you the way she does.

But Larry doesn't have to make up his troubles. He's seen enough for all of us. And tonight I was going to pay that girl the ultimate compliment – I was going to tell her things I hadn't told another living soul.

But you know, a decision like that, it's a hard one to make. And once you've made it, you don't much feel like beating around the bush, not when you've finally got her sitting there. The temptation is simply to turn to the old kid and say, 'All right Mandy, brace yourself. What do you think of a woman who lives with you as your lawful wedded wife for thirty-five years, then all of a sudden says she's off to live with a fancy man half her age in a caravan in Waltham Abbey? And as if that wasn't bad enough, the one person you'd expect to be on your side, namely your own daughter, lets you down. Turns out to be visiting them both on the sly. As if none of it had happened. I mean, I ask you, is that the sort of thing a man's expected to rise above, eh Mandy?'

The fact is, of course, you can't do it. You've got to choose your moment, hang on till the time is right. The trick is to bring the conversation round slowly to the object in mind. Then you let her have it. And that's what I did. I made her comfortable and carried on talking about this and that, but all the time edging closer and closer to the big moment. I even started to enjoy myself. It meant me telling her about the olden days, before the war, when a man could grow old with a bit of dignity intact. Granted, pensions weren't what they might have been and doctors wanted to see the colour of your money before they'd give you so much as an aspirin, but people knew how to look after their own. Compare that with today, I told her, and weep, because there's nobody left who cares.

A pause, and a sigh. I reckoned it was Mandy's turn. And sure enough, after a little start as if she's realized just that, she looks at me, eyes wide, and says: 'But Larry, don't you have any family?'

That was my cue. I took a deep breath – I'd need it. Because talk about Family, I could write a book.

'Amanda. There's someone on the phone wants a word.'

Made me jump. Made both of us jump. It was Ethel Duck's voice reaching up on the wings of a squawk from the very bottom of the stairs. A second later, Mandy has leapt to her feet. 'Sorry Larry,' I hear her murmur as she passes, and then she's gone, running down those stairs two at a time by the sound of it. That didn't even leave me time enough to warn her that if there's one thing Ethel won't allow, it's people using her phone. She'll be having a fit this very minute if I know her. But would she say anything to Mandy? It would be better if she did. Better than saying nothing, and simply chalking up a black mark against her – till the next time. I chewed that over for a full five minutes, until finally I managed to calm down.

'Just this once won't hurt.' That's what I told myself. 'And it won't happen again because you can tell her all about it when she comes back.' So I plumped up the cushions where she'd been sitting, got it all nice for her again, and started thinking of something clever and kind to say when her head popped up in my doorway again.

Only she never came. I must have sat there till going on midnight, just expecting that she would. I sat up until I heard her bedroom door closing for the final time, and realized it was no good.

So who do I blame? Myself for not jumping straight

62

in when I should have? Ethel for interrupting and ruining everything like she always does?

Or Mandy for asking a question, then not bothering to come back for the answer?

There's no sense in asking if I slept well. Disappointment has a way of ruining sleep. It was that lack of consideration more than anything. She must have known I was waiting. You don't run out in the middle of a conversation with a person and then just not come back.

Unless it was that Ethel kept her talking.

But even that was no excuse. I had her first. She should have thought up something to say and come away.

If I'd seen her this morning I would have said something to her. After the sort of night I had, I would have. Maybe that's why she took it into her head to leave the house even earlier than yesterday. She's the sort of kid who knows when she's done wrong, after all. It was just possible that she was ashamed to face me.

All the same, she was still going to have to come home. And explain. Because by then I'd realized for myself – a girl like Mandy would never knowingly have caused upset. If she didn't come back to hear the answer to her very own question then there must have been a reason for it, and knowing my Mandy, it would have been a good one.

That's why I must have nearly worn my ears out listening for her. But what do you think – I didn't hear a sound. Not a dicky bird. When nine o'clock came round I had to admit it was late, even for her. And just like you'd expect I started worrying about that too. Because there's other stuff I've never had the chance to mention to her either. About walking about after dark and Finsbury Park not a stone's throw away.

I'd been feeling a good deal better this afternoon; now all of a sudden I was feeling a good deal worse.

So that was my state of mind when late in the evening I pottered downstairs to answer one last quick call of nature before going to bed. Not that anyone would have heard a squeak out of me. Even if Mandy was out, it's hardly the sort of thing you want to advertise. So here was I, tiptoeing past her bedroom door when all of a sudden it opens, and there she was.

Well, I don't know who looked the more shocked – her or me!

'Oh, Larry,' says she, with a faint sort of smile.

'Mandy!' I reply. 'You're back, then.' Actually, I'm shouting at the top of my voice. Because the truth of the matter is, I'm that pleased to see her, everything else has vanished from my mind. 'You just got in?'

'Mmmm,' she replies – if a half mumble directed at her toes can be called a reply.

I could have left it at that, but there was something in the way she was standing clutching the door and looking at her feet, not me, that made me say, 'Get away. I bet you've been home all this time, and never let on.' I was joking of course, all I wanted her to know was that her absence had been noted.

But there you are with Mandy. Everything has to be complicated. I was only trying to be pleasant, and before my eyes she goes bright red, and doesn't say a word.

That's not the effect I'd been after, not when all I'd hoped for was to hear her chuckle as she said, 'Of course not, Larry. What a thing to suggest. I just got in five minutes ago.' Instead she was there, saying nothing that made any sense, practically turning circles on the spot.

Suddenly I wanted to end it, conversation and all, sign off with a few words that would help her to explain everything. 'Don't mind me,' I said. 'I bet I know why you were late. It's the buses. You're desperate to get home, and there they are, all heading off in the opposite direction to Finsbury Park. It's enough to drive you mad.'

All she had to do was nod. Then we could both have gone to bed happy. But not Mandy.

'Actually, I don't use the buses,' she says. 'Not unless I really have to. Most of the time I walk.'

And that stops me in my tracks. Makes me stare at her, wondering if I'd heard her right. That college of hers is a good three miles away. I know because being interested I looked it up in the telephone directory. It's right off down the end of City Road. People used to walk that sort of distance once, and not think twice about it, but not now, not in the days of the bus pass and all.

She's still talking, explaining. 'It doesn't take me that long, and it saves me pounds in fares.'

I daresay it does. But then, most people would be glad to spend all that just to save their legs. I mean – six miles.

'That's all very well, Mandy love,' I said, 'you walking like that, just to save yourself eighty pee, but have you thought about this? The longer you take to get home, the later it will be. I mean, half the time you don't leave that college of yours until it's way after dark anyway.'

She shrugs. As if to say, 'So what?' Starts fiddling with the handle on her door. As for me, I just watch her for a moment, then say quietly, 'Oh Mandy love, you've got to believe me. You're playing with fire. This is no place to be swanning around after dark.'

There must have been something in the way I spoke that caught her attention then. She left off fiddling and looked at me properly for the first time. 'I don't understand, Larry. What do you mean by that?'

'I mean, Mandy love,' I was still keeping my voice

quiet, not wanting to panic her with what I had to say next, 'I mean there are facts about this area that you just don't know. See, things happen around here that, not to put too fine a point on it, hardly bear thinking about.'

'What sort of things, Larry?' At last she's beginning to sound serious.

'Well there was this woman for starters,' I said.

'Yes?'

'Killed,' I said. 'They found her less than three hundred yards from where we are now. Not a breath of life left in her.'

Her eyes shoot open at that. 'Larry, no. Really? When?'

'Let me think, eleven, twelve years ago . . . ?' I was still trying to get it right, answer the question properly, when what does she do but interrupt. And believe it or not, she's laughing.

'Twelve years ago. Oh God, Larry. You had me worried for a minute. Now if it had been last week . . .'

'No, no, wait,' I said. 'That's only one. I haven't told you about the other yet. Someone else was found almost in the same spot, exactly the same thing happened to her as to the first one.'

'Oh yes, and when was that, Larry? Nine, ten years ago?'

I don't mind saying I almost lost my temper with her then. This wasn't what you'd expect from a girl like her. Just for a minute I might have been talking to June. Then suddenly she wipes the smile off her face and it's back to the old Mandy.

'I'm sorry, Larry. I didn't mean to laugh. It's just you really did scare me for a moment. Then when I heard it was all those years ago . . .' Seeing the look on my face she stops, and starts again. 'And the other one. When did that happen?'

To be honest, I had a good mind not to answer, but

66

being the man I am, I go ahead anyway. 'Six, maybe seven years ago.' This time I don't look at her. 'Go ahead, laugh, but that doesn't mean it won't happen again. If a woman's going to go out night after night when it's all dark, in a neighbourhood like this, what can you expect? Someone's bound to get the wrong idea. All I'm saying is, a young girl like yourself should be taking a lot more care.'

Silence then. At least she's not laughing. 'Thank you, Larry,' she says at last. And for a moment it all seems worth it.

But there was still one more thing at the back of my mind.

'What I don't understand, Mandy love, and I'm sure you'll excuse me asking – how come you're so hard-up? What about your dad? He must have pots of money. Enough surely so you don't have to be walking the streets of London at all hours.'

That's all I said, honestly. Just those few little words, but talk about blue touchpaper! Nothing intentional, of course, but you should have seen the effect. That sweet little face of hers goes all hard, like water freezing. And her eyes! No exaggeration, you could have lit a match off them.

'Listen Larry,' she says. 'The last person in the world I'd take money off is my father. I don't need him, and haven't done these last two years. All right?'

And there's nothing I can say, because she's slammed the door in my face.

The funny thing is, it didn't bother me a bit – for the simple reason it wasn't me she was upset about, but him – her dad. Either I'm no judge or there's an almighty difference of opinion there. And it's not just a case of all those thousands of miles between them getting in the way, we're talking about a major gulf. Did you hear the way she snapped at me? Seems as if you only have to mention his name and suddenly you're swimming in shark-infested waters. If you ask me, something's gone terribly wrong in that family.

Now for all I know, it may be her fault. But Larry's not one to take sides, especially not in a case like this. Because we're in exactly the same boat, Mandy and me, cut adrift and left to sink or swim. And who's done it to us? Family, that's who. Which makes you think – there never could be two people with more in common.

It would explain all those blips, as she calls them, though! Poor girl just hasn't learned to get angry, that's her problem.

Still, I didn't want to leave on an unfriendly basis, so I knocked on the door, just softly, and called out to her. 'I can see you're busy, Mandy love, but listen to me. I don't want you worrying about what I told you tonight, about the women? You stop at home and nobody will touch you. Larry will see to that.'

All very interesting, you might say. But it goes downhill after that. You'd hardly have expected to see any more of her that night, but what about the next night, and the night after? To make matters worse, Friday night is Harry's night.

Harry. He calls in on his way home from the stall. Has done every single Friday, barring accidents and holidays, for twelve years, ever since Doreen left. It's the guilt, what with her being his sister and treating me the way she did. I reckon he only meant to come the once to talk about it, get it out in the open, maybe do a bit of apologizing on other people's behalf. But then he should have realized the first time, wild horses wouldn't have persuaded me to mention that woman's name. Yet he keeps on coming, as if he's still waiting.

That being the case, though, it doesn't leave us much else to discuss. Nowadays he can't even talk about Molly. After years of being a creaking door she surprised us all by finally pegging out last year. I was sympathetic, naturally, but there's only so much you can say. And at least she stuck by him, right to the end, so he can hardly have anything to complain about there. All he's got now, though, is the stall, and that's hardly a topic for debate. Conversation, therefore, is — to say the least — limited, generally proceeding on the lines of Harry lifting the lid off his sandwich and saying: 'Egg again, Larry?'

'Egg again, Harry.'

I didn't say a word about Mandy, though. Partly because I'd expected her to find her own way up here, so the introductions could speak for themselves, and partly because if she didn't, then I would have looked a right Charlie, going on about this girl who can hardly keep away from her old Larry. And I was right, wasn't I, because there was no sign of her. Yet she must have known we were here, both of us.

The next day, Saturday, I did see her, but from a distance. She was on the other side of the road, marching off in the Archway direction. My guess was she was making for one of the parks. But why go by herself, I wondered. If she wanted a walk, I would have kept her company. And I could have told her this — it was hardly the weather for it. It may only be October, but you should feel that wind.

One thing will come out of this, however. I'm going to tell that Harry what I should have told him years ago — namely that he can find something else to do with himself on a Friday night. It's not as if he's a friend or anything. See, I've been thinking. I reckon he gave Mandy the wrong impression, coming here that night. I mean there was I, making it quite clear that Larry Mann didn't have a soul in the world, and then up *he* pops, making her think there's hardly a word of truth in it. No wonder she steered clear of me all through the weekend. Now she's probably telling herself that

Larry's got pals all over the place, and the last thing he needs is another one.

So no more Harry then.

All the same, even Harry can't be the only reason. What about us being neighbours? I've seen more of Ethel this weekend than I have of her, and the last thing you could call Ethel is a friend. Honestly, if I didn't know better, I'd think she was trying to avoid me.

Chapter Six

Isn't that just the way? You can live with a problem night and day and still not see the answer even when it's staring you in the face. Come last night, it was a relief when finally it got too late to stay up, meaning I could relax, stop the waiting and the listening, and think about getting some much-needed sleep. And it's only then, as I'm climbing into bed, with my mind on something completely different (whether a hot-water bottle was called for, to be exact) that the answer hits me, bang, right between the eyes.

It was the phone call. Of course. One moment she had been sitting there, full of friendly interest, practically pleading with me to tell her my life story, and the next moment she's gone. Vanished. And what took her away? The phone call, that's what. I have to say — I laughed out loud then. I did! It was so obvious, yet I hadn't given it a thought. Only it's then the next logical thing occurs to me. What could there be in a phone call that could make a friendly old kid like Mandy suddenly become all retiring?

Bad news, that's what.

No doubt about it — she heard some terrible news that night, and that's the reason she hasn't been up. Because she doesn't want to let on. I tell you, that girl is the mirror image of me — a very private person not given to airing her problems. I reckon she's been down there, huddled away in those rooms of hers, mulling it over and wishing there was someone she could turn to. Too shy to go bothering the one person she knows would care. That would be my Mandy all over. It's enough to make you weep, really it is.

I got to sleep, no problem, after that, but naturally she was the first thing on my mind when I woke up this morning. And by then, one thing was for sure: it couldn't go on. The poor girl could waste away before anything could be done for her, and whose fault would that be? Mine – for not doing anything about it.

Which is why the first words that entered my head when I woke up were: Something Must Be Done.

Only what?

I can tell you what I would not be doing for a start. That is, marching downstairs, banging a tattoo on her kitchen door, and yelling, 'Now then, Mandy, hows about telling your old Larry what's up?' And why not? For the simple reason that Larry Mann is not the sort to go poking his nose anywhere he's not wanted. It's just not in my nature. Another person's life is their own, and you don't go barging in, trying to take over if they don't want you to.

On the other hand, what could you do? You couldn't just sit around, waiting for her to tell you, because that might never happen. What I needed was a clue, the merest hint as to what was going on. That was the only way I would be able to help. And if I couldn't get that clue from her, then the only sensible solution was to look elsewhere.

Which is a roundabout way of explaining why it is that at half-past ten in the morning, long after Mandy has gone out, and Ethel has done her rounds, I'm here, outside Mandy's lounge, my hand on the door knob. There's no-one in of course, but that's the whole idea.

I'm looking for clues, that's all.

The problem is now, when it's time to turn the knob and walk in. You may laugh, but it's not as easy as it sounds. All this time I've been making her welcome as can be in my own place, yet she hasn't once returned the compliment. I haven't seen downstairs since she moved in. And now here I was, all set to enter un-invited.

Daft, I know. Like a second home these rooms should be, seeing as I must have been in and out of them hundreds of times over the years. No-one has ever thought twice about calling old Larry down when there was a hairdrier that needed fixing or plug that wanted changing. Then there have been all the times Ethel has sent me in with an errand of her own. So what was the difference now?

Hardly any. That's what I said to myself. Hardly any, and with a good firm grip on the handle I opened the door.

Even so, it comes as a shock.

These rooms have always been dingy, and the lounge the worst of the lot. Decrepit, damp, neglected are words that spring to mind. Old rooms in an old house. It would take an awful lot of good money to turn them around, but you can't expect that of Ethel — not when it's someone else who'd get the benefit.

So why the shock?

Because looking around me now was like seeing the place for the first time. I've never had to think very hard about what it would be like to live here. After all, if it's Indian girls you're talking about, these rooms might not exactly be your ideal home, but they're still a darn sight better than what they must be used to on the Subcontinent. I've yet to hear whether they have wallpaper over there. But now, looking at it, as it were, all through Mandy's eyes, you start seeing things afresh.

It's a case of copping the wallpaper, trying to remember when it first went up, and failing, it was that long ago. Yet it was me that put it there. One thing I was fairly sure of, it wasn't brown in those days, and nor is it because of me that it's coming away from the

73

ceilings. Those great spreading dark patches are responsible for that.

The plasterwork is just as bad. I reckon you could hoover up twice a day here, and you'll still find it scattered like dandruff over the floor. It's a shame that, because it was on the plaster that I remember Ethel gave me free rein. 'Do what you want, Mr Mann,' she said. So I went ahead and painted the rosettes and garlands in colours I reckoned would brighten up the place. They're still there, the lime greens and the oranges, but they don't do me credit, not with all the cracks and gaps everywhere.

Mind you, I don't suppose Mandy gives two hoots about the plasterwork. I reckon she'd be happy if there was just some way of stopping the wind howling through the gaps in the window frames. It doesn't matter where you stand, you can feel the hairs on the back of your neck lifted by something stronger than just a draught. What I want to know, though, is why Mandy has tied back the net curtains. They're not going to keep out the wind like that, and don't try telling me that Ethel approves.

Then there's the furniture. The wonder is that any of it is still standing. You won't believe it, but most of it used to be mine – till I got shot of it along with Doreen. Gave the whole lot to Ethel, I did, job lot for ten shillings. Couldn't wait to get rid of it. The settee was a disgrace even then, which was hardly surprising seeing as we'd had it for over twenty years, and it had been Doreen's Aunty Freda's before that. Looking at it now, you'd never think we'd been grateful to have it at the time. The main thing about it was, it had a little lever you could pull down to make the whole thing into a double bed. I never quite got the hang of it somehow, but Doreen knew how to use it all right. Anyway, it's on its last legs now. The leather's showing its real age and there's horse-

74

hair falling out of places where it's worn away.

It's a miracle Mandy spends any time down here at all, when you think about what she's welcome to upstairs.

Nothing new then – in all senses of the word. Except that there *was* something different about the place, it's just that it took those first few seconds to see what it was. She'd gone and moved it around – settee, table, everything. Everything was in its natural place before, now it's all out of kilter. She's pulled the two armchairs and the settee right up to the fire so she's made almost a little room within a room there. Which is all very well, only what about the rest of it? Now there's a great open space in the middle of the floor, and nothing to fill it with. You wouldn't believe how bare it is. And that's not all. Look a bit closer and you start noticing that the walls seem awfully blank as well. She's taken down every one of the pictures – even the nice ones like the one of the skinny kid with eyes nearly bigger than his face.

Still, I wasn't here to check out the furniture. I was meant to be looking for clues. With that in mind, I headed over to the big table. She'd moved it from the side over to the window and covered it with books and bits of paper, and more books – in short made an awful mess. Lord only knows what Ethel thinks. All the same, there was enough there to make you think there must be something useful amongst it all – if you could ignore the straightened-out paper clips and elastic bands and empty biros with the ends chewed off. And I'll say this, when I picked up the first bit of paper that came to hand, and started to read, I actually thought I'd hit the jackpot. There it was, a whole page of little tiny writing (not that different from mine!) where certain words just seemed to jump out and hit you in the eye – words like Love and Desire – even the little word that begins with S and ends in X. Honestly, I didn't know where to look. Then gradually, it dawned on me. She wasn't writing about herself at all, but about the people in some book she was reading. Well that was a relief, but it took a minute or two to get over the shock.

I was still a bit shaky when I moved over to the mantelpiece. But it was no better here. Ethel's knick-knacks had all completely disappeared. Instead there were postcards, tens of them, arranged higgledy-piggledy along the shelf. Well, you can guess what I thought. Whatever else she was short of, it wasn't friends willing to remember her when they were off on their hols – or maybe it was just one special pal suffering from a travel bug. In other words – precious information. But when I looked at the back of one, and then another, and yet another, they were all blank. She must have bought them herself and stuck them up for show. In fact, looking at the pictures on the front, there wasn't a beach or palm tree in sight. They were all what some people like to call 'art', meaning they were mostly blurs and blobs and sawn-off guitars.

I can tell you, it almost made me cross, having my hopes raised like that. I thought I was going to learn something at last, and all I'd found out was that Mandy was odder in some ways than I like to admit.

In a nutshell then, I didn't find a single thing in that sitting room that was of the slightest help. So there was nothing for it but to proceed to the kitchen. Even here, though, I had a shock. It's only been four days since I was last in. Surely not long enough for all this. I'm talking about those blooming postcards. They were here as well, only worse, stuck to the wall wherever you looked like some creeping plague. You couldn't even open the fridge door without some nasty little figment of an artist's imagination practically biting off your hand.

Was this what one lone phone call could drive a girl to do? Namely turn her kitchen into a chamber of horrors overnight. Those pictures were the sign of an unhealthy mind. And when a girl starts posting this sort of stuff up beside her sink, it's a sign that she needs help, fast.

Unfortunately, that's just about all I did find there. If I told you her cupboards were bare as Old Mother Hubbard's it would be no more than the truth. All she had were these little bags of beans, all dried-up and nasty, and no difference between them and the gall-stones Harry had taken out and would insist on showing folk for ever after. Apart from that, not so much as a tin of sardines. I mean, even sardines might have been a clue to something – if you thought about it hard enough.

So there you are. I was afraid it would come to this. All the time I had been looking through her sitting room and kitchen there was always the hope that I would find something, anything, which would mean that I could leave it there and not look any further. But what was the use? Neither room had come up with a sausage. There was nothing for it now, I would have to carry on, open up the last door.

I suppose I must have known I would end up here, outside Mandy's bedroom. Remember June? If there was the least little thing she wanted to keep hidden, it was off to the bedroom every time. You always knew where to look. And if I was ever going to find anything to help me now, there really had only been one place all the time.

The trouble is, if I had any hesitation about walking into her lounge those few minutes ago, it was ten times worse now. I mean to say, bedrooms are private places. Call me over-sensitive, but nothing could have made me barge in without a second's thought. In the end I had to get a grip, even if it meant speaking sternly to myself. I actually said it aloud: 'All right, so it goes against the grain, but just you remember – this is for

Mandy, no other reason. So get on with it, Larry my boy. Open up the door.'

And that does it. Next thing is I'm doing what I should have done straightaway. I'm opening the door.

Only very nearly to close it again.

Did I say Mandy was odd? That was putting it mildly. And if ever proof was needed, go and stand in Mandy's bedroom. See what she's done to it. The ironical thing is, this was the one room you could almost describe as nice. The wallpaper here was roses, faded of course, but pretty enough. The curtains had roses on them too so you could nearly say that they matched. There was a frill round the bottom of the bed and another around the dressing table. In fact, it was a proper girl's room, the one you'd least expect anyone to want to change.

As I said, you should see it now. Remember the pictures on the walls, the one of the cats and the other with the horses on a ploughed field at sunset? Gone. And not just them either. You can't see the roses any more. She's gone and pinned up these great squares of material that take up nearly the whole wall – all zig-zags and stripes, in browns and blacks. Like the colour of the people who wear them. Because I'll tell you what they were. They were exactly the same things you see native women wrapping themselves up in because the missionaries never taught them how to wear decent clothes. That's what she has chosen to cover up her walls, and if that wasn't bad enough, she's got them on her bed as well. Which, by the way, used to be June's – right from the time she was a child. Look at it now, though, and you might not even be able to recognize it. But it was her bed all right. You only have to touch it the once, and the whole frame begins to shiver like one great big creaking rusty spring. And what with my bedroom being right above hers (in fact we're practi-cally room-mates when you think about it!) that's the very noise I have to listen to if Mandy so much as breathes heavily. Lord knows how she ever gets to sleep.

You can understand my state of mind though. It's not every day you become fond of someone only to discover that they seem to be a completely different person in private. I could quite easily have walked away from it with just one question left in my mind: how Ethel could be such a snob as to allow all this.

This is what stops me: the second thing that hits you when you walk in, only it takes a moment to sink in. It's the smell.

It's lovely. That's what's so surprising. No, really. It's a smell of scent and soap and talc, mixed up, dare I say it, with all the soot and traffic fumes from outside. Because believe it or not, as if the place wasn't chilly enough, the silly kid has actually gone out and left the window open. But it's still lovely. Grown-up, yet at the same time youthful as bubble bath. You wouldn't believe the effect a smell like that can have – coming at you when you're least expecting it. And it's familiar. I must have been catching whiffs of it every day since she arrived, only so faintly I never realized it was there. But now, with it coming at you in waves, you couldn't mistake it. It was Mandy all over. Shut your eyes and you could almost imagine she was there, looking over your shoulder, close enough to touch.

Of course that was being a little fanciful – talking as though she was a bar of soap or something. More accurate would be to say it was due to what she had scattered all over her dressing table, to the jumble of bottles and jars taking up just about every square inch. Another small wonder when you think of Ethel, letting her get away with it. A real girl's mess, but there it all was – the reason my Mandy smells like she does. Clean and fresh and smoky as a rooftop garden.

Get on with it, Larry.

I didn't close my eyes – even if I was tempted. I came into this room with a purpose and I never once forgot that. I just wanted to say that it's true, about smells being the most powerful influences of all. After a few seconds, however, I was back on form and ready for a proper look round. For want of a better place, I started with under the bed, got down on my hands and knees and everything, and found – nothing, just a couple of pairs of shoes with no heels to speak of and looking as if they could have belonged to a kid. Having had no luck there, I inspected her bedside table and it was the same story, only a pile of books so high it would probably have wobbled if you so much as looked at it. There she was again, then, my Mandy acting just like June, piling up all her books because she never knew which one she wanted to read before dropping off. We used to tell her, June, that she would ruin her eyes but she never listened. Now here was Mandy, just as bad. So that really only left the dressing table.

I can tell you now what I was looking for. I didn't know before, but now I did, seeing I was standing there with the influence of Mandy all around me, inspiring me as it were. I was looking for a photograph, that's what. A snapshot, no matter how blurry or old, of her parents maybe, a little souvenir of hearth and home. It would mean that even if I never found anything else, I'd come away having learned something just from looking at their faces and the way they smiled for the camera. And so it hit me – absolutely the queerest thing of all – in amongst those bits and pieces, the bottles and the boxes and the scarves and the beads, there wasn't a single photograph.

That threw me, I don't mind saying it. I even set off around the room again in case I'd missed something. I know they had quarrelled and all that, but you always have something up, even if it's just for show. And then suddenly, I had another thought. If this was June we were talking about, where would be the first place you'd look? In the drawer beside her bed. She could keep any number of photos there. Handy for those occasions when she's feeling just that bit sentimental. All she'd need to do was accidentally-on-purpose open the drawer, and there they would be, her mum and her dad, smiling at her as if nothing had happened.

Well, you know how it is when you get a good idea – I mean when one moment you're at a loss, and the next, a light goes on in your head – you don't think about anything else. The second this one hits me, I'm over by that table, pulling open the bedside drawer, just to see if I was right. The only thing on my mind was the snapshots, how the moment I opened the drawer there they would be, staring up at me, the way they would at Mandy. It was only when the drawer was open and I found myself, instead, gazing down at a letter, lying there without an envelope or anything, that I realized what I was doing, i.e. taking a peek inside somebody else's drawer. Something I never meant to do, not in a hundred years. Cupboards maybe, but not bedside drawers ... On top of which, there was the disappointment. See, there wasn't a snapshot in sight. Only this one letter.

Hence the little voice, the one that never would have been there otherwise, whispering in my ear, 'Oh well, Larry boy. You're here now. You might as well.'

But here's the difficult bit. I'd no sooner than picked it up when something else happened. The door behind me opened and someone walked into the room. I thought of Mandy, and straightaway I panicked.

The silly thing, the absolutely ridiculous thing about it was, I didn't need to panic. I had a perfectly good reason for being there, one I could have explained to anyone who knows me for the man I am.

But what if Mandy hadn't known me long enough? What if she got completely the wrong idea?

I say this in retrospect, to explain why I did what I did. It wasn't even a case of me stopping to think. All I knew was I had to get the letter back inside and the drawer shut, and me away from the drawer, as fast as was humanly possible. The mistake, though, was in trying to do everything at once. I threw the letter into the drawer, shut it, and jumped back from the bed, all in one smooth movement. Yet what happens next is horrible. Instead of ending up innocently on the other side of the room, I find I'm down on my knees again, below the level of the bed, choking and making a horrible noise. Because along with everything else, I'd slammed my tie inside the drawer, gone pretty near to strangling myself to death. I had to start all over again – open the drawer, retrieve my tie, and close the drawer – just to be able to turn around.

And all this, just to find Ethel Duck scowling across the bed at me.

But it could have been worse. That's what I told myself as I went about straightening my tie and getting the air back into my passageways. Of course I'd have rather she hadn't seen me picking my hairpiece off the floor and putting it back in place, but it could have been so much worse. If it had been Mandy there, for instance . . . You don't need me to tell you what the young are like. They would rather believe in Santa Claus than the truth when it comes from those who are old enough to know. So it could have been so very much worse.

Then again, looking at Ethel now, perhaps not. Not with the face she was wearing, and a mouth set like concrete, all ready to ask the very same question Mandy would have asked if she were here.

Well go ahead, Larry, I can hear you say. Tell her the truth. At least she knows you. But you should know it's not as simple as that, not with Ethel. She has a way of twisting the plain honest truth into something far nastier than lies could ever be. Some of her comments about me and Doreen for instance . . .

But it was no good thinking about the past, not when we were in the here and now, and Ethel was standing there, about to put me through the mill. What was needed right this minute was an answer to that still unspoken question – to explain what I was doing there, rifling through Mandy's private drawers. Only there wasn't one, at least not one that would satisfy. The fact is then, Ethel hasn't even opened her mouth, and yet here I am, scrabbling about inside my head for the word, any word, that will take the look off her face, knowing all the while that nothing I say will make a blind bit of difference.

And then it happened. A miracle. One moment I'm gazing across at Ethel, helpless, quivering under the axe, and the next it's just as if someone has switched on a thousand-watt bulb inside my head. It was as clear as that.

In short, I'm describing the way things look when you shine the Light of Truth upon them.

Ethel might well ask what I was doing in Mandy's bedroom, but what was to stop me asking her exactly the same question? Because the pure fact of the matter was, she didn't have any more right to be there than I did. In actual fact, she had much less right. And why? Because her only reason for coming in here was to snoop and pry, to touch things that weren't hers, and leave her marks all over them. But me – I was there for a different reason altogether. I was there for Mandy's sake and Mandy's sake only. And *that's* what gave me the right.

The effect is like magic. I stand up straight at last and just stare right back at her, as much as to say, 'Fire away, I'm ready for you.'

Ethel is speechless. Nothing like this has ever happened before, someone turning the tables on her. There was no telling what would have happened next. There's a horrible look in her eye, but I don't flinch, not for a second. My blood was up and I was ready for anything.

Downstairs in the hall, a door slammed.

Say no more. We must have been out of that room faster than you could have said knife. Not bad for a couple of OAPs. Mind you it was a full five minutes before I got my breath back. Meantime, downstairs, Ethel is having a go at Gilbert for getting out of his chair without a doctor's certificate – and nearly giving her a heart attack.

Looking back then, you might say it had all been a bit of a failure. Only that is where you would be wrong. Something very important happened down there in Mandy's bedroom. Today was a turning point. From now on, things are going to be different around here, because I've discovered a way to help Mandy more than she could possibly guess.

You see, as from today, Ethel isn't going to find it so easy to poke her nose where it doesn't belong. Why? For the simple reason that I'm going to be on the case. The moment Ethel finishes her rounds, I'm going to be straight down there after her. And whatever she touches, whatever she moves, Larry will be there, putting it all back where it belongs. I'll get to know the place like the back of my hand, learn where everything goes. That way, when Mandy comes home, she'll hardly know Ethel's been in. Of course, Ethel herself will know all about it. But what can she say? She can't even lock the doors. Larry's had his own keys since before she ever came. And she's never going to ask for them back. In the event of a fire and a locked door, who's going to break it down – Gilbert? Hardly. Who knows then, given all that, as well as our little meeting just now, she might even abandon the visits altogether. But Larry won't. He'll keep on coming, just to be sure, traipsing up and down those stairs for as long as his old legs will carry him.

And the result of all this? Mandy will be able to call the place her own again. Not that she'll know a thing about it. Because Larry will be going about his work in secret, without thanks, without praise, just doing what friends are supposed to do.

And one more thing. That letter, the cause of all the trouble; it wasn't very long. Short enough, luckily – or maybe unluckily, depending on your point of view – to take in at a glance, and think about later.

'Dear Ms Tyson,' was what it said. 'We regret the problems you describe at your present address, but we are unable to offer you anything by way of an alternative at this time. We can only suggest that you count yourself fortunate in the current climate in having anywhere to stay at all. Yours sincerely, etcetera etcetera, University Accommodation Office.

Or words to that effect.

Well of course it was a blow. You can see what she's been up to. I could have sworn the old kid was all settled. But I hadn't counted on Ethel, had I? Obviously she's driven the poor girl half out of her mind. They've given her short shrift, though, at that university of hers, telling her to be thankful for what she's got. All the same it's going to keep me awake tonight, knowing she's not a hundred per cent happy. It comes from thinking I must have let her down in some way. Quite clearly, she still doesn't know how much she is appreciated. Otherwise she'd never want to leave.

It's not something I like to think about, Mandy not happy, down there, by herself. Mandy always on the lookout for somewhere else to live. It's time she knew who her friends are, and fortunately Larry's got just the idea to put her in the picture.

Chapter Seven

Mission, as they say, accomplished.

You can say this about Larry Mann: he's only got to have an idea, and he'll be up and at it, making it happen. In other words, I'd no sooner made up my mind after that little showdown in Mandy's bedroom, than I was reaching for my coat. Not to mention my wallet. I didn't even stop to have my lunch.

I've been spending money. Not on any old rubbish though, forking out just for the sake of it. Larry knew what he had in mind before he so much as put a foot outside the door. After that, it was just a case of finding the right place.

Lucky for me – bearing in mind that I hadn't had that bit of lunch – I didn't have to go far. Two stalls up from Harry's pitch to be exact. You can find just about anything there, under the covers where Harry operates. You only need to know where to look. The other side of the coin was I had to go all the way round the world so as to avoid being caught by Harry, but that was no great hardship, considering the time I would be saving.

You see, there were other things I learned this morning as well, even if it didn't all register at the time. But later on, back upstairs, they were blindingly obvious – a couple of clues about the old kid that were just about as telling as anything she could have put into words. To wit, she's filled those rooms of hers with all sorts of awful junk – postcards, native clothes, books galore – yet she still doesn't have one or two items that most folk simply couldn't do without.

I'll give you an example. Half the world would never get up in the morning if it weren't for the old alarm clock banging away in their ear. Probably carry on and sleep till noon. But once they are awake, what's the first thing most people reach for, to make up for the fact? The radio, that's what. A little bit of music is a must. Most folk would just roll over and go back to sleep otherwise. What I'm saying is, show me one person who doesn't have a clock or a radio.

Well, I've found one. None other than our Mandy. Unbelievable, but true. And I tell you what, it explains why she's up at all different times of the day – and then is looking so down in the mouth for the rest of it. The poor girl hasn't got the barest essentials for living!

So having found this out, what does Larry do? Only march straight out and buy her the two of them combined. In other words – a clock radio. To be serious, it's a lovely little thing. Compact? You've never seen anything like it. And cheap. It's Japanese of course, but what can you do? They all are nowadays, and anyway, so is my organ, but that hardly detracts. The main thing is, it *looks* as if it cost a bomb. It's all in the design. Anything black, and you're made. To me, though, that's almost the best thing. If you want someone to know they're appreciated, it's no good giving them something that looks as if it just cost a few bob. It's got to look special. Because that's what I want Mandy to know – that she's special, and Larry thinks the world of her.

So what do you think? Will a girl like Mandy be able to ignore a present like this? Of course she won't. In one fell blow, the old kid is going to know who her friends are, once and for all.

Mind you, it went to my head a bit, handing over the money and getting such a thrill because of it. I didn't want to put my purse away after. I was a fool to myself really, going around just looking for something else to spend my money on. They can see you coming then. Anyway, all I did was stop to have a listen of the canaries – about fifty of them – singing their little hearts out on the pet stall, and the next thing I knew, I was opening my purse again. What you could sincerely call an impulse buy. The man said I should have two, to keep each other company. But I knew what he was up to, and besides, I'll be there, won't I – better than another bird any day. Mind you, I hadn't quite banked on the rest – the cage and the feed and the mirror etcetera. On top of all that, another blooming bird would have been almost incidental.

Still you've got to treat yourself now and then, and we're all home now. He – Joey – is on the organ next to the woodland animals, getting used to his new surroundings. Only trouble is, he doesn't seem too keen on singing at the moment.

But that's just by the by. The important thing is that right this very minute, sitting on Mandy's kitchen table is one small – or not so small – item that's going to change everything. And if I could have one wish now, it would be to see her face when the old kid gets home.

Then again, when does anything ever turn out the way you think it will? The answer, in Larry Mann's experience, is never. Yet as the person who knows her best in this house, I really should have suspected it. Never expect the obvious from Mandy.

There was something odd just in the way she came in this evening, something very unlike the Mandy we've got used to by now. It was there in the way she let the front door slam behind her and then came up the stairs with a racket you'd never think was her. It was as if she was letting on that she was home and didn't care who knew it. And you'll be telling me I'm daft now, but just for those few seconds I found myself thinking that if this was a normal night, and there was nothing waiting for her on the kitchen table, I wouldn't be seeing hide nor hair of her this evening either.

The funny thing is, though, right at the very top, she stopped, hesitated as if she was listening. It was as if she had sensed for herself that something was up. Then I could almost hear her shrug, open up her kitchen door, and walk in.

I was in my kitchen at the time, and I can honestly say that for the next three or four minutes I don't suppose I moved a muscle. I stood there with a dishcloth in my hand, straining for the slightest sound from downstairs – such as a squeak, or a squeal even. But that was just it. I didn't hear a thing, not even a whisper. In the end I couldn't bear it any more, and I knew I had to do something, anything, to take the stress out of the waiting.

Thankfully I had just the thing for occasions like this, and the only silly part was that I hadn't thought of it five minutes ago. I hurried into the lounge and lifted Joey out of the way. A touch of the switch and that wonderful organ of mine shivers into life. Lights glow and there comes the low hum that tells you it's awake and ready to go. The question now is what to play for her, but even that's not hard. A moment later the whole room, the entire house is swinging along to the only song for Mandy, the one that goes: 'If you were the only girl in the world'.

The effect is instant, magical and romantic. Not that romance figured, naturally. I'm only talking about the music. But the fact is, I forgot about what I'd been listening out for all this time, and gave myself up to the enchantment of the melody. And when that song ended, I launched into another, no! a whole medley – off the cuff – of all the old favourites: 'Moon River' and 'Yesterday' and 'Tie a yellow ribbon', while under the music, the organ hummed and winked its lights at me.

Then suddenly, the mood changed somehow. For no

reason at all I had the feeling that I wasn't alone. I stopped playing and turned around. *She* was standing there, had been for Lord knows how long. I'd been so lost in the music, I hadn't even heard her. And don't laugh – it gave me a real jolt, because it was just like a film, where someone plays his heart out for someone else, never realizing she's there all the time.

Then I saw her face, and before I know what's happening I've braced myself. Her face was wrong. The way I'd imagined things – and imagined them I had, down to the last detail – she was supposed to come running up here, the clock radio clasped in her arms, her face lit up with girlish joy. Well, she had the clock radio all right, but she wasn't holding it. It was there on the coffee table between us, closer to me than it was to her. And of course there was her face. The one thing I could say for sure about that was, girlish joy simply didn't come into it.

If only she had said something it would have helped. But that was the whole problem. She wasn't saying a word. She wasn't even looking at me, not as such. Having someone stare at the level of your cardigan is not the same thing. Just for a second then I had the wild hope that there was simply something nasty on my tie, but of course, when I took a quick peep, there was nothing. Mandy was just being Mandy – only more so.

And still she wasn't saying anything. I waited and waited, but nothing came out. It was up to me then. Trouble was, I didn't want to be the first. In the end though, there was nothing for it. We couldn't stand there for ever.

'Hello, stranger,' I said. 'What's this you've got here then?'

'You know very well, Larry.' Not a hint of a smile. She didn't even look up. My cardigan was still all that interested her. And that is when I realized that something had gone horribly wrong. But you know how it is when a situation begins to go haywire. You press on anyway, because you can't think what else to do. Trying your best to sound normal and cheerful when everyone else is acting like strangers. Sort of hoping that if you can only carry on regardless, it will all sort itself out . . .

So I said, 'Oh, you must mean the clock radio.' I think I even attempted a chuckle. 'What do you think of it then?'

And there it was – her last chance to turn all this around. Because that was her cue to say, *'Oh Larry, of course I mean the clock radio. As for what I think about it, what can I say? How can I ever thank you?'* Which would have been my cue for all sorts of things.

But I knew the moment the words were out of my mouth that it wasn't going to turn out like that. She didn't even try to answer me. She just moved forward a little and pushed the radio even closer to my side of the table.

Which all but did for me. Yet even then it didn't stop me trying to keep things on a level. 'You don't want to do that, Mandy love. It's yours, didn't you know?' Then, laughing to show I was joking, I gave the radio a little push back towards her and said, 'You're not trying to make me change my mind, are you?'

You know what she did as it came towards her? She jumped back, fast, as if it was all set to bite her.

Well, that was it. Finally I lost my nerve. 'Oh for Pete's sake, Mandy love, what's got into you? You're going to have me in all sorts of trouble in a moment. When a person doesn't know what to think there's no knowing where it might end. You don't realize what the strain can do to some folk. Say something, won't you?'

After which I don't know when I've ever heard such a silence. As far as I was concerned though, I'd said all

91

I had to say, I was that distressed. If Mandy didn't speak up, then that would have been all there was to it. There's nothing you can say when someone's refusing to take part.

As it turned out though, even Mandy couldn't leave it like that, and finally speak up she did.

'You're very kind, Larry,' I heard her say – just. She was that quiet. She sounded like she needed to clear her throat. 'You're very kind,' she said again. 'But I'm giving this back, do you understand?'

Well no, of course I didn't understand. How could I? In a normal world, you give a person the present of their dreams, and they come at you with thanks flying, not this, pushing the present back at you like it was the last thing they wanted.

'The radio's for you,' I said again. It was all I could say. 'That means you keep it.' It was like trying to explain something for the twentieth time to a backward kid.

'No, Larry,' she says. Now her voice is fainter than ever. 'It doesn't have to mean I keep it. I've tried to explain before, but this is worse than anything. You're making me feel . . . Oh how can I explain?'

'Try me,' is what I say.

Two little words, and yet they do the trick. For the first time she looks me in the eye, sees the expression on my face. And this is Mandy we're talking about, remember. And suddenly, out it all comes, enough words for a week. You could see that she had it all planned, but it didn't come out that way. For one thing, she was mumbling and muttering that badly it was just one great jumble. She was barely making any sense. But the point was, I'd got her talking.

It was exactly then that I started to feel a lot better. Give me a Mandy muttering, getting herself all confused, any day. It's a lot less worrying than the same girl standing there, not saying a word. You don't know what she might have stored up then. But now she'd got started, and what did it amount to? Precisely nothing. All you could see was someone getting herself into a right old state, talking about needing more space, or some such nonsense, as if she thought I could do anything about it. If the old kid felt she didn't have enough room, she should speak to Ethel. In the end, I did what anyone would have done. I put her out of her misery. Interrupted her before she broke down altogether and turned us both into nervous wrecks.

'Oh cheer up,' I told her. 'What do you want to go making such a fuss for? It's just a little present from Larry, that's all it is. Just take it in the spirit it's given.'

Harmless enough words, you may think, but you should have seen the effect on Mandy. All of a sudden, she stops her muttering and looks at me, straight in the eye. And *shouts*. 'Big, little, it's all the same. You keep on doing it, giving me things. It's driving me mad. Can't you see, what you're doing, it's not ordinary?'

Talk about the mouse that roared! Quite took me by surprise it did, Mandy suddenly upping the volume like that. Naturally, I was taken aback, but one of us had to stay calm. So I kept my cool, looked right back at her and said quietly, and maybe a little sorrowfully, 'I'm not with you, Mandy love. What is it that old Larry's been doing?'

And that, if I say so myself, was what you could call a reasonable question. Because if she answers that one, what can she do but go ahead with a little list of everything that's been done for her since the very first day she arrived? As for ordinary – well of course it's not ordinary. But imagine, trying to accuse a person of kindness! You'd sound as if you really had gone mad – or bad. Of course there are plenty of folk who can throw any number of good deeds back in your face and laugh while they're doing it – I was married to one – but not Mandy. Not my Mandy.

And sure enough, she stops right there, eyes wide like the proverbial deer. And while she flounders, trying to think of something to say, I watch and wait, patient as the day, for the answer to that one simple little question. Inside though, deep down where no-one else could hear, my heart was beginning to sing. Already I was making a mental journey to the cocktail cabinet, bringing out the sherry, settling down to a long lovely evening up ahead. You see, already there was a look in her eye that belonged to the old Mandy.

Then suddenly, she turned and ran out of the door.

Just like that.

For a second, it was as if I'd been turned to stone. All I could do was stare at the spot where she had been standing, too shocked even to think straight. It was the unexpectedness of it: one moment she had been there, on the very edge of turning back into her old self again, ready to thank me for her lovely present after all, and the next, she was gone. End of conversation.

Only it wasn't just a conversation that was ended. As the seconds passed I could see it all more and more clearly. Every friendship has its ups and downs, and they hardly mean a thing. You make up and it's all forgotten the next minute. But this friendship hadn't even got started, not properly. The fact was, we didn't know each other well enough to quarrel, not yet. A quarrel now would mean the end, full stop. No more Mandy, no more rosy evenings.

Yet we were meant to be friends, Mandy and me. We had too much in common not to be.

And that is when I really started to panic. And could you blame me? You can't plan for the unexpected, for sudden explosions that send all your hopes and expectations sky high. The only thing I knew for sure was, it was slipping away from me, all that future, all that friendship, going to pot.

Unless I did something to stop it.

And the truth is, even while all this was going on, and everything was chaos and confusion, I still managed to listen out, straining for the slightest sound that would tell me in which room she had ended up. At the back of my mind, something was telling me everything depended on that. If she was in her bedroom, then that was it. I couldn't follow her in there. But if she was somewhere, anywhere else, then I still had a chance.

A chair scraped along the linoleum. She was in the kitchen. That was all I needed. I snatched the clock radio from off the table and fairly threw myself downstairs.

Outside her kitchen door, I stopped, took a deep breath, and knocked, very gently. When there was no answer I knocked again. And when there was still no answer I opened the door anyway. She was standing beside the window facing me, as far away from the door as she possibly could be, and – silly girl – she was crying. I stayed where I was in the doorway but held the radio out towards her.

'I wasn't sure if you'd heard me knock, love,' I said. Then, quietly, 'I don't know why you had to get all upset there, I really don't. All I've ever wanted is for you to be happy here. In which case, what's wrong with old Larry trying to give you the odd present now and then? He's just trying to cheer you up. After all, that's only what friends are for.' And I looked at her, and this time I really let my feelings show – all the hurt, and the disappointment and the upset. I didn't try to hide a thing.

The next few seconds are almost more than I can bear, then suddenly it's all over. Mandy sighs – such a big sigh you'd swear that all the air was going out of her. To my way of thinking, it was as if she was breathing out those bad thoughts and feelings that had forced her to act the way she did. Then she raised her hand, just a little bit, before she let it fall, as if it was too heavy for her.

It was all the answer I needed, though. I walked in, put the radio on the kitchen table, and walked out again. All on tiptoe. Shut the door behind me.

I think I'll leave her for a while, just to get on with things. I do believe the poor girl may be having one of her blips, so-called. The bright side is, she's got the radio now. And try telling me that won't cheer her up.

Chapter Eight

I'll tell you in one word what it's been like since then. Lovely. And I mean it. Mandy and me, we've been getting on beautifully.

She comes up just about every night now. Got her own little routine and everything. First she has her supper, after which she does some work on those books of hers, and then, at last, it's up to see her old Larry – who will have been sitting counting the minutes. In fact, if Larry had any say in the matter, she'd be walking in the front door and straight up here. It's all waiting for her – light, heat, a proper TV, everything. She could have her bit of supper with me, and then do her homework in the corner under the light. Try suggesting that to her, though, and she'll start to get bashful, coming up with all sorts of excuses. Still a touch flighty is our Mandy.

I won't hear a word against her though. It's just that it upsets me some nights when it's arctic cold outside and I know she's down there, huddled up next to a gas fire that's barely on, due to her economizing. Those are the times when she should be up here with Larry, snug as a bug. And it would save her having to wear those big ugly jumpers of hers.

But there you are. That's girls for you, isn't it. It's bound to come out even in the best of them now and then. Most nights, though, she's a perfect dream. She'll come here, and before she does anything else she'll make for Joey's cage. It just so happens that the very first time he sang was when she was there goggling at him through the bars, and now she thinks she should take all the credit. So the first few minutes are about the two of them chattering away to each other as if they could understand every word. Like a big kid she is really. In the end, I have to be firm and throw the cover over the cage otherwise they would be there all night, leaving a certain other party unable to get a word in edgeways.

But it's when she comes and sits down, next to me at the other end of the settee, that the evening really begins. I wish someone could see us then, with the gas fire flickering, and the TV on, high or low depending on what's showing. It would be a picture, I reckon, the sort a man like Harry could only dream about. Then we'll stop here and chat for ages, forget all about the time.

I say 'we', but of course it's me really, doing all the talking. She doesn't say much as a rule. You have to understand that that is her choice, though. She knows she'd only have to open her mouth and Larry would be all ears. But that's not her way. You see, my Mandy is that rare creature – a woman who wasn't simply put on this earth to talk. I don't mean I'm the sort who always wants to hold the floor. There are a fair old number of things I'd like to ask her myself – like what she was doing in Edinburgh, what she gets up to when she's at home with her mum and dad, who was that person on the phone – just the normal polite run-of-the-mill type of questions. And I keep on meaning to ask them, honestly, but it's the time – always against you. I'll look at the clock on the mantelpiece, and blow me if another hour hasn't passed and already she's getting up to go.

But you know what? I reckon the real reason she doesn't say much isn't because of me or the time. I reckon it's all to do with the type of girl she is. Never the sort to keep bringing the conversation round to herself. And quite right too. I mean, what would she have to talk about? She's got to be twenty-two, twenty-three at most. She's a blank page, one of Nature's innocents. And that's what makes her so different.

What's harder to put into words though, is the *way* that she listens. Women like Ethel and Doreen, they'll only stop quiet long enough to give a man time to make a fool of himself. Their brand of silence is the sort you learn to watch out for. And then you have Mandy, and the way she has of never saying a word. How can I describe it? It's like an invitation, drawing you out, making you say things wild horses wouldn't drag from you normally. And the result? I've been telling that girl things I've never put into words before.

For the first time in twelve long years, Larry is giving his side of the story. It's his turn now and he's hardly begun. And I don't mince my words, oh no. When it's a woman like Doreen you're talking about, there's no sense in coming on all forgiving. If the thought of her is alone enough to make your blood boil, then why hide it? Mandy, bless her, she just listens. The only sound you'll hear from her is that first one, that little squeak cum sigh that's like ointment on the ears.

Except that one time. Our one and only misunderstanding.

I suppose I'm talking about two nights ago. We were sitting up here, chatting away as usual, but this time things are even more conducive because earlier on I'd actually made a tape of me playing the organ, so – voilà! as they say on the Continent – I was able to talk and give us something to enjoy at the same time.

There was only one tiny fly in the ointment. The old kid clearly wasn't herself. I'd have said she was quiet, except 'quiet' would hardly be the right word, given that she's always that. But it was there all right. Something to do with the way she was sitting, maybe. Sort of fidgety, not at all restful. What's more it was distracting, trying to go on chatting while someone acts like they can't keep still long enough to hear what you've got to say. In the end, I just thought she must be sickening for something – a cold most probably, which would hardly be surprising when you think of all the times I've warned her about not coming upstairs to the warm like she should. What she needed was something to take the edge off it before it got started. And there it was, right on the tip of my tongue – *care for a whisky, Mandy love?* All I had to do was get to the end of what I was saying first. Only I never had the chance, did I, because for once, the unexpected happened. Mandy goes and interrupts.

Now, before you say anything, I am well aware that interrupting someone in mid-flow is not a criminal offence – at least, not in my book. But it wasn't the fact that she interrupted that shook me; it was what she said. Listen to this:

'Larry?' she says. 'Why do you have to keep calling her that?'

'Calling who, what?' I replied. You see, I hadn't quite got her drift, not yet.

'Doreen,' comes the answer, cool as a cucumber. 'You've already told me it's been twelve years since she left. Yet all the time you're talking about her, it's always "my wife" this and "my wife" that. I mean, you're probably divorced or something by now, so why not just call her by her name? It might be easier like that. You know, a way of . . . letting go of some of that anger. You might be happier then.'

I leave you to imagine the effect. For a few seconds all I could do was stare at her. That's how shocked I was. What did she think I'd been telling her about all this time, I want to know. Someone stepping on my toes in the bus queue? I'm talking about a way of life. Of slights and torments and someone queening it over you for thirty-five years. Not to mention the ultimate betrayal. You don't 'let go' of something like that as if it was just a snapshot of somewhere you didn't much like. And I was about to say so, in no uncertain terms. Only then in a cold flash it hits me: Mandy and me, we haven't even been speaking the same language.

I must have got to my feet, then, all set to show her the door, and maybe a side of Larry she'd never seen before. That would have given her something to think about. Then I saw it, the look on her face. By which I mean a look that was nothing but pure Mandy. She didn't have to say a thing. Biting her lip she was, and no doubt wishing it was her tongue. In short, the girl did understand and was sorry, really sorry.

All right, I'll own up, I was soft. I didn't throw her out. I sat down, gave it a few seconds, then carried on just as if nothing had happened. And that helped, because if it's Doreen you're in the middle of discussing, anyone else is going to shine by comparison, even Mandy. And what I want you to remember is this: she's only a kid, and what's more important, a kid with a heart in the right place – most of the time. The fact is, we all make mistakes, even the best of us. What's needed is a bit of tolerance and understanding. In other words – forgive and forget.

And I'll say this for her, she's been as good as gold ever since.

So no complaints then. Just a few suggestions as to how she could be even better. The first being that she could surely spend less time shut away in that college of hers. She talks about having to go in for lectures, but that doesn't mean she has to be there all day. In fact, there's nothing to stop her being home by lunch time, back here, where she belongs. According to Madam, though, she needs the rest of the time to prepare – in other words, to do her homework. But this is what I'd like to know: what is the point of homework if you don't do it at home? If you asked me, she'd get more

101

done here, in her own environment, than staying there with all the riff-raff that hang around the place to distract her.

But what really bothers me is the way she's still coming in at all hours.

I've tried to tell her how I feel. She knows I sit here worrying when it's way after nine and still she hasn't showed up. But I've yet to see it make a difference. It's the little kid in her of course – too young to understand what there is to worry about. I could talk till I was blue in the face about the dangers out there, but you can see the way her mind works, whispering it will never happen to her.

I tell you what, though, one of these days I'm going to have a good hunt through my drawers. I'm sure I've still got some old cuttings from the time. Both times. You never know, reading about it for herself, hearing about all the hoo-ha it caused, what with Ethel going on about how no-one was safe in their beds – as if it had actually happened inside this very house – it might just bring it home to her.

Then again, there's usually a bright side to everything. The fact is, if she was here more, I wouldn't get half as much done. This is the bit about the last two weeks I've kept till last, the bit I'm most proud of. I mean the work I do for her, for Mandy.

Not that the girl has any idea. It's the sort of work they used to talk about all those years ago in Sunday school, the left hand not knowing what the right was doing. In other words, she doesn't know a thing about it. There's no other way it could be, bearing in mind that my Mandy must be the only girl in the world you can actually embarrass with kindness. So I do what I do, and spare her the rest.

First job of the day then: to keep a good ear out for the front door in the morning, followed by the sound of Ethel on her rounds. After that it's my turn. I start off in the kitchen. To my mind it's always the kitchen that's the problem. If Ethel's been moving it all around, there's hardly any way of knowing how to put it back. But that's only one of my jobs. The rest has nothing to do with Ethel. It's a case of checking the plugs and making sure nothing's been left switched on. The last thing she'd want is to cause a fire. We'd all be burned to a crisp and she would have to live with that for the rest of her life. Then there's the pilot light above the sink to see to and after that a quick peek at the contents of her fridge. If she's low on anything like milk, or marge, it's a warning to me to get something extra for upstairs, just in case . . .

After that it's on into the lounge for more plug checks and what you could call the real fine-tuning, the bits and pieces that Mandy herself would never think or know about – because she doesn't have to. But one of these days she should ask herself why it is she never needs to go looking for a biro or a hanky or that bit of loose change like most of us have to. The reason of course is Larry, down on his hands and knees often enough, fishing them out from between cushions and under chairs where they would be lost for ever otherwise. Little things in themselves, but it all adds up. She'd soon notice if I stopped.

And that just leaves the bedroom.

I come to that last. You'd hardly credit it now when you think of the shock of the first time, but it's my favourite room. I've even got used to the junk she has hanging up – well, nearly. And there's no nonsense now about being shy of going in there. I walk in and out as natural as the day. Because I know exactly what she'd say. *Thank you Larry, thank you so much.*

Not that there's ever anything to do when I get there. Apart from the awful jumble on her dressing table, you can't fault her. The bed is always made, shoes tidy, drawers closed – in other words, ten out of ten. I come away saying to myself, 'Well done, Mandy girl. Keep up the good work.'

But I'll never stop going in there. Because one of these mornings, she's going to be so dozy or in such a hurry she'll forget to make that bed. Or else leave a hairdrier switched on, or the electric blanket – if she had one – something, anything that would be guaranteed to have Ethel down on her like a ton of bricks. And that's when Larry will come into his own, putting it all right before anyone knew it was wrong, saving the day. In the meantime, I'll stay with it, keeping up the good work, and let that thought be its own reward.

The best times though are when I accidentally on purpose meet up with Ethel, there on the middle landing. I'll tell her I've come to check a plug or mend a fuse, and there's not a word she can say. She can try to carry on with what she's doing, pretending that she's the queen of all she surveys, but it's never going to work. Not when Larry's there, a living reminder that these rooms belong to someone else, bought and paid for.

You must be wondering how I find the time really, but you know what they say: if you want something done, ask a busy man. And the result? I'll tell what it is. At long last, the old kid has got some privacy in this house. No-one goes in those rooms without her say-so, poking and nosing through her belongings on the sly. In short, her life's her own.

Thanks to me.

Chapter Nine

So now I bet you're thinking old Larry is a right idiot.
Well, laugh as much as you like, only excuse me if I
make one thing clear. All that about Mandy, about her
breaking the mould and not being like the others —
well, I knew it wouldn't last. And more fool you if you
thought any different. You had only to ask and I'd have
told you. Larry's seen too much not to know something
was bound to come along and spoil it all. But if I do
seem a bit dazed just at this minute, blame it on her.
Because after the show she put on, she very nearly had
me wondering.

The point I want to get across is, I might not actually
have said anything at the time, but I had my doubts, I
did really. Look at the people she was being forced to
mix with for a start, up at that college of hers. Her
seeming to be so nice herself only made it ten times
worse. Bad always wants to go after good. It's the way
of the world.

That's why I didn't worry about the fact she never
brought folk back here. I just liked to think she was
choosy. Added to which it was a relief, not having the
house deluged by strangers, never knowing what they
might be carrying away with them in their pockets.
Thinking about it now though, I reckon 'choosy' didn't
come into it. The girl is as poor as a church mouse, and
you need money for friends.

Of course once or twice she's tried to make out that it
hasn't always been like that, going on about some pal
of hers up in Edinburgh, as if the whole place was

queuing up to know her. To tell the truth, though, I couldn't bring myself to show that much interest. She was talking about people hundreds of miles away, and besides, she had me, didn't she. There wasn't any call for anybody else. No, it was present influences I was losing sleep about at nights.

And I was right, wasn't I? There's influences every- where, even in this house.

I'd better start at the beginning. Go back a week, to just after the time I talked about everything in the garden being rosy. We were up here as usual, settling down for a good old chat before bed. It all started off normally enough. I'd been sorting through some drawers earlier on and come across an old photograph I didn't even know I still had. You can more or less imagine what I'd done with the rest. Anyway, it's there in front of her when she sits down, and sure enough, she picks it up.

'What's this, Larry?' she says. 'Are you here?'

'Mandy love,' I say, all surprised. 'You weren't meant to see that. But since you ask, it's me all right. Me and a few others. Go on, see if you can guess which one?'

She's got about ten to choose from, all of us in uniform, so it takes a little time. Finally she points.

'That one,' she says.

And that was my Mandy for you. Spot on. Fifty years and she still knows her old Larry. A couple of seconds pass and then she says, 'Good grief, Larry. You were quite handsome.'

'That's what they used to say, love. But only look where it got me. A little bit less of the handsome, and maybe there wouldn't have been so much of the Doreen. Know what I mean?'

Well she doesn't answer, because already she's staring at the rest of the picture. Not much of an attention span, has our Mandy sometimes. 'What about

106

the rest of them, Larry? What happened to them?'

'All dead, love,' I said. Well, it was simpler that way. Otherwise she'd have wanted all their life stories, and look at the time that would have taken. But the effect is exactly what you'd hope and expect.

'Oh Larry, I'm sorry. How terrible for you. Where did it happen – North Africa?'

Well hardly. It's the sand that's got her confused. That was taken on Bridlington beach, and we were the catering corps. The war ended before we ever got posted. But there's no time to say a word about this because a certain young lady is still talking.

'All so young, Larry. Were they very good friends?'

'Best friends a chap ever had, love.'

Actually, Harry's there if you look close enough. But she's not to know that. The thing is, what should happen next but she reaches forward and touches my hand, just like that.

And that really did take me by surprise. I was still trying to think of something polite that wouldn't have offended, when all of a sudden comes the Voice from Below, to ruin everything.

'Amanda! Telephone!'

Telephone! Would you believe it, I'd forgotten all about warning the old kid that the last thing she should be doing was telling people to ring her here. Ethel would really go mad with her now. But again it was no good. The girl had vanished before I could open my mouth.

This time though, I decided to keep calm. She was gone now, but she was going to hear it from me straight the moment she got back. Then I remembered: the last time she went to answer a phone call, I didn't see hide nor hair of her for days after – and nearly made myself ill fretting about it.

Well, this time, it was going to be different. I decided to do what I should have done before if I'd had the sense, namely, to follow her downstairs and wait for her in the hall. That way, when she'd finished getting herself into trouble with Ethel, I'd be right there to keep her company back up the stairs. Then we could have that cup of tea I'd been on the very point of offering her. And most important, I could tell her all she needs to know about Ethel and telephones.

So that's what I did. I left my nice warm lounge and lumbered all the way downstairs just so as to stand sentry by the hall table. That's friendship for you; hundreds I could mention would have felt one blast of that draught blowing in through the front door and been back up those stairs like a shot. You could hardly blame me for hoping she wouldn't take all night about it, though. Quite apart from the draught there was Ethel, like there always is. If she came out while Mandy was still on the phone, there would have been all sorts of questions. Quite simply, there is no limit to the woman's nosiness.

It was only natural then that I'd be anxious to keep an eye on what was going on at the end of the passage leading to the kitchen, not knowing if it was Mandy who was going to appear any second, or Ethel. And that's when I noticed that the door was open, that I could see straight in. That was unusual for a start. Ethel guards her kitchen like Fort Knox, only just now she wasn't there. She must have carried on into the scullery beyond, leaving Mandy to let in all the cold air – which would be something else they'd be chalking up against her. Of Mandy I couldn't see a thing. The Ducks keep their phone up on the wall behind the door, and that's where she was now, murmuring away on the other side, apparently not short of something to say for once. The one person I could see, and see all too well, was Gilbert, sitting next to the fire, facing me. In normal circumstances he would have seen me too, eyesight or no eyesight, but not today, for the simple reason that he was making a great show of reading. It was laughable really; he had his book held right up in front of his nose – *Tales of the South China Sea* – but the only wonder was that he'd remembered to keep it the right way up. See, he didn't fool me for a second. What he was really doing was listening, getting an earful of every blessed word.

So there you are. The poor girl couldn't even have a phone call to herself without one or the other of the Ducks having their pennyworth. Which was bad enough when you think about it. It's just that it wasn't a tenth as bad as what happened next.

I heard the phone go 'ping', meaning that she must have finished at last, and sure enough, a second later she appears from behind the door. The surprising thing was, she was beaming all over her face, which was hardly what you would have expected from someone who had just been forced to share a private conversation with some nosy old goat under a tartan blanket. Nor would you have expected her to waste any time getting out before Ethel popped up to call her to account. Yet the silly girl did no more than go straight over to Gilbert and stand there for a good minute smiling and chatting away as if he was her favourite uncle. He loved it of course. You could see the old buffoon just lapping it up. And it was that, I reckon – I mean her being so pleasant – that must have given him ideas. Because just as she was turning to go (and another minute and I would have been in to drag her out myself) the book he was holding suddenly slid off his lap and to the floor. It landed at her feet, far too conveniently to have been an accident, and like a flash, Mandy, being the girl she is, was bending to pick it up.

And that's when it happened. The thing I'm talking about. He goosed her.

Blink, and you'd have missed it, it was that fast. One

second he's sitting propped up with cushions on all sides and a blanket on top, and the next he's there with his hand right up her skirt. If I say I was shocked beyond words, you'll understand, but the effect on Mandy was almost too painful to describe. Her head shot up from where she was bent over the book with the result that she must have been looking straight at me, yet she was too flabbergasted to notice a thing. All I could see was her face as it was then, mouth shaped into a perfect 'O' and two bright red cheeks flaming up like matches on either side. Just for that one second I was certain she was going to scream, faint, shout, do something that would bring Ethel scurrying in from whatever she was up to in the scullery, and with it the world down upon her head.

I knew then I had to warn her, tell her not to do it, let her know that if she made a sound, Ethel would have her out on the street so fast she wouldn't even have time to pack. But somehow or other, the words wouldn't come. The shock was too great.

Then suddenly, there was no need. Mandy closed her mouth, snap! just like that. She stood up straight and handed the book to Gilbert, as politely as you please and yet without so much as a word or a look. Then slowly she turned her back on him and walked towards the door — and me. For my part, I'd already backed off so as not to be seen by Gilbert, was standing flat up against the wall in the gloom. But that could hardly explain how she could have walked straight past me, and yet not said a word. The fact was, she didn't even see me. And why not? Because she was too busy laughing, laughing so much, and at the same time, trying so hard to keep it quiet that the whole of her body was shaking with it and tears were forcing themselves down her cheeks. She laughed all the way up the passage and into the hall, and continued up to the top of the stairs. And all this time I was right behind her, watching, too stunned to say a thing. Before I was even halfway able to speak she had disappeared into her kitchen and closed the door behind her, leaving me standing there, wondering if the entire world had gone mad.

Of course, I thought it was nothing but a nervous reaction on her part. People do the strangest things when they're in shock. Especially the innocent ones. See what I mean about Bad going after Good, though, corrupting it? Making a young girl laugh because she's been indecently assaulted? And in this house of all places. I could always have told you Gilbert was rotten – I just didn't know how rotten.

You're not going to be surprised to hear then that Mandy didn't come up again after this. I hardly expected her to myself. But then again, Gilbert's behaviour had left me in a terrible state. I couldn't get the picture out of my mind, of hands disappearing under the pleats of her skirt. Right up it was, right up between her . . . it's no good, I can't say it. But it stayed with me all evening, no matter what I did to try and forget. And you know what made it ten times worse? It was the thought of that poor girl, all by herself downstairs with who knows what thoughts going through her head, and no-one to confide in. In the end, round about eleven, I heard her footsteps on the landing, and couldn't bear it a moment longer. If I did nothing else this night, I had to remind the old kid that there's still some decent folk left on this earth.

The upshot was I just about collided with her on the landing. She was coming out of her kitchen wearing nothing but a dressing gown and a towel over her arm.

'Can't stop Larry,' she said as we both stepped back from each other. 'My bath's going to be ready in a sec.' And with that she made to walk past me towards the bathroom as if nothing in the world was the matter. You should have seen the way she smiled, though. It was heartbreaking, that's what it was. You could see she was trying so hard to put a brave face on everything, fighting not to let her real feelings show. All the more reason, it seemed to me, for not simply letting it go at that. So instead of allowing her get past, I sort of spread myself across the landing a bit, just to make her slow up a little, give us both the chance to talk.

'Everything all right, then, Mandy love?' I said, as casually as I could. Yet if only the light had been better, she could have seen the worry and concern written all over my face. As it was, she didn't seem to notice.

'Fine,' she said. If I'd asked her about the weather, she couldn't have given much more away. 'Thanks for asking.' And with that, she actually tried to squeeze past me.

Well I had to do something. I caught hold of her arm, looked straight into her eyes and said, 'Now just stop there, Mandy love. Listen to your old Larry for a minute. Are you sure you're telling me everything? There's nothing happened to ... to upset you recently?'

The straightforward questions are always the best. This one wiped the smile right off her face. But even then she didn't say anything, just stared down at her arm where I was holding it as if something about it was different. Then her face lit up and she was all smiles again.

'Oh, I see. You're talking about the phone call. Did you think it was bad news? Honestly, I don't know why you had to go worrying yourself, Larry. It was good news, the best I've had in I don't know how long. Remember that friend I told you about once, the one who lives away up in Edinburgh?' She didn't even wait for me to nod – or shake my head, for that matter. 'Well next weekend I'm having a visit. Just four days from now. I know it's not long, but oh, I can hardly wait.'

'Oh,' I said. 'Oh.' And after that I couldn't think of a thing to say. Until finally I came up with, 'Coming all that way just for the day, this pal of yours?'

That wasn't meant to be a joke, so there was no need for her to laugh like that. But laugh she did. 'Four hundred miles, just for the day? Oh Larry, of course not. How could you think such a thing? I'm talking about the whole weekend – Friday to Sunday. It wouldn't be worth it otherwise, would it?'

'No,' I said faintly. 'No I suppose not.' And it was then, laugh or no laugh, that my heart started to bleed for the poor kid. 'Mandy, love,' I said at last. 'You know, I'm awfully sorry to be the one to tell you this, but Ethel's not going to have it – not if your friend's planning to stay here. It's just not her way, love. You thinking otherwise, well, it just shows what a lot you've got to learn. Why, I can remember . . .'

She never even let me finish. 'It's all right Larry. You see I've already had a word with Mr Duck. He says there'll be no problem. He's going to talk to Mrs Duck. But he said she wouldn't mind at all. So you see, nothing to worry about.'

And with that, she gave her arm a little shake and squeezed right past me into the bathroom. Shut the door behind her. A few seconds later you could hear the water heater explode with the sort of racket that would have sent all the other girls flying back into the passageway. Not Mandy though.

In other words, I'd been given the brush-off, had all that sympathy and concern thrown right back in my face. Yet would you believe it, even now, I couldn't shut off worrying about her. The next thing is I'm standing with face pressed up against the door trying to make myself heard above the roaring and hissing from inside. 'Mandy, love,' I said. 'You just watch out with that Ascot. If it starts playing up, you give me a shout. I could even wait out here if you like . . .'

But there wasn't any answer. I suppose there was too much noise for her to know I was there. But downstairs, the kitchen door opened, and there was that quiet which comes over the house when Ethel's on the prowl, wanting to know what's going on. Come to think of it, I could have told her a thing or two.

Still, if you think that was bad enough, wait for the rest. Because that was when the rot really set in. Nothing between us was the same after that, and I'm not just talking about Gilbert.

The problem was the girl herself. Mandy. It's no use making any bones about it. She was the one that got me worried. Only how do I explain what nobody else would understand? You would have had to know her the way I do. To see her in those next few days – it was a case of bright eyes and a smile for everybody, never a frown or a cross word. You'd have thought it would do your heart good seeing her like that. But what you've got to remember is, there's a difference between controlled high spirits, and the state she was in just then. It was unnatural. She couldn't stay put more than five minutes. Sit her down, and she'd be up again, looking for an excuse to get going. Wednesday night, I don't know why she bothered coming up at all. She'd no sooner arrived than she was leaving, going on about all the college work she had to do so she could have the weekend free.

Of course, it all came down to The Weekend. You'd have sworn it was a mixture of Christmas and birthday rolled into one the way she was behaving. Pretty soon it was starting to loom large in my eyes too, but not in the same way. Right from the start I was wishing we'd never had it crop up. Half the problem was having to watch the girl act in a way that's just not like her. And the other half was concern. She hasn't lived long enough to know what Larry found out half a century ago – namely, the more you let yourself get excited about something, the bigger the let-down.

But one other thing couldn't help but cross my mind, watching her struggle home last night, Thursday, with a load of shopping on each arm: she'd never gone to this much trouble for anyone else. She's never even offered a certain person so much as a biscuit. Now here was this friend of hers about to get the whole treatment, by the look of it.

But it was her I was thinking about really. Worried all the time that this friend of hers might cancel, and what I'd have to do to cheer her up. But come this morning, Friday, I decided a new attitude was called for. Now that the big day had arrived and it didn't look as if there was going to be any cancellation to disappoint, maybe it was time to start giving this friend the benefit of the doubt. In other words, it was time to think in terms of there being the three of us here instead of the two. After that, it only took a bit more effort to start looking on the bright side. If this friend – who *was* a friend of Mandy's after all – turned out to be only half as nice, the chances were the three of us would get on like a house on fire.

That's why, just before lunch, I popped out and did some shopping for us three – just in case.

Only, what is it they say – *There's no fool like an old fool*? That's it, isn't it?

Coming home, I reckon I was more loaded than Mandy was last night. I couldn't have got any more into my carrier. Chock-a-block it was with all the things that young girls like. Angel Delight (various flavours), gypsy creams, French fancies, Viennese whirls – it was all there. Not that Mandy is all that easy to tempt when she's by herself; it's hard enough to get a cup of tea down her normally. But I thought, once

115

she saw her friend tucking in, the chances were she might do the same.

So I'd done my bit in one sense, then. But there hadn't been time to get downstairs for my rounds this morning – though doubtless Ethel would have been in before me – so the first thing I did was nip back down to the middle landing to see if there was anything for me to do. And straightaway I noticed. There were flowers, everywhere, stacks of them, stuck up in jugs in every room. Don't ask me how many there were or what kind, just ask yourself the number of bus rides she could have had for what they must have cost.

What I do know is, the moment I set eyes on them, and caught the whiff of them in the back of my throat, I could feel myself getting unsettled. It was so – how can I put it – out of character for Mandy.

And that wasn't all. There was the sheer amount of stuff on her larder shelves, half of which I'd never even seen in the shops before. I mean, anchovies. What would young girls want with anchovies?

After that, the day just seemed to go on for ever. I've never known one like it. Then, as if she was trying to make matters worse, Mandy seemed to have forgotten about coming home. All I could do was sit here, watching the clock, waiting for something to happen.

Then at last, on the dot of ten, I heard it – the sound of the front door. I could hardly have missed it. The wind must have snatched it out of someone's hand, and slammed it shut with an almighty crash that shook the entire house. Not that I minded. You could forget the din, at least the waiting was over.

Then there's Mandy's voice in the hall, not just talking, but chattering away, nineteen to the dozen, and *every word clearly audible* despite there being two flights of stairs and a landing between us. And the first thing that hit me was – this was not the Mandy I know, the one who tiptoes between rooms as if she's scared of disturbing the mice. This was a different Mandy altogether.

If you'd heard her, you would understand why it was I couldn't move, why I just stayed where I was, clutching the side of the sink wondering what to do next. The plan had been to toddle on down the moment I heard them, introduce myself on the stairs and save Mandy the embarrassment. But suddenly I couldn't do that now, not with a Mandy I didn't know.

Then, blessed relief, she actually stopped talking. Maybe she had run out of breath, or even – and here was a thought to brighten me up no end – that was the end of it; she had calmed down. Excitement over. In which case, I could go and shake hands all round, offer them a warm fire, even a cup of hot chocolate seeing it was so late . . .

And then it happened.

Another voice, picking up where Mandy's had left off. Not saying very much – no more than half a dozen words. But that's all it took to turn the world upside down.

You see, it was a man's voice.

It was no good trying to think. Thinking was the last thing on my mind. 'Mandy,' I shouted. 'Mandy love is that you? Are you all right?'

The words were out before I could stop them. Downstairs everything went quiet. Then Mandy's voice floated up, awkward, like you'd expect, scarcely loud enough to be heard, yet at the same time, clear as a bell. 'Of course it's me, Larry. Who did you think it was?'

And that was a small shock in itself. Because it was exactly the sort of thing Doreen would have done – answer a question with a question. Twisting your words right back at you. You can't win.

And she knows it. A second later there comes her voice again, only louder this time. 'Larry, that friend of mine is here. Would you like to come down and say hello?'

To which the answer was most definitely, most emphatically and positively 'no'. Larry had been all set to meet a young woman. Had waited here all day to make her welcome for Mandy's sake. A girl, that is, not a man. Never, for one second, a man.

But what could I do? I let go of the banister, said goodbye to the good times, and made my weary way downstairs.

Chapter Ten

At first all I can see is Mandy. For the simple reason it's impossible to take my eyes off her. I'd seen something of the way she could change before this – quick flashes of temper lighting up her cheeks, the same when she's excited. But it never lasted. One well-chosen word, and all that unnatural colour would simply drain away and she'd be her sweet pale self again. Not now, though. Even in this light you could see it was here to stay. She was rosy as a child who's run all the way home from school, the exact same colour Doreen used to be when she'd go out night after night and tell me she had been visiting her cousin. The trouble being, her cousin didn't know anything about it. Her eyes are as bad, still sparkling from the cold and the traffic fumes – and something else again. For the first time ever you could imagine men noticing her in the street. Only what I would say to them would be: walk on by. Because I know all about what goes on behind those sort of eyes and that sort of colour. Better not to look. Except I have to, just in case she's still there, somewhere, Mandy, my lovely pale girl.

And then she smiles at me, and straightaway I know she's gone. My Mandy never laughs at me when she smiles.

So it's almost a relief to look past her, and see who's there instead. As if even a stranger would be less strange than the girl who was standing where Mandy should be. Besides, it might only have been a minute since the whole world was turned on its head, but I was already getting used to the idea. I knew what to expect – a boy, the same age as her, another kid.

It was a small certainty – I hadn't even put it into words as such – but it was comforting in its way. Knowing what to expect in all this mayhem. And at least we knew where those jumpers of hers had come from.

Which only made it worse when I saw what was really there.

There was no boy here. Standing behind her was a man, I repeat, a man. By which I mean not a day under forty, older than that even.

'Larry,' says Mandy. 'Larry, this is Francis. Francis, this is Larry.'

I didn't shake hands. What reason was there? He didn't make a move towards me. In any case, I was too busy looking. Trying to get it straight. I can only seem to take in the bare essentials. He's tall and dark, with a lot of hair. His own.

But I still have ears. In a crisis they can sometimes tell you more than eyes. So I don't miss a trick when he casts a look in my direction and says, 'Aha. So this is the famous Larry. Amanda's told me all about you.' He's doing an impression of a man who's just lifted the stone off some interesting wildlife. And to go with it, the voice. Fancy accent. Officer class. Although this man has never been in the army.

I expect Mandy's waiting for me to say something, but she can wait for ever as far as I'm concerned. I'm still too busy, listening to that voice, trying to see my way past it, and what I suppose would pass as good looks, all the time trying to get through to what's really there. And it's coming, it's dawning on me. I'm beginning to put him together. His eyes are set too close, his nose is too long. When I said he was dark, I meant it. There might even be foreign blood there. What's more, that tweed jacket of his might set off his shoulders just nicely, but I reckon there's not an ounce of muscle on him. And I'll tell you this for nothing – Doreen wouldn't have thought much of him, not after the first impression.

But what you can't get away from is the fact that he's so sure of himself. Confident. That's what they all are, men like him. He knows what I'm doing, but he doesn't give a monkey's. He's said his hello, now he's just pretending that I'm not there, the way these people can. Namely, the upper classes. In others you'd call it plain ignorance. However, he can't move while I'm still there, taking up all the space, not budging till I've looked at him, and then looked at him some more, searching till I've found something I can pin on him.

It takes time though. Beside me, Mandy is clearing her throat, wondering how to get past. But it's no good. Not when I've almost found what I'm looking for.

And suddenly, there it is. It was staring at me all the time, in the set of his shoulders and the crease in his shirt.

Married.

The satisfaction is wonderful. Suddenly I feel as if I could almost laugh in his face, because it cuts him right down to size. It's enough to cheer anyone up. After that it's almost a pleasure to step aside and let him pass, because now I know what we're dealing with. What's more, I reckon he knew it too. I'd no sooner got out of the way than he was hurrying on into the sitting room, propelling Mandy in front of him. And me, I'm letting them go, all buoyed up because I'd got his measure. Then the door closes and half a second's satisfaction dissolves into nothing. Because if he is married, then what does that make Mandy?

Fifteen minutes pass, and I hear them on the stairs again. You couldn't have missed them. He was taking her out to dinner – at this time of night. But then, you could tell he was the sort who could make places stay open. And you could just imagine the place they'd be going to now. Somewhere where the waiters look down their noses at you, and ask you to test the wine, just so they can see the look on your face. Only not him. They would be all over him. He was the right sort.

Oh yes, you could imagine it all right. Big hellos, then on to the wine and the steak and the gâteau, and mints and Cointreau. After the last tipple and the taxi home, what would you say would be coming next?

I saw them walk along the road together on their way out. From up here, in the gloom, she even looked like my Mandy again – no more than a kid – going out for a late-night walk with her dad. Then all of a sudden at the end of the road, she stops and throws her arms around his neck, and because of it their faces meet and merge, and it's no good thinking of fathers any more. Fathers get arrested for less.

You won't believe this, but after all that I never did hear them come in. I was asleep. Oh I meant to listen out for them all right, and when I finally did get to my bed, sleep was the very last thing on my mind. There was that one fact I needed to know, and I was only going to discover that by staying awake. But maybe that's what happens when a thing is that important: your brain plays you false and sends you off to sleep before you even know what's happened. Added to which there was the shock of it all. It takes it out of you.

The upshot is, I'm sound asleep within minutes, and there's Doreen. She's standing in front of a mirror putting on a scarf. Orange lipstick and a mouth that says, *I told you so, I told you so.* Women and their mouths. Some things never change, no matter what you do. Still, at least she should have been some kind of preparation for waking up, for all the unpleasant-

122

ness ahead. But she wasn't. Nothing could have prepared me for that.

At first I thought I was still dreaming, or that I'd woken up in the wrong place. Other people's voices shouting to one another. Her voice, his voice, and no attempt to keep a lid on it, not letting you get away from the truth for a second: there was a stranger in the house. Two strangers. And of course this was no dream.

Having fallen asleep, I hadn't learned the answer to my question, either.

The fact was, even now, twelve hours later, the shock hadn't gone away. It took until they went out again for the second time – to some art gallery on the other side of town, as if we had wanted to know – for the rest of it to sweep over me, the sorrow and the anger, the disillusionment. In one word, the disappointment. It made no difference which way you tried to look at it, the truth always remained the same, blinding from each and every angle. Mandy had lied. No more, no less. She had led me, led us all, in one long merry dance up the garden path with all that talk of a 'friend' and so on and so forth, yet somehow forgetting to mention that this 'friend' of hers just happened to be a man. It didn't matter that nothing was said as much in words; you can lie by omission every bit as well as by other means. Ask any woman. And that's what she had done. She had lied. Lied to her Larry.

If it weren't for that one question that remained to be answered, it would all be very simple. In short, she never was any different. All you had to do was trust Larry to find it out.

Then again, I'd forgotten how other people would react. Reminder, when it came, was like another explosion, smaller, but at closer quarters.

'Mr Mann? Cooee, Mr Mann, are you there?'

Ethel. Yes it's true. In all this, I really had forgotten Ethel. My heart heaves itself out of the pit of my stomach with a mighty bound. Whoever would have thought that the mere sound of Ethel's voice could, out of the blue, lift a chap's spirits like that? But it did, because it changed everything. As if Ethel would ever put up with a man in the house, for a single hour let alone a night. The very idea was laughable. There couldn't be a moment's doubt what she was calling me for now; she wanted him out. Only she needed someone there to help – just in case it all turned nasty. Now it was a case of plans having to be made, the police called even, just to be on the safe side . . .

'I'll be down in two shakes, Mrs D,' I called out, loud and clear. The woman must know that she could depend on someone. She deserved it. For once in her life, there could be no faulting her character. And for the first time that morning, there was something close to a smile on my face.

I was halfway down the stairs before it hit me. What about Mandy, though? It was all very well chucking him out – the sooner the better for all concerned – *but what about Mandy?* She was the one who had gone ahead and done It, broken the very first Law of Ethel Duck, and of all landladies of the old school. No Men in the House. Ever.

Only when it came to this one, he wasn't the problem, not really. All she had to do was close the front door and lock it. No, there was another reason for wanting me. Age had finally caught up with her. The good old days had gone when she could haul suitcase after suitcase into the street all by herself. She needed help for that. In other words, it was Mandy she wanted out.

And it's then, just to add to the chaos, that something else occurs, not so much a thought but a face – Mandy's, the way it is usually, when he's not there.

Mandy's face, turned towards yours, listening to every word. I reckon I've come to know that face as well as my own – and the person who goes with it. And suddenly, that's all it takes – one flash of those sweet features, and I'm seeing clearly again. My Mandy could be naughty, she could come out with her little fibs and think she was fooling us all, but she wasn't the sort to bring men home just so she could ... do whatever it was Ethel had in mind. Surely not. Not my Mandy.

Not my Mandy.

What was needed here was a second chance. A bit of give and take. Not that anyone would suggest that she get off scot-free, but several sharp words should be enough, resulting in a few tears maybe, proof that she realized how serious it was. After that, a fresh start, a new beginning all round.

Only someone would have to tell Ethel.

Ethel. She was always going to be the problem. You do not lightly set about persuading a woman like Ethel Duck to change the habits of a lifetime. Because that's the way of women, always wanting to think the worst of others like them. And nine times out of ten they'd be right. Unless it's my mother you're talking about, in which case make that ten out of ten. She saw through Doreen from the very start, and it's matter for thankfulness that she never lived to see herself proved right. But it's Ethel we're talking about now. The very thought of her would be enough to drive most men back up those stairs. But not Larry, not when there was Mandy's face, lighting every step of his way.

At the bottom, Ethel is actually smiling.

In the circumstances, I found it rather confusing, but this was no time to be sidetracked by small things. Not when I needed to plan what I was going to say. There were the sentences to be shaped and got into line, polished and stored up ready to be trotted out no matter how thick the enemy fire. And most important of all, there was knowing when to choose the moment.

In the kitchen, Gilbert waves a hand (and both of us know where that's been) and Ethel folds her arms across her pinny. For a moment not one of us says a word. The temptation is to throw caution to the four winds and go in all guns blazing.

'*. . . Only young, Mrs D. That's all . . . Just needs a second chance . . . We all need to learn . . .*'

Willpower triumphed, however. Somehow I managed to hold my fire and in the event, it's Ethel who speaks first.

'We need a few moments of your time, Mr Mann . . .'

I nod. But the words keep trooping through my head, threatening to spill out if I so much as open my mouth. '*Mere slip of a girl. No doubt about it. Needs a mother's hand . . .*'

'I hardly have to tell you, at our age, some things will always need another pair of hands.'

'*Of course you're right. You need help. And she's been naughty, I'll not deny it . . .*'

'Just look at it. You can blame the frame of course. Adds to the weight no end.'

'*I'll speak to her though. Strong words, mind. A week from now we can forget this ever happened.*'

'There's no way we could manage, not with Mr Duck in his condition. But you can see, we have to get it down. It's been up there so long. And what with all the dirt that blows in . . .'

'*A wise heart knows how to forgive . . .*'

'What we need is someone strong enough for the task. So there you are, Mr Mann. Would you, Mr Mann? Be so kind?'

She's waiting for an answer. Which can only mean that it can't be put off any longer. It's time to grasp the nettle. Grab the bull by the horns and give it to her straight.

I look her in the eye, and say: 'Oh come on, Mrs D. You can't want to throw her out just like that. I mean, where would she go?'

A dead silence. Ethel stares at me as if all of a sudden I've broken into purest Turkish, then looks at Gilbert, who looks at her. Then with a dreadful effort (unlike the last time) leans forward in his chair, and rotates a single bony finger against his temple. And for the first time it strikes me that there's been no mention of Mandy, or fancy men, or anything you could recognize for that matter. The only clue is Ethel and the fact that she's forgotten to lower her hand from where it's been pointing all this while, namely, towards the picture hanging above the gas fire. It's a three foot by three foot expanse of mountain scenery, complete with sky-blue lake and sunset. In the present situation all it does is add to the general confusion.

'Ah,' I say. 'You're probably talking about the picture.'

Ethel narrows her eyes. Obviously thinks I'm trying to have a joke at her expense. All the same, she answers me, slowly, as she would for a dying idiot at his last gasp of understanding. 'Yes, the picture, Mr Mann. It wants cleaning. We have to get it off the wall. Mr Duck can't do it. So we're asking you.'

What comes next is a final desperate attempt to enter into the spirit of the thing. 'Cleaning,' I say. 'Well I don't know about that. It looks the same as it ever did.' I should know, seeing it was me who had to lug it home for her from Woolworths all those years ago.

'Well that's just where you're wrong, Mr Mann. We were talking about it when Francis was here. I said the colours weren't what they were, and he said all it needed was a touch of white spirit. Five minutes and it would be as good as new . . .'

The rest of what she said just seemed to trail off into nonsense. And it didn't matter how hard I listened, it only got worse.

'. . . He said in a few years' time, a picture like this would be a collector's item, so it was only sensible to take care of it. Apart from which, it gave a whole new vista to the room. Told us he could practically feel the alpine breezes in his hair. Lovely way he had of speaking. I don't suppose Amanda's had the chance to introduce you yet?'

She was asking me a question, and a serious one at that, namely who'd been first in the introduction stakes. But it was no good trying to answer her. The words wouldn't have come. All I could do was stare blindly from one to the other, until I finally came up with a question of my own.

'Mrs Duck. You've got to put me straight. Are we talking about the same person here? You've actually met, I mean, had words with this man, this so-called friend?'

Ethel bristles ever so slightly, a sign of worse to come. 'Well of course. Amanda brought him straight down this morning, just like she said she would. And really, since we're on the subject, I can't see any call for rude names. And certainly not when it's a man of his sort . . .'

This was too much. 'But Mrs D. That man stayed here last night, here in this house. Are you telling me you didn't know that?'

I was shouting by now, a thing unheard-of in Ethel's domain. The effect on her is frightening to behold. She has a way of literally expanding before your eyes, like a great she-cat lifting her fur, turning itself from a fireside tabby to a wild thing red in tooth and claw.

'Mr Mann.' The sound of her voice is the hiss in the undergrowth, the noise that tells you not to take one step further. 'Mr Mann, I hope you're not trying to suggest that anything *immoral* has been going on in this house.'

If I tell you the very room had shrunk around us it

would be no lie. Even Gilbert was disappearing into his chair. Yet I held my ground. Waited for what was coming next.

'This is a respectable household Mr Mann, and I'll thank you to remember that. There's never been anything of that nature gone on under this roof, not ever. Do you understand me. Only once have I ever had to worry about such a thing. Only once, a long time ago. But of course, you would know all about that, *wouldn't you*?'

And suddenly everything went quiet. Ethel, who you might have expected only now to be getting into her stride, had stepped back and folded her arms. A moment before she had had an entire book to throw at me, now, instead, she was satisfied just to leave it there. All she needed to do was sit and wait for what she had said to sink in. Gilbert too. The pair of them were looking at me with the self-same expression on their faces. Smug, that's the only way to describe it. The look of people who know something you don't. Then all at once it clicks. Something that happened here once, something that I should have known all about . . .

Out of the blue then comes the old cold feeling, the one that used to come and go, but mostly stayed. Doreen – did she, did she ever, here, with him? The one in Waltham Abbey. Maybe even not just with him either. What about Gilbert? He'd have had a lot more strength then. And I'd seen where Gilbert's interests lay. Suddenly what I needed was to sit down.

The good Lord only knows where all this might have led if Ethel hadn't butted in, ruining her own triumph so to speak. Surprisingly, it was to return to the original subject, as if none of the past few seconds had happened. What's more there's not even any malice left in the voice, or none so you'd notice. 'What I'm saying, Mr Mann, is, you're not to go thinking the worst. It does you no credit at all. But then again, if Amanda hasn't told you, then you're hardly to know. That young man of hers couldn't be more respectable if he was the cousin of the Queen herself. Doctor, he is. Surgeon. Like her father.'

Oh, this was the worst trick of all. Of course he was a doctor. What else could have had this effect on Ethel? He must have walked through the door with his testimonials round his neck. Ethel would have been there, laying down the red carpet.

And as for me, it's back to the old days, of feeling like the only decent person left on earth, the single righteous man, the only one who cares about the difference between right and wrong. And whose fault is it? His fault, that's whose. He turns up, and in one short night tips the whole house and everybody in it on its head.

There was no sense in staying, no sense in talking even. I got the picture down for them and went back upstairs. But there was no peace that day. How could there be? With a man like that in the house. But really, you could almost forget about him; it always came down to Mandy. The best you could say for her was that she was taken in, like Ethel and Gilbert. But the worst . . . ? It's not that hard to put into words. That she'd gone the way of all women, and Larry was right all along.

But there's one more thing before you think the worst, before you raise your voice to call her rotten like the rest of them, before you go telling Ethel you don't mind whose suitcases you help drag down into the hall and out the front door.

Which is why I'm lying here in my bed, doing what I should have kept myself awake to do last night. Listening.

Remember what I said about June's bed? The one you only have to touch to have creaking and groaning like a train grinding to a halt? Some nights I've lain up here counting the times Mandy turns over. If she turns over tonight, if anyone turns over tonight, I'll hear it. It's as simple as that.

They came in about an hour and a half ago, just as I was climbing between the sheets. They made a lot less noise than when they went out, but I could hear them all right, strolling back and forth on the landing like it was the middle of the day, before, almost the last thing of all, one long whispered conversation outside the lounge. But it's quiet now. A couple of doors closed for the last time, getting on for an hour ago, and after that, nothing. Not even a squeak. The only sound is of the lorries rumbling away in the distance, ironing out the litter that drifts across the Holloway Road, heading north.

Half-past two – that's what it says on my clock (digital, like the one I bought for her, only the numbers on mine are green and instead of standing still, turn somersaults all the night long). And it only goes to show. It doesn't matter what others would have you believe, you really should always think the best of people.

Chapter Eleven

Waking up this morning, it's as if nothing has changed. The same din as yesterday, with the conversation at full volume, and doors banging loud enough to wake the dead. Yet instead of jumping out of bed and fretting, I just lay there and let them get on with it. Hardly surprising seeing as it must have been well after four when I finally did drop off. Shocking, but there you are: some things are worth staying awake for.

So that was one reason for feeling better this morning, but there was another to go with it. Today was Sunday, and Prince Charming had to go home to his wife. And his children. That's what I decided last night, with all those hours to think about it. There are bound to be children, after all. We're talking about a man of over forty, and just in terms of statistics, there are bound to be kids. Pretending otherwise isn't going to make things any easier for Mandy.

Two children then. Boys. Ten and Twelve. Poor kids.

I've decided Mandy doesn't know about any of them, not the wife or the children. You've only got to think about it calmly for a minute. There's no way a girl of her calibre would be going about with a man she knew was married — even if she is completely different when he's around. The tragic thing is, it won't always be like that. One day she's going to have to find out, and that will be the day we see a sadder and wiser Mandy.

In the meantime though, lying there in bed, with all the clatter going on, it seemed that the best way of getting through the rest of the day was by seeing as little of the two as possible. Him especially. No point in letting them get under my feet.

Then again, it was just as well that things went wrong. Otherwise I would have missed the one bright spot of the weekend.

Hearing the front door slam, I naturally thought they'd gone out, and that was my chance to creep downstairs so as to get a breath of fresh air and the newspaper. I was only halfway down the hall however when suddenly the front door bursts open, and it's him, breezing in with what looks like a ton of newspapers under his arm. Apparently some folk can't make do with just the one copy of the *Sunday Express*. They have to go and buy the whole shop.

The thing is, then he tries to carry on breezing, right on past me without so much as a good morning. Now call me old-fashioned, but that is not the sort of behaviour you expect in your own house. What you would term insult added to injury. Then outside, in the street, I had a thought. What if Mandy had been telling him about the two of us and what we get up to when we're by ourselves? It would be all Larry this and Larry that till he was sick of hearing it. Which means you could see now why he would do all he could to put me down, in other words, ignore me the way he just did. The man was eaten up with jealousy.

So there you are. If I hadn't met him, how else would I have known that – or been able to picture his face as Mandy chatters nineteen to the dozen about none other than her old Larry?

Which brings me to the best part of all – namely this evening. Half an hour ago I heard Mandy come in, and this time she was by herself. I don't think she can have raised so much as a particle of dust on that landing, she was so quiet. And that's how I knew his nibs had gone home, leaving the real Mandy behind him.

Already there's a different atmosphere in the house. Well nearly. It's not what you'd call perfect silence, not with all the racket coming up from a certain room that just happens to be situated below mine. It's Mandy of course. The silly girl is down there sobbing her heart out. Apparently it hasn't occurred to some folk that there are people trying to get some sleep in this house, people who might even be tempted to pop downstairs and point out that a little consideration in this area might not go amiss, but Larry's not like that. The way I see it, girls will be girls, and there's no call to gripe just because they like to act daft every now and then.

I don't know how long I can keep this up though, making excuses for her. Listen to this – it's been three days now – that's Monday, Tuesday, Wednesday, and has there been any sign of Madam? Has there ever. Yet she's been home – I've heard her, creeping around like she always does. Quite active really, so she can't even give the excuse that she's ill.

You know what's happening of course. It's him up there, His Lordship. He's got to keep her away from her old Larry or she'd start enjoying herself again and forget all about *him*. You can just imagine him, trying to think of all kinds of ways to keep us apart. The worst you could say for her is that she's just doing what she's told.

But it's not good enough. Simple decency should be reminding her of who her real friends are. And they could be lying up here dead for all she knows.

Added to which, I can't stand waste. I've still got half the stuff I bought when I thought – thanks to her fibs – we were expecting another girl. I can't keep it all for very much longer. As it is, she's missed her chance of a Viennese whirl. I polished those off last night. And was I sorry? Not a bit of it.

Put simply, the worm's finally beginning to turn. A man can only take so much. Then it's time to start thinking about dealing out a drop of the same medicine. If she wants to turn the cold shoulder on old Larry, then he can do likewise, and every bit as well as she can. Granted, reserve isn't in my nature, and it's not how you'd want to behave to a friend in the normal way, but there, sometimes it takes a friend to point out the error of your ways.

Starting from tomorrow, Mandy's going to see another side of Larry, one I daresay she never dreamed existed. No more smiles, no more asking her how her day has been, no more offers of sherry. She'll hardly know what's hit her. I'll be polite, but distant. And dignified. I'll keep it up for days if I have to, until finally, when she can't stand it any more, she'll turn on me and beg to know what it's all about. And that's when I'll tell her. The whole story. There'll be no mincing of words, just the plain truth – pure and simple.

I reckon we'll need a few handkerchiefs around here then – a box of them probably. Rainbow colours. Because there's no getting away from it. Sometimes the truth hurts.

Now do you want to hear what actually happened?

In the first place, I had the best night's sleep I'd known in days. Then I spent the entire morning working out how I was going to say this to her, and then how I was going to say that, until by lunch time she was standing right there beside me, tears starting out of her eyes, her little voice breaking as the words come out: *'Larry please oh please oh please Forgive me I have done such Wrong'* and so on. It was after lunch though, that we came to the nub of the matter –

about what to think of a young person carrying on with a man who was twice her age, and Didn't She Know He Was Married? I was in the butcher's by then, treating myself to a bit of steak and it's there, as I'm tucking the meat into the side of my carrier, I had second thoughts, told myself that maybe I'd do better to strike out that last question.

The problem was this: I could picture her apologizing for everything else, for all the noise and commotion, all the fibs and general lack of consideration, even for not bothering to come and say hello to her old pal, but try as hard as I might, I couldn't imagine what she'd say to that last thing, about his being married. Doreen now – she would have been easy. She'd have just laughed, which shows the sort of woman she was, a perfect example of the breed. But Mandy? The shock might well kill her.

Better to stick to the essentials then, carry on with giving her a bit of the old harsh medicine – and when it was all over, switch right back to the Larry she knows and loves and not one ounce of hard feeling between us.

So there you have it – nicely worked out to a tee.

Switch to this evening then. What happens is, I'm standing in my kitchen, by the stove. The steak is sizzling away beautifully in the pan, the chips have turned the right colour and all I'm waiting for now is the peas. Then from downstairs comes this little knock on the wall.

It's a miracle I even heard it actually, I was that busy. Besides which, I simply hadn't been expecting her, not after the record of the last few days – which was partly why I was treating myself to a slap-up meal in the first place, a sort of consolation. The result is, hearing her now, not knowing she was coming, gave me a real shock, which goes a long way to explain what happened next. Without even stopping to think what I

136

was doing, or why, I simply grabbed every blessed thing off the stove and threw it into the oven, out of sight. I was still turning off the knobs when she appeared in the kitchen door, with that sweet old Mandy-smile I hadn't seen in days.

And me – what did I do? Nod and carry on as if she wasn't there? Offer a curt good evening and then start to let her have it – all the stuff I'd been rehearsing from the moment I woke up (barring the bit about married men), or in short order, simply tell her to get lost? Did I do any of these things?

'Hello stranger,' is what I said. 'Fancy a cup of tea?'

Two reasons: the first being that all it took was the sight of her, out of the blue like that, to make me forget everything I'd wanted to say; and second – she was standing there holding up a great big white cake, all icing and cherries round the top as if she'd copied it from a picture in a kiddies' comic. And no prizes for guessing who it was for.

It's not often that Larry's at a loss, but I'll own up. I was completely knocked out. 'Aye aye Mandy love,' was all I could manage, followed by, 'and what have we got here then?'

For an answer she just looks at me, only it's in such a way I would never be able to put into words. Suffice to say it was between her and me only, and it was a look that said more than a hundred folk all speaking at once could ever say. It was a look that said, 'I'm sorry.'

After that, her actual words, when they eventually came, seemed unimportant. 'It's a cake, Larry,' she says in that soft little voice. 'I made it for you.' I suppose I nodded, but to tell the truth I was barely listening. It was more the tone of what she said that captured the attention – contrite and sad. She should have left it there, really, with that impression fresh in my mind, instead of adding, 'I just thought, seeing everything you've done for me since I came here, that it was time I paid you back.'

'With a cake,' I said. 'How very nice of you, love.' At the same time, though, already beginning to run through my mind was a whole list of other things offered in the other direction. Like fruit, cigarettes, cold platters, a clock radio. Now we have one cake. ..

But there you are, as I always say, it is the thought that counts, and what was more, there must have been a fair bit of work gone into that cake. If she hadn't cheated and used a packet mix. For the moment, I didn't say anything derogatory. Besides, I reckoned I knew what was coming, and sure enough, as if to prove me right, she hurries over to me and plonks the cake down on the side – exactly where I would have been doling out the steak and chips if she hadn't turned up at just that minute – and says, 'Well, I'd better go, Larry.' And starts heading back for the stairs. But I was ready for her. One little hand on her arm was all it took to stop her.

'Now just you hold your horses,' I said. 'You're surely not leaving already. What about this cake? I can't go and eat it all by myself.'

'But Larry,' says she. 'I can't stay. You were all set to have your supper.' With that she waves a hand in the air where the smell of sizzling meat and chips is so thick you'd need a knife to cut it.

And that's when there washes over me the queerest feeling I can ever remember. If I had to put a name to it, I'd call it Joy. Pure Joy. 'Mandy love,' I said slowly, savouring every word. 'Look around you. Can you see any sign of supper here?'

She looks at me, and then all around, looks everywhere, and what do you know, there's nothing there. Just bare kitchen, and not so much as a frozen pea.

And that feeling of mine? I'll tell you where it came from. It came from knowing as I never had before that there wasn't a soul in the world who knew my Mandy like I did, not even Mandy herself. It wasn't shock that had made me shove my supper out of sight, it was me, thinking ahead for us both. The naughty girl had hung on until supper time, waited till she could practically taste my supper in the air, and *then* come up. That way she'd thought she could dump the cake and run. But there was me, reading her mind, and not even realizing I was doing it, getting rid of the evidence, and with it, her excuse.

The joy comes from feeling so close to her, feeling I've climbed inside her very skin.

So what can she do but lead on when I give her a little push towards the lounge, with me behind, knives and tea plates at the ready?

The cake was all right – a bit sweet for my taste, and what's more, I told her so – not in the spirit of criticism, but so she would know for the future. She tried to explain it away by saying she had had to measure it all out in tablespoons because there were no scales downstairs, to which I replied she could come and use mine any day of the week, I'd be glad of the company.

In any case, I left a good half of it on the side of my plate, said I was sorry, but I hadn't had much appetite these last few days. That was an obvious cue for her to ask me why, but she didn't, she went straight on talking about all the work she had piled up to do for college, and I took that as a clear sign of a guilty conscience.

Seeing she was taking that attitude, I began to think it would do her no harm to hear a bit of what I had stored up for her after all. It was either that or have her go off thinking she could do the same thing again whenever she felt like it. Added to which, the cake had made me remember I was hungry, and there was a perfectly good steak dinner going to ruin in the oven.

I began with a sigh. 'Mandy love, you know me, I'm

the last person in the world to complain, but why oh why haven't you been up to see me all this long time? It's been ever so lonely up here.'

Well, I could say this for her, she blushed – red as a schoolgirl. But apology? not a word of it. Just a few mumbled excuses about being so busy. Strange to say though, I wasn't disappointed. No, really. You see, in a funny way, it was like being taken back to the old days, and instead of Mandy, it was June sitting there, a nipper still, little round cheeks getting redder by the minute. June as a naughty girl.

Now I know there are folk who swear that nothing teaches a child as well as the back of your hand. Well good luck to them. We're all entitled to our opinion. But me, I never lifted a finger to June. For the simple reason it's all water off a duck's back to them. It's words you want to use. A clip across the ear is never going to keep a kid awake at night, but a few well-chosen words will. Which is the best thing you can say about them, kids: they'll believe anything if you tell them often enough.

Know where I learned that from? The same place we all learn. From my mother. She never laid a finger on us either. She didn't have to. *It's all in the eyes of God* – that's what she used to say – and we'd believe her too. After that you're never going to go far wrong, not when you know there's someone up there watching all the time. Never taking their eyes off you.

She'd have smiled if she could have seen June sometimes, face all screwed up, trying to convince herself to the bitter end it was her and not me who was right. Which was when like as not Doreen would barge in and spoil it all. One half-hearted clap around the head, and that was June, off scot-free.

(Yet why is it, when I never lifted a hand to June, it was her mother she sided with in the end?)

What I'm saying now is, though, with Mandy sitting

140

there, it was like being given a second crack at the whip. The challenge was the same, namely to persuade her – gently – to behave like a good girl should. And this time, no Doreen to butt in at the crucial moment. It's the angle that counts. See now, Mandy was probably expecting me to tell her off, and was all ready for that. But that's not what I had in mind. Oh no.

'You know,' I said. 'You don't have to worry about keeping on the right side of Larry – I mean with cakes and so on. It doesn't matter what you do, he's still going to be here for you, ready and waiting, whenever you think you might have a few minutes to spare.'

'Larry . . .'

'Of course, I'm not saying I'll always be my old cheerful self. I've seen too much trouble, and when you're alone so much, you're bound to dwell on things.'

'Oh Larry . . .'

'But what I want you to know is, Larry understands. He knows you've got a life of your own, and it's too much to expect a young girl to spend her time worrying about her old pal missing the only bit of company he's got the right to hope for. What I'm saying is – don't think about us. Joey and me will get by somehow.'

'But Larry . . .'

'No buts, Mandy love. The main thing is that you enjoy yourself, while you're young. Some people never get the chance.'

If I could only have had a picture of her face as it was then. Eyes bright with unshed tears, lower lip all of a quiver. I'd known this moment would come – but not so soon. Yet this was my Mandy for you – all sense and feeling. At least, that's what I thought.

'Larry,' she said. And this time, it only seemed right to let the old kid speak. After all, I thought I knew half of what she was going to say – *Larry I'm so sorry so very very sorry . . .*

In fact, I was so sure of it, it took a few seconds to

realize what it was she actually was saying, and even then, I could hardly believe it.

'Larry,' she was saying. 'Larry, thank you. I should have listened to Francis, and Ethel too. Both of them said I was coming up too much. They said you didn't need me. Only, silly me, I didn't believe them. And the cake – well that was Francis's idea. He said all it needed was a gesture. It would show you that I *do* care and I *do* think about you. Then maybe you wouldn't mind if I made more time for the rest, for making friends. After all, you know me. I'm never going to find it easy. You remember I told you a little about what happened before, up in Edinburgh? It could so easily be like that again. But I've been so frightened of making you unhappy. Because I know how it feels – we both do, don't we, Larry . . . ? Oh, but I don't have to explain. You've just told me you understand. Thank goodness you understand.'

And then would you believe it, the girl leans forward and plants a kiss on my cheek.

A Judas kiss. Because we know who put her up to it. He did, and probably Ethel as well. Now I'm meant to take the cake, and watch her walk away. Then if she has the time, and if I'm lucky, I'll see her for five minutes in the middle of next week.

Ever heard of brainwashing?

But we've been here once or twice before, haven't we. There's been the Mandy who's been doing all the talking, and the other Mandy, deep down inside, telling her what she's doing is wrong. The true Mandy, the one I know better than she does herself. And she's still there, just. Bad Mandy is smiling at me, and the look in her eyes tells me she thinks she's already out of here, but watch her closely, and you'll see someone there who's not quite sure.

And that's who I talk to.

'Well love, that Francis of yours, you've got to hand

142

it to him. He certainly knows all about the old folk. Where did he learn it from? Some poor old soul tucked away in a home somewhere? His ma, I expect. I mean, he knows all about the "gestures" as you call it. I expect he told you it's the little things that count, and all. And he's right, of course. You'll never catch an old person complaining. They wouldn't dare. Better something than nothing at all. Eh, Mandy?'

'Larry . . .'

But I haven't finished, not by a long chalk. 'The funny thing is though, love, you never do learn to live with the shock.'

'Shock, Larry?' Whatever she meant to say is gone. She sounds now as if she needs to sneeze, or cough or something.

'The shock, love. What comes after years of struggling to do your best, only to wake up one morning and find you're on your own. Not a blessed soul around who gives a damn. All there is to look forward to is *the little things*.'

I stop there. No need to go on. Look at her, just look at her. It's all coming rushing to the surface. Those eyes. It's only a question of seconds now. Deep breath, count the moments until . . .

'Larry, oh Larry. I'm sorry. I wasn't thinking. I didn't know.'

And finally, whoosh! Here come the tears, streaming out of her eyes, pouring off her cheeks. Guilty tears, and tears of something else, unless I'm very much mistaken. But mostly guilt. She can't speak, can't even utter a word. Sentences are quite beyond her. Mandy is feeling really awful.

I can let her go now, see if I can rescue that dinner of mine. She'll be up again tomorrow as usual and the day after, no two ways about it. That's my Mandy for you.

So you tell me. Who knows her better – him or me?

Chapter Twelve

After that, what can I say about the last three weeks that you won't have guessed already? That we haven't looked back since? That we get on like a house on fire? That we're as happy as two bugs in bed? Well all that. But I'll tell you what it's really like. It's feeling that for the first time in his life, Larry's got everything. When Mandy's sitting up here, and there's me there beside her, you could offer me the moon and I wouldn't take it. Because it's all here. The place is complete. I even thought the other day about that ornament of the porcelain girl with the wind up her skirt, and you know, I had to smile. She's not needed any more. You can't add to perfection.

And Mandy's happy, you can tell. She hardly says anything now that's worth the mention. What she likes doing is sitting on the settee next to me, listening to me chattering on. She doesn't even seem interested in Joey any more, which annoys him no end. He sits there on his perch practically shouting for her to come over and talk to him, till in the end I have to throw the cover over the cage, which serves him right for trying to muscle in on what has nothing to do with him. She comes up here to see her Larry, not some old bird.

Of course there's another reason. There always is, even with the best of them. She comes to take her mind off other things. Such as the fact that in all this time she hasn't received so much as a letter or a card from his nibs. I know she's thinking about him, sitting there with a tiny part of her listening out all the time for

Ethel at the bottom of the stairs, telling her there's a phone call for her. But there never is. Or hardly ever.

So a new Mandy then – regular, reliable, a little quieter if that were possible, ready to listen all night long if you asked her. But that's not all; there's been another development. Those little treats I keep putting out for her, stuff she never touches when she's here, have started turning up downstairs in her cupboard. And don't look at me. She's been buying it all herself. Packets of fig rolls and Battenberg, glacier mints, what have you, all appearing and disappearing a lot faster than you would expect. What beats me is why she can't come out and admit she's developed a taste for them. Because give credit where credit is due, none of it would be there if it weren't for Larry putting ideas in her head. You'd think she'd start filling out a bit really, but there's no sign of it yet.

Which brings me up to the middle of this week, and the one little wobble we've had so far. But before anyone wants to go saying I told you so, wait till you've heard the whole story. It all turns out beautifully in the end.

On Tuesday night we had that telephone call we've been waiting for all this time. Well that was it – our Mandy was off, down those stairs so fast you'd have thought there was someone handing out free five-pound notes at the bottom. And – you've guessed – I didn't see hide nor hair of her for the rest of the evening.

As for the next night, forget it. Her mind was somewhere else completely. And this time, in view of the circumstances, I wasn't prepared to be that forgiving. What's more, she didn't even come out and tell me she was expecting a visitor. She just sat there with a half-baked smile all over her face, and let that speak for itself. Thursday morning I had a peek in her cupboards. No sign of the Battenberg now. It was all man's food – gentleman's relish and Stilton and little bits of upmarket snacks, all salt and foreign flavours.

I shan't even bother telling you what was going through my mind. Suffice to say, come Friday morning, if I could have gone to sleep and not woken up till the Monday I would have been happy. Bumping into Ethel in the hall, then, only seemed like the final straw.

The two of us don't talk much now; apart from when she needs something. But sometimes she gets desperate – and who wouldn't with only the Living Skeleton for company? And then, as in this case, there's always something cropping up she wants you to know about. She must have been lying in wait because the second my foot comes off the bottom step, there she is beside me, beady little eyes gleaming with what she's got in mind.

'Mr Mann,' says she. 'I'm in such a state, you can't imagine.'

That was a matter of opinion. The woman was visibly shaking – and enjoying every minute.

'It's bad news for Amanda. I just don't know how I can tell her.'

You can imagine the effect that had on me. News for Mandy, and Bad News at that. Before I knew it I was opening my mouth to ask for more, but I'd forgotten: Ethel has a couple of scores to settle, and this was her chance. Without another word she sweeps straight past me, up the stairs to the middle landing, as if daring me to follow her this time. As it happened, just this once I had a few important errands to run outside, so I let her go, but there's no denying it, she'd left me in a proper stew – exactly as she'd intended.

Bad news for Mandy – whatever did she mean by that? Well, the choice was endless. Family's what you think of first, or maybe not if you're Mandy and me. The fact is, there's a whole world of bad news out there, and it was useless to try and guess.

'Never mind, Mandy love.' I actually said it loud. 'Larry's here. Whatever it is, this will only bring us closer together. We'll be happier than ever after, just you see.'

And with that, all I could do was wait until Ethel saw fit to let me in on the secret.

She took her time though. In the end, we met — almost by agreement — at three o'clock in the afternoon in the hall again, though I might add I'd been in and out of the front door at least five times by then. Fortunately, there was always going to be a limit to how long Ethel could restrain herself.

I opened the batting. 'So what's all this about bad news for Mandy?' I said. 'Nothing too serious, I hope.'

'Who knows, Mr Mann? You must know how girls do take on. I'm not sure what she'll make of it.' After that, a brief struggle to stretch it out. Which she lost. 'It's Francis,' she said, and now it all came out in a rush. 'She was expecting him to come tonight. But he telephoned this morning, just after she'd gone off to college. Left a message to say that he can't make it after all. Said he'd phone again tomorrow to explain.'

You know how it is when you hear good news when you've been expecting bad. It takes a minute or so for it to sink in. I must have been a complete blank to look at until slowly, I felt a great big grin spreading all over my face. Daft is how I must have looked, and Ethel when she sees it starts climbing up on to her high horse.

'Well, really Mr Mann. I wouldn't have thought it was any laughing matter — not with Mr Duck looking forward so much to seeing the young man again himself. And as for Amanda . . .'

I can't remember the rest. I don't know if I even stopped long enough to listen. It was the best news I could ever have wished for. Sad for Mandy, naturally, but if it helped her see the sort of man he was —

namely, unreliable, not be trusted – then I could only rejoice.

And rejoice I did, all the way up the stairs and back to my kitchen. I even poured myself a little glass of port, and toasted the man who was so far away and couldn't be bothered to make the journey.

And there was more, though you must believe me when I say I never would have wished this part upon Mandy. Remember last time he came she never bothered to come home until after he'd arrived? Well it was the same today. She must have stayed on until it was time to meet his train, then gone straight to the station. So she never got the message. She must have waited for the next train too, and the next, because it was well after eleven when finally I heard her little footsteps on the landing. Ever so slow they sounded, as if she was tired out. Closed the kitchen door behind her so quietly you could barely hear it. By now of course Ethel had gone to bed.

And talking of Ethel, that reminds me. When I said I'd gone straight upstairs after hearing the news, that wasn't quite right. Because now that I think about it, didn't I say something to her about leaving a little note on the kitchen table for the old kid, just in case? I did, you know, and blow me if it hadn't clean slipped my mind.

No point in disturbing her now though. Mandy is down there, sobbing away about something. If you ask me, she must be having one of those famous blips. Which means she'll just have to hear about it in the morning when she's feeling a bit more herself.

But you know how it is: you spend the whole day meaning to get round to something, and you never quite manage it. That's exactly what happened to me today. I don't know how many times I thought about her down there, and reminded myself that I had something to tell her. Still I just couldn't seem to find the time. And anyway, what was wrong with Ethel? She could have given it to her straight from the horse's mouth. Only I had forgotten, you see. Today was the one day in the month she goes off to see her sister in Greenwich.

So I did feel bad about it, but then, she couldn't have it all ways, could she? One of the reasons I was so busy was because I spent half the day making sure that, come this evening, I'd be able to surprise her with the nicest tea she could possibly imagine. I reckoned she'd forget about moping the moment she set eyes on what I had for her: all the old favourites – fig rolls, Battenberg, gypsy creams. And if she turned her nose up at that, I had half a mind to ask her why, seeing as I knew she was eating exactly the same on the sly.

Come seven o'clock then, it was all waiting for her. Tea *and* sympathy. Then again, when I heard her knock, I thought she must have rallied a bit. It was louder than usual, as was the sound of her feet on the stairs. Probably just the thought of her old Larry had cheered her up no end.

Then what happens but I turn and find it's not Mandy there in my kitchen door, but Harry! Harry who'd sat there like a big lump all those weeks ago when I'd said to him, 'Why not drop the visits for a while, eh?'

'Ethel let me in,' he says, as if that explained everything. And if that wasn't enough, he walks straight past me into the lounge and sits down as if it was any normal day of the week. Starts eyeing the cake and plates of biscuits spread out in front of him. Of course, what I should have done was point out that we don't hold open house here. People come by invitation only. But the trouble is, when you're confronted with that sort of brass neck in someone, words have a habit of failing you.

My way of dealing with it is to say quite politely that I'm expecting a visitor any moment. To which he nods, and stays sitting there anyway. I didn't say a word after that, thinking if I kept quiet he'd get the message. But that was always the problem with Harry, sitting in silence never did worry him one jot. All that happens is that after five minutes he leans forward, picks up a gypsy cream and says, 'Where is she then?'

'Who?' I said, too busy wondering how I was going to get rid of him to think what I was saying.

'This friend of yours. The one you said you was expecting. Where is she?'

Now I knew what he was thinking; folk like Harry, they just love to feel they've caught you out.

'She'll be up,' I said. And left it there. You see I thought she would be, I really did. A while later though, after he's polished off another two gypsy creams, I couldn't help myself. 'She's not expecting me to have visitors, you know.' To which he says nothing.

Purely to take his mind off things, I switched on the TV and there we both sat. For two hours. In the end, I didn't have to say anything. He got up of his own accord, brushes the crumbs off that great belly of his, and says:

'Ah well, looks like she's not coming.'

You can imagine. I opened my mouth to ask whose fault he thought that was. Then I saw the look on his face.

Do you really need to hear any more of this? So far as Larry's concerned, wild horses couldn't make him waste any more words on Harry. All I can say is, who does he think he is? His life is a wreck, his wife is dead, he runs a fruit stall and he can't stand fruit. He looks ten years older than he is. Yet he thinks he can go giving me a look like the one he tried giving me tonight. Me. It's himself he should be feeling sorry for. That's all.

After he went – not long after, as you may guess – I cleared away everything that was there. Stuck it in the kitchen pail. He'd ruined it all anyway. But that wasn't the reason. The reason was that for the first time I was angry, absolutely stamping. And not just with Harry. It was Mandy. In a funny way this was the worst thing she'd ever done to me, not coming up when she was expected. Because just look at the result. She'd let me down in front of a no-hoper like Harry, sent him away thinking Larry Mann was no better off than he was. The way I saw it, the last thing she deserved now was tea and sympathy. She could just keep on moping as far as I was concerned. And I turned up the TV loud, so that if and when she did come knocking I wouldn't have to hear her.

She didn't, though. I never even heard her come out of her kitchen all evening.

Bang in the middle of the night I wake up, mind clear as a bell. The girl is simply feeling left out. First His Lordship fails to show, and then her old pal from upstairs goes and makes himself unavailable all evening. No wonder she was down there, too miserable to put in an appearance. Looked at in that way, it makes you want to jump right out of bed and put the smile back on her face.

And that's what I did. This morning, soon as I reckoned we were both decent, I knocked on the kitchen door and opened it, just a little. I must have made her jump, because she turns around, eyes wide, her mouth cram-full of something. Evidently I'd caught her in the middle of a little early-morning snack. At least, I call it a snack, but I doubt that anyone else would. The whole place was littered with all sorts of wrappers and papers, and I don't know what. The old kid must have been having a feast. Well, I didn't say anything. It was nice to see her indulging herself. And she certainly didn't have to look so guilty about it. So I kept it short. 'Morning, love,' I said to her. 'Missed you last night.'

Just that. But it was enough to let her know she's appreciated, that there are folk who notice when she's not there. And sure enough, round about seven she was up to see her Larry. She didn't say a dicky bird about His Highness, so I simply followed her lead, and kept off the subject. There was no point in upsetting the old kid, and it was hardly as if we didn't have lots of other things to talk about.

And if you'd asked if I thought anything was wrong, I would just have laughed in your face.

Chapter Thirteen

For those few days, though, after that weekend when
he didn't turn up, everything was perfect. Mandy was
her lovely quiet self – a little morose maybe, but I
didn't mind. You can't expect someone to be good
company all of the time, can you? And anyway, she
knew who to blame. I had a quick peek in her
cupboards on the Monday, and you'd never believe it.
All the stuff she'd bought when she thought she was
having a visitor had disappeared. There wasn't so
much as a funny-flavoured crisp left. It's as I was
saying about her and the fig rolls – you wouldn't think
one person could get through it all so fast. The Girl
With The Secret Appetite – that's what I should call her
really. Mind you, it can't have agreed with her. Last
night I heard her in the smallest room. The poor kid
was throwing up fit to drop. I had half a mind to catch
her when she came out and tell her to go easy next
time.

Then again, maybe she's just like I was with those
Viennese whirls. Eating it all because she didn't want
to leave him any – not if he can't be bothered to show
up when he's expected. Funny to think of the two of us,
isn't it though – both acting the same way when the
world lets us down. There must be a mould turning out
people like us – two halves of the same coin. Nice
thought, that.

But it doesn't make up for what comes next.

I should start dreading the middle of the week.
Really I should. It's always then that the rot seems to

set in. This time it was the Wednesday, and as usual it's Ethel and the phone that do the damage. Next thing we know, she – Mandy – is on the middle landing, singing – yes singing – at half-past nine in the evening. And believe me, if there's one thing that girl can't do, it's sing a note. Then as if that wasn't bad enough, the actual news has to come from Ethel the next morning. And that's only because somehow she has got it into her head that it's me who's all upset every time *he* gets a mention. She should see the effect on Mandy. Anyway, the good tidings is – he's coming down on Friday, just like he was supposed to do last week.

Well. I thought very hard about what I did next. I knew she wasn't going to like it, but at the end of the day there was nothing else I could do. Somebody was going to have to talk to her. So just to make sure – this being the Thursday, and he might already be having his effect on her – I left a message for her on her kitchen table. 'Mandy, see me. Important. Love, Larry.'

She didn't keep me waiting, I'll say that for her. She was up the minute she got home. I said hello as usual, but I didn't give her much of a smile. It was only fair to let her see that this was difficult for me. Strangely for her, she was quite chatty, falling over herself to tell me about what she'd been up to at that college of hers. Funnily enough, she can be quite thoughtless like that at times, wanting to talk about herself when she can see I've got something on my mind. Normally I would let her get away with it, but not today. So I interrupted her, gently. Told her to sit down because I had something to say.

First of all I told her how fond I was of her, how life had brightened up no end since she'd come. I also told her how it was difficult for a chap like me to go poking his nose into other people's affairs. A person's life is his own, is what I said to her, and it wasn't for any-one else to try and tell them how to live it. But – and this is how I put it, 'There comes a time, Mandy love, when you've got to say something.'

I think that's when she must have cottoned on to what I was going to say because she gave me this quick, guarded little look I'd never seen before. At least, not from her. If I hadn't been so sure of my ground, I might have wanted to stop there, before it got any worse. But Larry isn't one to backtrack, not when he knows he's right.

'Now then, Ethel tells me that you're expecting this friend of yours again this weekend . . .'

'She doesn't mind, though, Larry. I've asked her . . .'

'I wouldn't be so sure of that, love. She's got a funny way of showing things sometimes. Anyway, it's not Ethel I'm thinking about. It's you.'

'Me, Larry?'

'You, love. The fact is, I was at my wits' end last week, seeing you so unhappy, and not knowing how I was ever going to bring back a smile to that little face. And why? Because this Francis bloke tells you he's coming down and then never bothers to show.'

'There was a reason for that, Larry.'

'Oh I daresay there was. And he'll probably have a reason this week and all . . .'

You should have seen her face then. Talk about Jekyll and Hyde. Those sweet little features just seemed to vanish before my very eyes, and suddenly I wasn't looking at Mandy any more. She'd gone, and standing there in front of me, staring back at me, was every woman in the world. Nasty, spiteful. And a voice to match.

'The reason he didn't come down last week, *Larry*, was because he was saving lives. There was a huge accident outside Edinburgh – you must have seen it on the television. Every doctor in the region was working that weekend.'

Suddenly I felt quite ill. It really could have been

Doreen standing there, using her voice the way only women can, jabbing at you with every word.

Don't ask me how I kept my cool, not when there have been women who've been throttled for less, and rightly. But kept it I did. 'That's not the point, Mandy, love,' I began to say quietly, too quietly, because she simply jumped in on top of me.

'No, you're right. It's not. The point is, I would have been a lot less unhappy if *someone* had simply given me the message that was left for me . . .'

'Ah,' I said. 'Ethel . . .'

'No, not Ethel, Larry. I talked to her. She told me what you promised to do. You were meant to leave a note for me, and you never did.'

Well there was an answer to that, but would you believe it, she never gave me a chance. Before I could say another word, she got up from her chair, and walked out of the room.

So what sort of behaviour would you call that?

Funny thing is, the moment she'd gone I forgot all about taking umbrage. If she'd only let me finish, she'd have seen what I was trying to say. Which was simply this: where was her pride? It stands to reason: when someone lets you down, the last thing you do is welcome him back so he can do it again. It's the one way not to be disappointed. That's all I wanted to say to her. But she just didn't stop to listen.

So there you are, we've quarrelled, and she's gone and taken it personally. Only will someone please tell me what I said.

All the same, I knew he would turn up. Mandy wasn't going to change her mind, and there wasn't going to be a phone call like the last. People like him – they're born cunning. They know they can't chance their arm twice in the same way – not two weeks running anyhow.

156

So that's the first thing that hits me when I woke up
yesterday. But it got worse. Mid-morning I heard Ethel
downstairs, having a whale of a time by the sound of it,
pattering about, moving furniture would you believe.
Now normally I would have been down there before
you could turn round, but for once I decided not to do
a thing about it. It was hardly as if I'd get any thanks
for it. I mean, if Mandy thought that much of her
privacy, she wouldn't be having that man here to stay
for the whole weekend.

Come the afternoon though, I couldn't resist it. I had
to see what Ethel had been up to. If it was something
awful, something that was really going to upset
Mandy, maybe I'd be able to sort it out for her before
she got to know about it.

And here was proof if ever it was needed that Ethel is
the strangest woman alive. A girl brings a man to stay,
not once, but twice, and what does Ethel do but start to
smarten the place up. That rug in front of the gas fire
was good enough for us, and later it was good enough
for the Indian girls. Not any more, though, not when it
comes to a certain cheeky young lady and her fancy
man. The very rug that has served faithfully these last
twelve years has been taken up and another one put in
its place. I even know where it's come from. I've been
seeing those greens and pinks staring out from the all-
purpose box in the junk shop round the corner for the
last two weeks. The point is, though, it looks new
compared to the old and by Ethel's lights, that's
pampering. When you think about it, it's no wonder
Mandy thinks she can get away with murder, because
there's Ethel practically telling her she can.

And after that it's just downhill all the way. He's
here, and you've guessed it, it's like living in a
madhouse.

He's even interfered with the air we all breathe. No,
really. You could still smell it – him – on the landing,

on the stairs long after they'd gone out. I'm not joking – the man wears perfume. You can't mistake it. And I don't mean aftershave either. There's a world of difference between a splash of Old Spice and this. It comes at you in waves – like the ones you're supposed to think of every time you catch a whiff of it – Mediterranean waves rushing over broken columns and all that. Well, it was bad enough on the landing, but when it started drifting up the stairs it was time to take Active Measures. I didn't have any air freshener to hand, but I had something just as effective. And maybe I did feel that bit dizzy after I'd sprayed it around everywhere, but I'll tell you something – I'd rather be knocked out by a respectable fly spray than nancy-boy perfume any day of the week, and I expect Joey would too.

I'll come clean, though, when I say there's a limit to how much you can lift your spirits with the liberal use of aerosol. Especially when this was only the Friday night and there was still the whole of the weekend to be got through.

Which probably means you'll be surprised to hear that I woke up this morning in soaring good spirits. And no, I haven't gone mad like the rest of them.

One reason you can maybe guess. It involved not getting a wink of sleep before three, listening to the silence, the perfect silence that tells a story in itself.

So that was one reason, but the other was almost as good, and only hit me in the wee small hours when nothing (and I mean nothing) was going on. I'll give you a clue if you like. It's all to do with the time of year, a time when everyone with a normal life is preparing to join forces and celebrate. Get the picture? In other words, did anyone mention Christmas?

Before you go asking what Christmas has to do with anything, consider this: husbands spend Christmas with their wives. Whether they want to or not, that's the way of the world. Likewise, children who get on with their mums and dads. And that, you may think, accounts for most folk when it comes to what the world is doing at Christmastime. But then again, what about those people who aren't married or who don't get on with their folks? What sort of holiday can they look forward to, once it starts rolling round to that time of year again? Says a lot about your life, it does, who you spend your Christmas with. Which brings us to Mandy, bearing in mind everything else we know about the old kid. What will she be doing for Christmas?

Well, there's an answer to that, of course. And I'll just say it involves a certain interested party and no end of goodwill.

In other words, nobody else might want her, but there's still someone up here who loves her.

But it's not going to be just any old Christmas. Any fool can buy a tree, put his turkey in the freezer, pick the Christmas cards off the mat and hope he's got enough milk to tide him over. Larry's and Mandy's Christmas is going to be something else again. The Christmas I've got in mind is going to take no end of forward planning, with lists and checklists made up and completed, down to the smallest detail. Everything in, nothing left out, and all so that Mandy can have a Christmas she will remember for the rest of her life.

Which quite simply means this is no time to dwell on the present. It's time to look to the future, the one that contains Mandy and her little face all rosy and glowing, gazing up and saying to her old pal, 'Merry Christmas Larry. And thank you, thank you for everything.'

Result — until dinner time, they might have been swinging from the lampshades as far as Larry was concerned. He was too busy sitting up to his elbows in lists, trying not to panic. Because no sooner had I started then it hit me. Already I've left it a bit late. They had their bigwig switch on the lights getting on for a fortnight back, and yet there was me, too caught up with other things to give it a second's thought. What I should have remembered was, switching on the lights is only the starting pistol. From now on, it's going to be dog eat dog out there, every man for himself, and what's needed now is some fast and efficient planning.

Think I'm exaggerating? Well, listen to this. Four weeks to go before the big day, and what should appear on the mat this morning but the first of the Christmas cards. It's a tradition all by itself, that one card, turning up like clockwork, a week before everyone else's.

It's from June, of course, showing a bit of the old forward planning herself. You could say that's the small bit of me coming out of her (the rest being entirely her mother). It's supposed to make me think I'm on the top of her list, as well as leave me plenty of time to send one back. And like a fool every year I open it in the faint hope that this time she'll have put something different inside.

And what happens – you give someone a second chance and you get the same old slap in the face. Nothing's changed. Open the envelope, and there it is: 'Hoping to see you this year. Love from June.'

And that's just what I'm talking about. It's always the same. Yet all it would take would be a couple of words to turn everything around. Despite everything. Larry's not the man to bear a grudge. All he wants to see is that 'Love, June' changed to 'Love June *and Bill*'. And you know why? Because that would show she'd worked on him a bit, made the effort. I'm not even after an apology, not any more – just his name at the end of a card, which would amount to the same thing.

Christmas seven years ago it happened. The fifth I'd spent on my own.

Naturally enough, I'd got my own little routine by then. Nothing fancy, just a nice quiet programme of innocent enjoyment, starting off with a decent breakfast while the oven got to work on the turkey. And let me tell you now, it was hot in that kitchen of mine -- a fact which explains everything else. After all, there are women who don't bother to get dressed on Christmas Day until they're about to serve dinner. And I never saw Doreen smarten herself up just to peel the Brussels sprouts.

Only how was I to know I was going to be receiving visitors? First I heard about it was an almighty racket on the stairs, the clumping and clattering of boots and the sound of 'Once in Royal David's City' being murdered by two voices. Next thing, there they were, June and that great hulk of a husband of hers, falling through the kitchen door like a pair of overgrown kids. Snow on their coats like *Christmas with Bing Crosby* and bottles under their arms. Grinning all over their faces.

'Surprise!' Her voice squeaky, a little bit nervous even. His booming, not even pretending to give a damn.

And me, standing there in vest and underpants and nothing on my head. You see, it was too hot even for the hairpiece.

Not expecting visitors, I'd left it by the side of the bed. And that's what they'd done. Caught me standing in my smalls, with a piece of bacon halfway to my mouth and not a hair on the top of my head. Someone in Waltham Abbey would be laughing from now until New Year about this.

And just for starters, June takes one look, and that nervous beam turns into a giggle. 'Oooh Dad. You don't half look a sight.'

The moment she'd spoken she could tell she'd said the wrong thing. Well, she could see my face, couldn't she? That grin disappears like I'd come along and wiped it off myself. A young face she had, even though she was well over thirty then. Always thin, was June, and never one for make-up really. So there was nothing to hide the expression that came over her now. I want to call it her *young* look, but I suppose the word for it really should be anxious. The girl was actually worried about what I was going to say. And that, I'll admit, stopped me in my tracks a bit. And so for a second or two we just stared, me in my underpants and she with her young look, and both of us with the good sense not to say anything, not straight out, not straightaway. And who can tell what would have happened next? It was only five years then and we'd still kept in touch, sort of, on and off . . .

And that's when *he* had to open his mouth.

'Well, go on June girl. Give your old dad a kiss and he'll be all yours again.'

That did it. It must have been the shock of his voice coming between us that brought me back to my senses. Suddenly I was seeing clearly again. Five years of her giving aid and comfort to her mother, keeping in with her and her fancy man. Five years of Fraternization with the Enemy, and she thinks she can come and blot it all out with a kiss, one kiss – because *he* told her so.

Then it was probably straight on from here to Waltham Abbey for Christmas proper. And a good laugh all around.

Surprise. I could do a bit of surprising myself.

I told her she could wipe that silly look off her face for a start. Told her she'd got the wrong house, the wrong man. Larry Mann didn't have a daughter. Not any more. That ended five years ago. Words to that effect. And, yes, a lot more besides.

To tell the truth, it was all a matter of planning again.

That's the only way I can explain what happened that day. I'd spent so much time planning what I'd say to her if I got the chance, it came out without me really having to do anything. Or think anything. All of it justified, mind, every word. Only. Only what I'm saying is, maybe I wouldn't have chosen to come out with it all at once, not then, not if I'd been really thinking about what I was saying. But you know what it's like when you let the water out of the bath and then can't find the plug when you change your mind. And when you do, it's too late – I looked at her, and saw she was starting to cry. Real tears and all. Even her mother could never fake those. I don't suppose she ever saw the need. And it was then that I found the plug. Stopped right where I was, in mid-flow. Didn't say another word. And I'll tell you what else. A moment later, me being the sort of chap I am, and seeing her like that, I might even have found myself taking it all back, well, some of it anyway. I might have. If I'd ever got the chance.

But that's just it. I never did get the chance. Because something happened then that never should have. All of a sudden there was Bill, jumping in where he had no business, between a father and his daughter, pushing her out of the picture and shouting – at me of all people, coming out with things I couldn't bring myself to repeat. Big fat finger, poking me in the chest, big red face, all bristles, shouting into mine, in my own kitchen. The very image of all those louts you see on TV at football matches, insulting decent folk they don't know from Adam.

But do you know the worst thing about it? She let him. Just stood there and never once raised her voice to stop him, not even to complain about his language. And believe me, there's not a respectable woman alive who would have put up with what he was coming out with. All she did finally was to tug on his coat, before disappearing away off down the stairs. One more jab of a finger after, he was behind her. I don't suppose the snow had time to melt on their coats.

Which was good enough for me.

The only thing I can say about it now is to wonder where she finds the raw cheek to keep sending the cards. Because that's not once but twice she's betrayed the last person in the world she ought. Even her mother only managed the one time. There's not a man anywhere who could take that lying down. Yet his name at the bottom, that's all it needs. The next best thing to an apology. I might even get round then to sending one back.

Anyway, where was I? Oh yes. That card of June's, it's a reminder, as if I needed one, that time is getting on. From now on every minute counts.

Chapter Fourteen

So here's the plan.

All weekend it took me in the end. I was so busy
with it that when it came to the time for his nibs to
depart, I didn't even notice. Well, hardly. There was no
way you could escape them completely, not unless you
were stone deaf. Mind you, it's Mandy who's the real
culprit down there, laughing all the time as if life with
His Lordship is just one big joke. Ha ha ha, she goes,
morning noon and night, ruining your concentration
until you find yourself wishing that someone would
come along and switch her off. Makes you wonder
what one person could say that's so funny.

But Sunday comes around once more, and believe it
or not, this time I'm almost wishing I'd seen a bit more
of him while he was still here. Know your enemy,
that's what they say. But with all the work of making
my lists and the fact that they're out nearly more than
they're in, you could hardly say I had the chance. And
anyway, you can hear all about him, just in that
flaming laugh.

I did listen out for her, though, after, in case she took
it into her head to come up once she'd got rid of him.
Not that I wanted her to, not really. Not when all she'd
be doing was seeking company for a mope. No, what
was worrying me was that she'd make her way up
when I was still sitting surrounded with my bits of
lists. One look at them, and she'd know something
was afoot.

But I needn't have worried. She was back here after

seeing him off and the first thing she does is close that bedroom door of hers and not come out till the next morning. Not that she was sleeping. You only had to step inside the bedroom and listen for the sounds coming up through the floor. Silly girl was at it again.

Anyway, here's the plan.

From now to Christmas is one month. Four weeks. That being the case, I've got four lists made out (with copies just to be safe) containing all the items to be gathered in by the end of each one. Are you with me?

List One (headed: Early Miscellaneous) is about the small stuff, plus various things that might be in short supply nearer to the time. So what I'll have by the end of the week are all the nuts, wrapping paper, chocolates — stuff that will keep. Not to mention those classy tree decorations that often disappear by the time you've made up your mind to splash out, the sort you would buy in June if you only had the foresight . . .

Going on to the second week, then, I want to have the tree, pudding, cake, order the turkey, oh, and find out the price of a second TV just in case. Third week will be for buying the liquor and some of the perishables, looking around for stocking-fillers — she's going to have a stocking, naturally, even if it's not her that hangs it up. And the fourth week . . .

Ah now, the fourth week. That's going to be almost the most important week of all. By that time, I reckon this place will be bursting. Christmas could be dropped on us from a great height and still I'd be ready. No fear of either of us having to turn to the other and say, 'Did you forget the . . . ?' It's just not going to happen. It will all be here. Except maybe for one thing. The biggest and the most important thing. It's not written down anywhere on my lists, because it's in a class of its own.

If I haven't found it already, the fourth week is reserved for one thing, and one thing only. Mandy's present.

What are you going to get for her then, Larry? I hear you ask. Well, that's just the point. I don't know. I don't even have the first idea. But between now and the big day my eyes won't have a moment's rest. They're going to be looking looking looking all that time. And when at last I see something that's right, I'll know it. There'll be nothing left to do then.

In other words, I've got my work cut out!

In the meantime though, there's the question of whether to tell Mandy. At first I thought to myself: why not? The old kid is bound to be miserable, faced with a Christmas all by herself. You might say the kindest thing would be to tell her everything's taken care of, that she isn't going to be alone and friendless, that she's going to have Christmas after all, thanks to Larry. Added to which there's the thought of the two of us, filling up the long winter evenings here in front of the gas fire, with all the stuff laid out around us, ticking it off our lists as it comes in, me pouring out the Christmas cheer, and her trotting out her mother's handy hints for turkey leftovers. I mean it's a pleasant picture, you'll admit. Sort of brings Christmas that much closer.

In which case you're probably amazed that I haven't gone ahead and spilled the beans already. Well, I'll tell you why not. He left on the Sunday, and I didn't even catch a glimpse of her until the Wednesday. And that was an insult in itself, her drifting through the door without so much as a word of an apology. You'll forgive me for thinking we were back to the bad old days. But the crowning moment comes after I've finally got her to sit down, and say to her, just by way of testing the water, 'So what have you got planned for Christmas, Mandy love?'

Do you know what her answer was? 'Mmmm?' is what she says. 'Mmmm?'

She wasn't even listening! Sitting there on my settee

in front of my gas fire, and she wasn't even listening to a word I said. It would have gone in one ear and out the other.

No, she's got to wake up a bit first. Wait till she starts noticing the Christmas trees blocking up the windows, and 'Silent Night' piped in at her from all sides. And later, the Sally Army, doing their bit, shaking their boxes under her nose, after what little bit of money she's got. Even those funny types at the college will be handing out the Xmas cards and talking about going home. It'll sink in soon enough, you mark my words. And we'll see what she thinks then, faced with a Christmas without so much as a turkey drumstick.

But you know something, even then I'm not going to tell her. I'm going to wait, hang on till the big day. By then I reckon the poor old kid will be beside herself. But imagine the look on her face when Larry steps in and shows there's been a Christmas waiting for her all along! It'll be like a dream come true. Of all the surprises I've planned for her, this is going to be the best one ever.

But what if she's one of those funny types who don't care if it's Christmas?

The answer is – no chance. I know my Mandy. Even when she's acting up like she has been lately, I know my girl. I've seen what she's like when she's properly alone, when lover boy hasn't been in touch and the last visit begins to wear off. In no time, she'll be up here to see the only friend she's got, listening to all the friendly chat and picking up ideas for that little larder of hers. My Mandy will be back to herself in a twinkling, and she's not the sort not to notice Christmas.

And I was right. Of course. In the end it hardly took any time at all. Friday night she must have been overdoing the snacks again because there she was down in the lav, throwing up like a big kid who's eaten too much birthday cake. And today, Saturday, she was right back to normal. Nice, quiet and attentive. A bit nervy, maybe, but that was hardly my fault, and I wasn't surprised when for the first time in ages she smoked some of the cigarettes I'd put out for her. But more of that later.

First, let me tell you about this morning. I reckon I did my own little bit to press home the point about Christmas. By the purest chance I was in the hall picking my cards off the mat. Thick and fast they're coming now, even for Larry. And that's when she arrives down the stairs, panting slightly as if she'd run all the way.

Well, maybe I shouldn't have done it, but I couldn't resist it. I counted out the cards right there in front of her. Four for me and seven for the Ducks. 'Why Mandy, love,' I said, sounding all surprised. 'There's not a single card here for you. You are Miss Popular, aren't you. Never you mind though. There's plenty of time.'

Now you can tell me I was seeing things, but just for a second there, I could have sworn she looked a bit lost. What's more, she didn't say a word. Just turned and ran back upstairs, which was proof if proof you needed that she'd only come down because she thought there might be something there for her. Only who from? Not from Lover Boy, that's for sure. He never writes.

After that little tête-à-tête it was straight out for the real business of the day. In case you've forgotten, today was the end of week one of the Plan, and Oxford Street was waiting.

Even if I hadn't met up with Mandy, I would have been in a good mood. It's being out that does it, seeing the shops all done up for the Christmas spree. You'd never guess there was a recession – or maybe you would. Maybe that's why they're trying so hard.

Whatever, the effect is lovely, and they're all doing it, even the second-hand shops on the Holloway Road – as if a few bits of tinsel is going to make someone cough up their last five quid on some fleasy old bits of junk. But it helps, doesn't it, reminding you what Christmas is all about. It's the same when it comes to fighting your way through the crowds, putting up with rudeness in the bus queue and so forth. You're all in it together, because you care. The ones who don't care stay at home and don't spend their money. And the shops (at least the ones in the West End) understand that, and make sure to give you the welcome you deserve with their decorations and carols over the intercom. Makes it more tasteful, more like it should be all the year round.

Tired out I was by the time I got home, though. Tired out but happy. There wasn't one single item on my list that wasn't where it should be, namely sitting on my kitchen table, ready to be ticked off and put away.

The wonder was that I still had the strength to talk when Mandy appeared, but once I'd got started there was no stopping me. Somehow I brought up the subject of Christmas, the way it was before Doreen left. Naturally I made it all sound a lot better than it actually was, didn't say a word about the trials and tribulations of spending the season of goodwill with people who are thinking only of themselves. The truth is, I could have gone off on a different tack altogether, mentioning how it was around Christmastime it happened, with Doreen buying in everything we needed, putting it all away, and then announcing that she was off. What sort of woman does that to a man? But I don't say any of this to Mandy. Don't want to give Christmas a bad press do we?

What's more, it was during this that she started to smoke, which makes me think that some of it was hitting home. And so, just to make sure that no chances were lost, I asked her, quite casually: 'And what about you, Mandy love, what plans have you got for the big day?'

Well, it was only the same question as I asked last time, but you should have seen the difference now. Red as a beetroot she went, straightaway. And it was seeing her blush like that that told me there wasn't a word of truth in what was coming next.

'I expect I'll be getting together with a few friends, Larry. Nothing much though. I mean it's not that big a thing, is it? Christmas, I mean.'

And all the time she was pulling at the flecks on her jumper, careful not to look remotely in my direction. And that answer spells it all out for Larry. For one thing, Mandy my girl, he knows when you're telling your little porky pies, because if you try talking about friends, then you've got to be telling lies. The simple fact is, you don't have any. In the first place, you can't afford them; you don't have the money to do anything they do, and in the second place, you haven't got the time. You've been too busy thinking about lover boy, saving it all up for him, with just enough left over for that so-called work you're doing. You're only lucky you've got Larry to understand you. Who doesn't go on to ask why you've gone the colour of a Jersey tomato when he asks a perfectly simple question.

So, a far cry from a few days ago when all you could manage as answer was 'Mmmm?' Oh it's sinking in all right. I reckon there's no way anyone is going to be forgetting about Christmas around here.

Anyway, I didn't push it. I mean, it just wouldn't have been right to go depressing the girl too much. That's not old Larry's way. Besides, now that we'd dealt with Christmas, I had something else to talk about.

I'd found those cuttings, you see, the ones from the newspaper. It took that long in the end, I was

171

beginning to think I'd got shot of them. Searched all through the drawers I did, not to mention the cupboards. I must have emptied the cocktail cabinet twice over and still no joy. Finally it was only by a bit of good luck that I found them at all. I was moving the wardrobe in the spare room, which was a job in itself. And there it was, the old brown envelope I'd forgotten about. I reckon it must have fallen down the back, and even then I only found it because the wardrobe snagged the carpet up and there it was, sandwiched between the lino and the rest. It couldn't have been more hidden if someone had put it there himself, but I wasn't surprised. You can't live in comfort in a small place like this unless you keep things tidy. I reckon I've got all sorts tucked away in surprising places and then just clean forgotten about them.

The point is, I was glad I found them. I can go on till I'm blue in the face about the dangers of stepping outside your own front door, but there's nothing like a bit of newsprint to hammer it home. Makes it more official. So purely to take her mind off Christmas a bit, I leaned over and picked the envelope off the coffee table and handed it to her.

'Look what I just happened to come across yesterday, Mandy love. I know you're always thinking I fuss too much. But take a look at what's in there and maybe you'll understand why your poor old Larry gets in such a state sometimes.'

So of course, being the sweet kid she is, she goes right ahead and opens it, didn't even seem to mind me getting a bit closer while she was at it. The truth was, I'd sort of forgotten myself exactly what it was inside.

Well, newspaper cuttings, naturally. That was the whole point. What I hadn't realized, or at least had forgotten, was how many. Not just the local stuff, but from all of the big newspapers as well. But then, it was hardly that surprising. When something like this

172

happens practically on your front doorstep, you're bound to take an interest. I daresay Ethel's got a pile of her own twice the size.

Anyway, I let Mandy sort them out, separating the first lot from the second on the table in front of us while I tried not to breathe down her neck. Normally I wouldn't sit so close as to have to worry about something like that, but I had to be able to see, didn't I. What's more she needed a bit of help now and then. 'She was the first one,' I'd say, recognizing the photo, and hand it to her so she could put it in the first pile, then go on to find something for the second pile. But mostly I left it all up to her. Then we sat there and read, cosy as you like with not even the TV on to interfere, just the two of us and the gas fire popping in friendly fashion.

After a bit, when I was sure she'd read all there was and was just filling in time by looking at the pictures, I said, 'Well then Mandy, what do you think?'

For a second she didn't answer. Too busy staring at the photo of the older woman. Not that she could have seen much. You know what newspaper pictures are like. A blur of female, with hair much too fancy for her age, leering out at you with a glass in her hand. Why do they always show pictures of the deceased that must have been taken when they were at least one over the eight? One of life's mysteries, I reckon.

'So go on, what do you think?' I said again.

'Well,' Madam says at last. 'It's very sad. Both strangled like that, and no-one ever found. And of course it must have been worrying for you – and Mrs Duck especially. She must have been the same age as the older one when it happened.' Then she stops. 'Oh!'

'What?' says I.

'Nothing,' she says. 'I was just wondering if they knew each other, she and Ethel. That would have made it really sad, then, wouldn't it?'

173

'Well, you can stop wondering,' I tell her. 'Nobody knew her from Adam. Not a soul came forward. See it's all there, in writing. Ashamed you see.'

'Ashamed?' says Mandy, all innocent, just as you'd expect. Ashamed of what?'

Well, even I had to blush a bit. Still, an honest question demands an honest answer. 'Well, it's obvious isn't it, Mandy love. She was one of those, you know, women who are no better than they should be. That would have been why he caught her.'

'Oh, you mean a prostitute. She died because she was a prostitute. Oh Larry why?'

Well, there was no answer to that one. Last thing in the world you'd expect was Mandy coming out with a word like that so matter-of-fact. Twice. I was still coughing to cover up the embarrassment, when what must she do but carry on, and on the same theme, no less.

'The other one wasn't though,' she says.

'What other one?' says I. So you can see the state I was in.

'The younger one. The second one who died, all those years after the first. She was just a local woman on her way home from her friend's. No way was she a prostitute.'

'Oh no?' I was that surprised I forgot to blush any more. See, somehow or other I'd always thought she was. But Mandy was holding up the cuttings, the one from *The Times* on top, and sure enough, it didn't say anything there about her being one . . . you know, one of those.

Then I stopped being surprised. In fact it only went to prove my point. And I said as much. 'There you go, Mandy love. That's what I've been saying all along. The sort of person who did this wasn't to know that. All he saw was a woman out on the street when she shouldn't be, and made a perfectly natural mistake. So

174

what did he do but go straight ahead and do her in anyway. Silly woman had it coming if you ask me.'

Well, she doesn't like this, you can tell from the way she shifts around a bit on the settee next to me and says, 'Larry, I don't think . . .'

But this is my chance, the opportunity to say what I've been trying to get across all along. 'No, Mandy love. You listen to me. Now can you see why your old Larry worries so much. You don't know what's out there, yet you waltz along those roads after dark like you owned the place. Someone, some day is going to get the wrong idea.'

'But Larry, it was such a long time ago. Look how old the cuttings are. I mean, it's not the sort of thing that happens every day, now, is it?' Then all of a sudden, she goes quiet, adds, 'Oh look, I never noticed. It happened at Christmastime, both times.'

Right out of the blue, you can see the fight has gone out of her. And what could be more fitting? It was that mention of Christmas you see. The conversation had gone full circle, and here was Mandy suddenly looking all mopy again, without yours truly ever having to mention the C word.

What more was there to say? Nothing, that's what. These things have a habit of sinking in by themselves, I reckon.

You know what? I'm going to have a good night's sleep tonight. I just know it.

Chapter Fifteen

In the end, I gave her the cuttings. Absolutely insisted that she have them, and you know, she's been in before eight every night for the past week. So there you are, I reckon the penny has dropped at last.

Having said that, maybe there is another reason after all. It's a proper routine with her now, looking for something in the post. She comes home, rushing through that front door as if she can't wait, only to stop by the hall table. Then, seeing as there's nothing for her there, it's a case of padding off down the corridor to the Ducks' kitchen to ask if there's been any mail at all. They're getting fed up with her already, coming in with the same question night after night. Yesterday I just happened to be in the hall myself when I heard Ethel tell her in no uncertain terms that if someone gets a letter, it's no concern of hers. It would be sitting there on the hall table, and Why Should She (Mandy) Think Otherwise? I don't think the old kid will be asking again.

But you know, it's a minor mystery. It can't just be Christmas cards she's looking for surely. So who *is* she waiting to hear from? Keep ruling out Francis, is my opinion. You can learn a lot about a man from the way he spends his weekends, and he is not a writer, you take my word for it.

Another time, it might be one more thing to keep me awake at night, but not now. It's the end of Week Two and Larry's been falling asleep the moment his head's hit the pillow. Hard work, that's what it is, but I'm not complaining. It's all gone like a dream – up to a point.

There's been the weather for a start – good crisp London weather, as if someone had taken the lid off the city and all you could see when you looked up was blue sky, pale and clear as a glacier mint. Even the traffic has a ring to it. Mind you, it hasn't half been cold. Open your mouth to speak and you can feel your gums dry up. Better not to say anything at all if you can help it. Not even when you start noticing faces you haven't seen for years popping up on the Holloway Road with Christmas carriers in their hands. It's got to be the weather, bringing them all out in their droves.

As for keeping to the timetable, nothing could have been smoother. Last night, Friday, I looked at my list and every mortal thing that was on it was sitting there in front of me, waiting to be put away. Not surprisingly I went to bed a happy and contented man.

And then, long before I was ready to drop off to sleep, it starts. The nagging doubt. And what begins as a niggle grows bigger and bigger, until I'm there, wide awake, tossing and turning like a nervous wreck.

It's been two weeks of serious shopping, but always at the back of my mind has been the thought of that one important object still to find. Mandy's present. But that's the trouble – two weeks and I haven't seen a thing. I've told myself I'll recognize it when I see it, that it's just out there, waiting, but nothing has even come close. So now the question is: how long will it take? Followed by: and what if I don't find it at all?

Needless to say, I didn't get a wink of sleep all night. The only thing I could do in the end was to promise myself that first thing this morning I would take myself off to the West End again, and forget about everything else.

Mistake Number One, though, was not stopping in long enough for a proper breakfast. If there's one thing I've learned today, it's that a couple of slices of bread and marmalade are not sufficient for a man with a mission. I'd no sooner stepped off the bus when the old stomach starts to growl. And so on to Mistake Number Two. Instead of popping right then into the nearest café for a snack, I just decided to keep going. Decide is the wrong word. It simply didn't occur to me to stop. All I could think of was Mandy's present, how I had to start looking, how time was getting short.

But then the problem was, where to start. The trouble with lists is that you get used to them telling you exactly what it is you're looking for. If suddenly you don't have one you can feel completely at sea – like I did. I mean, I knew where I was all right – in the West End – but without one of my little lists in my hand pointing me in the right direction, I might as well have been in the jungle.

Jungle – that's a good word, considering where I ended up first of all. Fifty yards from the bus stop I passed a record shop – you couldn't miss it. There was music blaring out on to the pavement in all directions, but at least it gave me an idea. Because there was June all those years ago nearly driving us out of our minds with the noise of her little portable she got after her Aunt Dolly. Mad she was about her records. Didn't have very many, but what she had, she played over and over again. I don't think we knew a moment's peace until finally it broke down under the strain. (It was only a cheap little thing, nothing like what I've got up there now.) But June was broken-hearted. The point is, if it was June as a young girl that I was buying for now, I'd know exactly what to get for her.

Well, it was worth a try, anyway. I reckoned I could at least step inside and ask for something to appeal to a nice quiet young person with refined tastes. Which brings me back to what I meant about the jungle. If the music had seemed loud on the street, here it was deafening, banging away like there was a war going on around us. And as for the shop assistants – don't remind me. I took one look at them and walked straight out again. They were just a load of black kids most of them, straight off the street I'd say, standing around as if they owned the place. The thought of having one of them laughing in my face, or worse still, not taking a blind bit of notice when I talked to him was too much. Better to get out before I gave them the chance.

And it was only when I was outside that I remembered: in any case, Mandy doesn't have a record player.

You can see how this day was shaping up, then. Another experience like that and it would have finished me. As it was, with my legs beginning to wobble, I had the sense then to walk back to the Tottenham Court Road and find myself that café and a timely cup of tea. But even there, things were no better. I sat with the cup in front of me, imagining how it was going to be. Never mind the expensive tipple and Mandy and me in funny hats. It would still be Christmas without a present. Or to be more exact, a present like any other, that didn't tell her anything about what she meant to me, and me to her. Just an expensive bit of nothing wrapped up in fancy paper. Even Francis could do better than that.

Two cups it took before I started to calm down, but still I didn't feel any better inside. It was all I could do to get myself outside again. I had to tell myself there was Mandy to think about, and I couldn't let her down. Out on the pavement though it all hit me afresh. Here I was with only thirteen shopping days to go, and I didn't have a clue what to do next. For a minute I just stood there, watching the world go by, watching the youngsters especially. Honestly, I was in such a state that if I'd seen a girl who looked remotely like my

Mandy, I might have gone up to her and asked straight out what she wanted for Christmas. Mad, that's what she would have thought of me. Probably would have run off to the nearest policeman and had me reported. But I didn't do any such thing, for the simple reason that I could have stood there all day and not seen anyone who was a bit like her. That's the thing about Mandy. She's a one-off. And all Larry wants to do is show her he knows it.

And then it came, a small miracle in itself. Illumination.

Nothing had changed. I was still standing there like an idiot, when out of the crowd there walked a woman. But not just any woman, none of your Doreens or your Junes or Ethels. The first thing you noticed about her was that she was smart – by which I mean beautifully dressed, hair done all nicely and held back by velvet band, and with a face that could have been any age between twenty-five and forty. A cut above the rest is how you'd describe her, definitely not the sort you see on the Holloway Road on a Saturday afternoon. But the next most noticeable thing about her was the way she managed to walk somehow without getting pushed and jostled like everybody else. It was almost as if she was creating her own space just so that for a few brief seconds she could stand out enough for me to notice her – and what she was carrying. A little plastic carrier bag, hardly bigger than her own hand. One look at it and you knew that inside was something small, and very expensive. A Harrods bag. A second later she'd passed me, and a second after that she was swallowed up in the crowd like everybody else. Another moment and I wouldn't even have registered her. But that was all I needed.

Harrods is where people like her always go at Christmastime. Where, I bet, Mandy's mum does all her shopping – when she isn't in Hong Kong. I mean it's supposed to be the place where you can find anything, isn't it? So where else should I look for Mandy's present?

Salvation, that's what it was. There had been two problems with Mandy's present – firstly where to look and only then what to get her. And here was the first problem solved.

And what that boiled down to was knowing, suddenly, that everything was going to be all right. So what did I do? I turned around and went straight back inside the café and had another cup of tea. Only this time I enjoyed it – and the custard slice that went with it. See, I had all the time in the world.

But when did I last set foot in Harrods? I tried working that one out on the bus on the way over. I reckoned it was years even before Doreen upped sticks. She never did like the place, and I'll tell you why. She never had the vision. She'd walk around the displays telling anyone who'd listen how she could get it all in Selby's on the Holloway Road, and cheaper. In the end, even June would have to grab her by the coat and beg her to put a sock in it because of the looks we were getting from the staff. When you bear that in mind, it's hardly any wonder that I've never been back. She was a woman who simply didn't have it in her to rise to the occasion.

So today was proof to end all proof that I'm better off without her. Do you know, it was a thrill in itself just walking through one of their great double doors and knowing this time I wasn't going to get shown up. And you could feel the difference straightaway. Welcome – that's what the place was saying to you from the very first blast of hot air as you came into the shop. Welcome, you look like our sort of customer, the sort who appreciates the finer things in life, namely quality merchandise for quality folk. '

Fanciful? Not at all. I tell you, that shop has an

atmosphere of its own, and perhaps it's just that you have to be a special type of person to feel it. Nothing else could have explained the sense of – what's the word? – wellbeing that simply came over me as I stepped inside. I took one look around me, heaved a great sigh of relief, and said to myself, Larry my boy, you've come to the right place.

And after that? I just wandered, didn't even look for anything, not as such. Now that I knew where I was, there was no need to rush. This first visit could be an indulgence, I could stop and look at everything, or nothing, marvel at it all, like I was at a museum. Only the difference was, here, they don't charge.

Having said that, even in a place like Harrods, there's only so much you can do when you reach my age. Suddenly, after three hours of heaven, it was getting on for five and I hadn't made it off the ground floor, and there was me, in the middle of Accessories discovering I was on my last legs. Although firm common sense told me to leave it for now, to stop where I was and go back the way I came, I still couldn't bring myself to hurry. In three hours, the place had done all it could to make me feel part of it.

Which is to say, even in the last moments, coming through Perfumes, I was dawdling, breathing in the most expensive air in the world. I mean, have you ever looked at the prices on those scents? And besides, I've got a sensitive nose. Ask anyone who knows me. Coming at me from all sides it was, as shop staff sprayed bottles of the stuff into the air or on to the wrists of anyone who asked. And that's when I smelt it. *The* scent.

What happened next is . . . well, difficult. I don't mean that it was awful, only that it was unlike me. Just one of those things that happen when you're too tired to think what you're doing, or why you're doing it. You get carried away on the spur of the moment. And anyway, no-one could have said there was any harm in it.

The scent that I caught was not like the others. It was familiar for one thing. But it wasn't until I turned and tried to follow it around with my nose that I realized why. There on a counter was a framed picture of broken columns and the waves rushing in, and I knew. It was his smell. The one he insists on leaving on the landing of decent folks to kill the flies. And here was gallons of the stuff, standing around in bottles, and calling itself Andrex or whatever. You could even try it on if you wanted. There was one of those bottles with the word 'tester' round its neck which could only mean one thing. What's more, the kid behind the counter wasn't going to object. If all of the seven dwarfs had come up for testing he would still have been too busy ogling himself in the mirror to see. It has to be said, they don't have the same calibre of staff working there any more.

Finally, I noticed this. Here in the atmosphere of the place, it didn't seem to smell quite so bad, not when you consider the effect it had at home. And that, you could say, was what made me curious.

Well, you've probably guessed what happened next – when you bear in mind that everything there was telling me to have a go, and that when a place like Harrods tells you to have a go, that's what you do. The long and the short of it is, before I'd even thought about what I was doing, I'd reached out a hand for the bottle and started splashing it on wherever appropriate. And when that didn't seem to make much difference I did the same all over again until it was running down my neck, down under my collar and I don't know where else.

And this is where the really strange thing happened. Now that it was me that was wearing the stuff, not only did it not smell so bad, it actually smelt quite nice. Not my cup of tea in the usual run of things, not by a long chalk. But it was something different to do with your time. And it was funny to think that everyone would be able to smell you coming. More than that, although it was just a smell, it was almost like wearing something that was solid, like a disguise. If Doreen or anybody was to catch a whiff of me on a dark night, she'd think I was someone completely different. And if it was Mandy on the that same dark night, she'd think it was . . .

Piece of fun, that's all it was, no different from trying on a hat. But I'll say this, it taught me something. I'm willing to bet anything you like that dressing up in fancy smells is half the secret of his success. No, really. Listen to this: there I was sitting innocently enough on the 104 looking forward to home and a well-earned rest, when up comes a woman who plonks herself down beside me without so much as a second glance. Next thing I know, before the bus has even moved off her nose is starting to twitch and – this is the honest truth – I'm suddenly aware of all these side-ways looks coming in my direction. In short, the glad eye.

Considering that she was sixty-five if she was a day, and painted up like a shop-front to boot, it was a relief to get off the bus when the time came. Who knows what sort of thoughts were going through her mind? And in a woman of her age. Makes you shudder, honestly it does.

All of which made the sight of Mandy and her sweet face standing there behind the front door, almost as if she'd been waiting for me, even more welcome than usual. Mind you, she looked as if she could have done with a bit of a day out of the house herself, she was that pale. Lovely little smile she gave me, though, when I said to her, 'Cheer up Mandy, love. It might never happen.'

Still, if she'd been hoping for a bit of the old tea and chat, she was going to have to be disappointed. The only thing on my mind now was getting a bit of hot food inside me after eating practically nothing all day. Then again, being the considerate sort, I didn't want to just leave her standing there with no explanation apart from needing my tea. It wouldn't have seemed nice somehow, and besides, she might have seen that as a reason for not bothering to come up later.

So what I actually said to her was, 'I'm going to have to get on, Mandy love. I don't know what it is, but I've just come over queer. Think I'll go and have a lie-down.'

Straightaway, she answers, 'Oh Larry, are you not feeling very well?'

That's my Mandy. All concern. I tell you that girl deserves everything that's coming to her.

'I'll be all right love. But I tell you what, drop in later when you've got a minute, just in case.'

So that was that sorted.

But there was one last thing. On my way upstairs, taking it slowly, naturally, I had a feeling that something was going on behind me, down in the hall. So on the middle landing I stopped, took a little peek over the banister ... and there was Mandy, down below, exactly where we'd been talking, only now her head was up, and that little nose of hers was twitching away like billy-oh.

Now, I know there were some nasty moments today, but when you think about the rest, I'd be tempted to say that this, the second Saturday before Christmas, was pretty close to what some folk would call a nearly perfect day. Mandy love, we're going to have a lovely time, such a lovely time.

Chapter Sixteen

Just give me a moment to think. That's all I need. A few minutes' quiet reflection.

There are things I've still got to take in. Letters coming out of nowhere. The sort that fly at you, wanting answers, telling you to do this and do that, and all by such and such a deadline, not giving you any time. The sort of letters you don't need, not on top of everything else. The sort of letters you don't want.

One letter to be exact. One letter too many, though. One bloody letter.

Excuse language.

It's what you get for letting yourself look on the bright side. Just for a little while, I had started to think that maybe somebody up there loves me after all. That after twelve long years of watching the bad prosper, maybe the tide was on the turn. Because all of a sudden you've caught a glimpse of pure goodness shining like a silver lining in a wicked world – and keeping its shine. People come along, try to put it out, try to drag it into the dark, and wonder of wonders, the good stays good. Keeps on shining, brighter than ever. And it's then you find yourself thinking: maybe you're not alone. There's another voice beside yours, crying in the wilderness. And this, finally, is your reward.

But it's all piss and nonsense isn't it? Another one of life's little jokes. Because out of the blue there comes a letter. And it's not even as if it's addressed to me.

But I'm the one who's got it. I can't put it down, and it's not mine to throw away.

It arrived this morning. The letter she's been waiting for. I came downstairs to find Ethel there by the hall table, a pile of cards beside her which she ignores while she holds a large white envelope up to the light, no doubt wishing she had X-ray eyes.

If only that were all, though.

Ethel has no shame. She put the letter down fast enough when she saw me, but there was no mistaking what she'd been up to. Yet she had the cheek to look me straight in the eye and trill, 'Morning Mr Mann,' as if I'd done no more than find her checking her pools.

'And good morning to you, Mrs D.'

The letter's lying between us, second-hand now, thanks to her. And all she does is smirk, and mince off down the corridor.

After she's gone, I check what's there for me. Two cards, both with the postmark of Reigate. And that's it, the whole year's news stamped on the outside of the envelopes. In other words, Aunts Gertie and Freda are still alive and kicking and fit enough to get out and buy a couple of stamps – and still refusing to do anything together. The insides of the cards themselves wouldn't tell you so much.

Then there was Mandy's letter. See, I knew straight off it was a letter not a card. Ethel never bothered to put it back on the table properly and it only took a slight brush of my arm for it to fall on the floor. Naturally I picked it up and it was the feel of it between my fingers that told me. Letter. No doubt about it.

And it was that, oddly enough, that got me wondering, even despite everything else, despite Mandy tripping up and downstairs to see if anything like it had arrived. It depended on the way you looked at it. If you thought it was normal on top of the labour of having to fill in hundreds of cards, for someone then to go to the trouble of writing a letter – and a thick one at that – all well and good. But if you thought it was a bit

187

odd to be making that much more work for yourself at a time like this, then you'll know why it bothered me. See, the way I looked at it was, you would only go to the length of writing a letter at Christmastime if you had something very important to say.

Postmark Hong Kong.

All the way from Hong Kong then. All this way just to be fingered and mauled by Ethel Duck in her nosiness. What had been meant for Mandy's eyes only practically had thumb marks all over it. I put it back on the table as it was.

It was as I was climbing upstairs again with my own cards that the picture came into my head, as clear as if it was right there in front of me. Ethel standing by her kitchen door, just waiting to spring out again and take up where she'd left off. Holding Mandy's letter this way and that, trying to make out something, anything, of what was inside. Have I not said it before? The woman's curiosity knows no bounds.

And I knew then, there was only one thing I could do. I went straight back down, doubtless disappointing a certain party poised to return to the snoop, and picked it up, to take to Mandy's kitchen. But it was as I stepped through her door that another thought occurred to me, almost worse than the one before. The only way I could leave Mandy's letter here, on her table, and keep Ethel away from it was by stopping in all day. That would mean a whole day's Christmas shopping lost. And I couldn't do that, I just couldn't. Not when we were into the third week of the Plan.

The upshot was, the letter ended up propped against my kettle in full view to remind me it was there, while I got myself ready to go out. Only it would have been better in a way if I'd simply shoved it into a drawer and tried to forget all about it until Mandy came home. As it was, it just sat there on the side, ruining my concentration. Even when I wasn't in the same room, I could feel it there, like another person. Like a warning almost. And all the time I kept coming back to it, looking at it, and wondering.

I could try to explain, I suppose. This may sound mad, but where Mandy is concerned, it's almost as if I've developed a second sight. Or you could simply call it instinct, popping up whenever there's anything remotely connected with her. I know now the reason she does things, often even before she's thought of doing them herself. She's become familiar ground, you could say. And that's half the beauty of her. Someone who's at all decent is almost bound to act in a certain way. That's why, when you think about it, the Doreens and the Junes of this world are so unpredictable.

I even know what makes her unhappy – Francis not phoning, Francis not coming when he promises, Ethel snooping and . . . And any mention of her mum and dad.

Well, surely you remember that time she nearly bit my head off just for mentioning the subect? I was licking my wounds for days after.

Which brings me back to the letter. There couldn't be any doubt who it was from, and what could be more natural – a letter from her mum and dad? Nothing, until you remember she told me that she and her father hadn't said a word to each other in two years. She never did go into details, and to spare her feelings, I never did ask, but you knew who was at the bottom of it. Francis, a man who could split a family apart. Francis who was still on the scene.

In which case, why were they sending letters now?

Do you see the way my mind was working then? Everything logical and thought-out, and all leading up to the certainty that this wasn't just any old letter.

So what do you put in a letter that no-one in their right minds would be sending unless there was something special they needed to say? It's hardly going

189

to be news about what the dog's been up to, or how too much rain recently has been ruining the dahlias. No, it would have to be something else. Something important. Something big enough to cross the Gulf of Discord.

I was sure of this, though. It's not good news. If Doreen won the pools, the last person she'd think about was me. Good news isn't important enough, not to other people, and least of all as a reason for making up a quarrel. So it has to be bad. Nothing else will do.

Bad news then. *Please come home, your father is dead.*

Yes well, we don't want to overreact. It doesn't have to be that bad, with Mandy disappearing off to look after her mum, whether she wants to or not. Better to be realistic, bearing in mind what they've all been up to already. Maybe something on the lines of: *Your father is very ill. Perhaps dying. Do not come home, though, as the sight of you would only distress him.* That would make sense. Putting her in the picture but making no bones about what they think of her.

Only, you tell me – what sort of thing is that for a young girl to have to hear two weeks before Christmas?

The effect on me was bad enough. But that's not what counts. It's her you've got to imagine – Mandy, reading something like that, on her own, when probably all she'd been doing was looking forward to a Christmas card from her folks. Mandy having to learn from cold print what should have been broken to her gently by a friend. *Sit down Mandy love. I've got a bit of bad news.* Mandy suffering because of it. Yet what have I been saying all this time? That Larry would do anything in the world to make her happy. Now here he was, about to hand over the one thing guaranteed to do the opposite.

What sort of man would that have made me? The kind who could happily go back on his word? The kind

190

who could take a letter like that, knowing what it might contain, and hand it over for someone to read cold and unprepared?

I don't think so.

I'll show you the sort of man I am. I traipsed back and forth across my little bit of kitchen, brewing up pot after pot of tea, moving the letter for the kettle to boil, putting it back again, supping tea I didn't really want, asking myself again and again what I should do. And that went on for two hours. Two solid hours.

So what happened then? Well, in the first place the kitchen pretty soon started to drip with condensation. Hardly surprising given all the steam that had been pumping out of the old kettle. I reckon by the end of the morning that letter was halfway to coming unstuck all by itself. In other words, what happened in the end more or less came about without any help from me. And when you consider how Ethel would have done the same thing without thinking twice merely to satisfy her instincts, my holding out till it was nearly the afternoon just seemed daft. In short then, two minutes after finally facing up to the inevitable, I had the letter lying open in front of me.

But would you believe it, even then I couldn't bring myself to read it. Not straightaway. The old hand started to shake – just like it did outside her bedroom the first time I ever went in. I'd had to give myself a good talking-to then, and it was the same now. After a deep breath I looked down and started to read.

The first thing I noticed was the date. Three weeks ago. It's Christmas. Everything takes longer.

'Dearest Amanda,

  Your letter arrived this morning. I don't have the words to describe how we felt. All I can tell you is that you have not been out of our thoughts for a single minute. Sweetheart, if you could only have told us where you were . . .

But already that sounds as if we are blaming you, which is wrong. Believe me when I say we blame no-one but ourselves. It is a terrible thing to be a parent and know that you have hurt a child. Especially when this was the last thing we intended.

I'm not going to waste precious words and time. The episode of your father and that woman shook us in ways we could hardly imagine. But whatever its importance then, it is over. Your father and I are closer than we ever were, perhaps because finally we understand each other a little better.

Amanda, I think what I am trying to say is, we are only people. Could you remember that when I tell you that all we want to do is hold you in our arms?

I would write more, but I have your letter here. It is too short. Every time I read it I feel there is so much you are not telling us. Are you in trouble? Or has someone else hurt you in any way, because if so . . .'

Do you really want to hear the rest? There wasn't very much. At least nothing that you could pinpoint as relevant. No mention of Francis. Not so much as a dicky bird. No real news even, not on the lines of how they both were and what the weather was like.

What had made the enevelope so bulky was a wad of something else – little bits of paper stapled together. It took me half a minute just to work out what they could be – not having ever travelled on a plane. You see, it was an airline ticket. And attached to that was another piece of paper that read, 'Heathrow–Hongkong, 23rd December. Please confirm A.S.A.P.'

That's what the letter was really about. They're trying to bring her home for Christmas. They want to take her away.

So.

So do you want to know what I've been doing for the past hour? Emptying the cupboards, that's what. Bringing it all out – the stuff I've been buying these past weeks. There's too much to go on my little kitchen table, so it's piled up on the sides, and that's not including the Christmas tree lying on the bed in the spare room just waiting for someone to come along and unwrap it. Seeing it spread out now, it makes you wonder how I managed to fit it all in in the first place.

It's all here, you know. Brandy, sherry, advocaat, ginger ale, glass balls, tinsel, Victorian crackers, brazil nuts, liqueur chocolates, liqueurs on their own, mint chocolate, white chocolate, wrapping paper, tangerines, novelty biscuits, serviettes with holly on them . . . I could go on and on. I haven't left out a thing, barring the fresh stuff, the vegetables and the brandy butter, but even that's all taken care of. Everything else is here, down to the last hazelnut whirl.

Only, I don't like hazelnut whirls. I got them just for her, for Mandy.

The funny thing is, all of a sudden, I've got the sort of ache in my guts that makes me feel as if I've eaten a whole mountain of them already. Why didn't she tell me that she's been writing letters too?

For the past five minutes though, I've been sitting here thinking I really should apologize to her. All this time, there's been me thinking it was her fault her parents weren't talking to her. Then what happens, it turns out they were the ones at fault all along. There it is, in black and white: 'Believe me when I say we blame no-one but ourselves.' See what I mean? The poor girl is innocent. She cut herself off because they were wrong. If you ask me, when it comes to families, I reckon hers are on a par with Doreen and June. Yet she never said a word.

The girl is a Saint. That's all I can say.

They're sorry now though – if you were to believe this letter. But are they? It occurs to me that you can read that letter any way you like, but you won't find one word of apology. A lot of beating around the bush, but look for one mention of the S word, and you'll look in vain. It's not there.

You know what it's all about, of course. It's the old story. Round about Christmastime, people develop a conscience, nothing too uncomfortable, just the odd twinge and the tiny worry of what they would say if anybody asks. Only they don't want to go putting themselves out too much, and as for an apology – perish the thought. So what do they do, they send a letter.

I bet they wouldn't even have got round to that, if it hadn't have been for Mandy making the first move. And we all know the reason for that. Ethel. Quite obviously, and despite everything I've tried to do to help, the girl has never been able to get used to it – all the snooping and the prying. So in a moment of weakness she writes. And the next thing we know is this. The last people in the world she wants to see, jumping on the bandwagon.

Sounds familiar? It's June and Bill all over again. Only in this case it's not even a visit. Just a letter if you please.

There's a word for that sort of thing. It's called Blackmail. It happened to me, Christmastime seven years ago, and I've never once got over it. June and Bill, invading me here in my own house, laughing in my face, so sure they could bring me round. Five minutes of them, that's all it took. A whole Christmas ruined. And thanks to them, untold hours of pain and suffering.

You know, I'd do anything to spare Mandy that. I would, honestly.

The question is – how far would I go?

I reckon the answer to that is easy. The next question is a different one entirely, namely: what would Mandy want me to do? Is this really the sort of thing she'd want to see? To which I would reply: I know my Mandy.

I'm putting the letter away. Not far – only behind the bread bin. You would even be able to see it sticking out if you look. There's a margin of white that's unmistakable. So there's no question of me hiding it, let alone getting rid of it. You see, she's going to have to read it in the end. You can only protect someone so far. There'll come a time when she'll have to decide for herself about some things. Naturally I would do my best to help, maybe make the odd suggestion, but what it comes down to is, there's only so much you can do. No-one should ever try to come between a parent and its child.

In the meantime however, let the old kid enjoy herself, have the Christmas she deserves. And just for starters, I'm going to be making out a card for her now – all robins and holly and snow. In a big white envelope and all. Then she can't say that no-one is sending her anything for Christmas.

As for me, I'm staying put. Up and down is how you could describe today. Happy one minute, tragic the next. Believe me, it takes it out of you. Right now, I'm back on the level, knowing I've done my best for her, for Mandy. But I don't think I could stand an afternoon at the mill. Rest is what I need now, a few refreshing hours in front of the TV with my feet up. I'm not going to lose by it. Today I looked with the eyes of a man who thought he was going to have to eat everything in sight, and it brought it all home to me – there's enough here to keep us going till Easter.

Besides, I took another blow this afternoon. Suddenly – round about two o'clock I suppose – I realized that with all the brouhaha, I couldn't remember when

I'd fed Joey last. Not that I'm entirely to blame. I mean, I know he's covered up a lot of the time, but surely it's not beyond the imagination of a bird to remind me he's there now and then. And he's been noisy enough in the past. Anyway, I took the cover off the cage, and there he was stiff as a peg beneath his perch. I gave him a little prod just to be sure. But it was no good. He was dead as a doornail. Mind you, he never was the same bird after Mandy stopped taking notice of him. All the same, you'd have expected an animal to have more staying power than that. Which leads me to wonder if there wasn't something wrong with him in the first place. Now if you ask me, there may be an interesting principle at stake here. If you pay good money for something – no matter what it is – you have the right to expect it to be fit for the purpose you bought it – which in this case was sitting on his perch and staying alive.

So what about it? What about me taking him back to where I bought him and telling them I got a bad bargain? Maybe they'd do me a part exchange – on a parrot, say. Mandy might like a parrot to talk to, and I don't suppose it would be that much more trouble to keep than a canary. Anyway, there's no sense in just throwing him away, not without giving him a go. So I've wrapped him up in a bit of the *Sunday Express* and popped him in the bottom of my shopping bag, all ready for the morning.

Chapter Seventeen

Here comes the nasty bit. You'd have thought nothing more could happen today after everything else, which only shows how wrong you can be. All I can say is, the sooner Christmas comes and puts us all in a good mood, the better. This evening it was Mandy who was out of sorts.

For a start, she was late getting in. Way after nine it was. The news had been on and everything. Can you believe it, after everything I told her, after all the trouble it took finding those cuttings, just so as to put her in the picture. Yet late she was. And what was her excuse? The same as ever: working all day, books she'd needed in the library and so on and so on. Well that's as maybe, and Larry's the last person to want to comment, but you could see it wasn't doing her any good. You know what they say about all work and no play.

As it is, she should watch herself. The fact is, she is definitely not looking her best, attractively speaking. I have never known her little face to look so pinched, and that's even with all the snacks that are still appearing and disappearing in her larder. I reckon she should be taking more rest, relaxing more with another certain party, or what looks she has will be lost for ever. She might be young, but nothing can age like a woman. Not that it would alter an iota of how I feel about her. I've always said I would love the old kid no matter what.

Mind you, you'd wonder if I still felt the same way after tonight's little performance.

It started off normally enough. I'd left her in the lounge while I went off to do the donkey work, i.e. putting on the kettle and laying out a tray. Just for a treat – as a taste of things to come – I shook a few Quality Street into a bowl. A girl couldn't have asked for more. Only it was while I was busying myself with all this that she was up to no good in the next room. When I returned, there she was next to the cage, cover in hand, and a funny look on her face.

'Where is he?'

'Where's who?'

Now I know that might seem a strange answer considering what she was pointing to, but to be honest, I'd had so much to think about today, Joey was never going to be the first thing to spring to mind. Besides, had I said a word to her about taking the cover off anything while I was off doing something else?

But you could tell she already had a bee in her bonnet from the way she snapped, 'The canary, Larry. Where's Joey?'

And that's when it hit me. 'Oh Mandy, love,' I said. 'Don't ask. I'm that upset about it.'

'Why, what's happened?' By now you couldn't help but notice that that funny look of hers had turned into something altogether sharper, and uglier. Still, I thought that would change once I told her, and let her see how I felt.

'He died, Mandy. Just like that. I found him lying there, poor little mite. Not a scrap of breath left in him.'

'Larry . . .'

'I know, love. The fact is, I don't know where to put myself. He was all I had, and now he's gone. It isn't half going to be quiet up here without him . . .'

And that's when it happened. She turned on me, no better than a wild thing, practically spat at me. 'If he was all you had, then why didn't you look after him?'

Well, that would have been bad enough in itself. But

it wasn't the end of it. While I stood there, too shocked to say a word, she was still carrying on. 'You killed him, Larry. You never took the cover off, you never talked to him. You stopped me going near him. I don't even think you could be bothered to feed him half the time.'

'Well, Mandy . . .'

But she didn't let me get a word in. 'That poor bird. Cooped up in that cage. Some people should never be allowed near a living thing.'

Some people. By which she meant me, I presume. The man who had kept her as much fed and watered as any old bird. Well, there was an answer to that, but I don't know if it was the shock, or the hurt, or both, the words just wouldn't come. Then suddenly I stopped floundering for something to say, and instead a quiet dignity took over. If this was the girl I'd been trying all along to help, then I'd been wasting my time. She didn't deserve it.

The next bit was going to be easy, a real pleasure: I was going to walk out of that room into the kitchen, get that letter out from behind the bread bin, come back and give it to her. Shove it in her face. With my compliments. Good riddance to it and her. We didn't need people like that around here.

Then she burst into tears.

Now what did she have to do that for? And as if tears weren't enough, she starts whimpering like some kid trying to stave off a rocketing. 'Oh dear, Larry, I'm sorry. I didn't mean to shout. It's just that I was fond of him too. Please believe me, I really am sorry.'

Well, I'd be lying if I said I'd ever heard an apology more heartfelt — even if she could at least have tried to meet my eye while she was about it. Anyway, it was a start. So I didn't make a move for the kitchen, not yet. I just waited and watched, wanting to be sure she meant it. But I have to say that after a minute I began to feel,

I don't know, embarrassed. If you're going to cry, you don't just stand there while the tears drip off the end of your nose, like you've got a bad cold and can't be bothered with a handkerchief. Not when you're a woman. And it's not even as if she was sobbing. It's as I said, she was just standing there, staring at the floor, arms hanging just any old how by her sides while the tears rolled down her face.

Suffice to say, it got to be enough to put me quite off my stride, until finally, more to try and find some relief from it all, I said, 'Something else upsetting you then?'

The moment the words were out though, I knew it was a mistake. What that girl needed was a good telling-off, not sympathy. But it was too late. She had already looked up, surprise all over her face. So you see, she wasn't expecting sympathy either, and no wonder.

'Larry,' she says. 'Larry.' And stretches out her hand. And that, I have to say, was the worst thing of all. I wouldn't have minded if it had just been for a straightforward handshake between friends. But she'd started to cry again and what with that and her hand still snaking around in my direction, it's like having a blind person groping towards you trying to discover if there's anybody there.

None of this seems to bother her though.

'Larry,' she says, the tears still rolling down regardless. 'Larry. I don't know what's happening to me any more . . . I don't understand . . . I thought there were people who loved me, even now. But it's nearly Christmas, and where are they? Where are they all?'

The obvious answer to that was – why ask me? She hadn't exactly been open with her old pal, despite all the concern shown, so how was I supposed to know about anything now? Bit late for that. Added to which, she could at least have tried making sense, instead of muttering on the way she was doing, never quite finishing what it was she wanted to say. I would have pointed this out to her, but I didn't have the heart, not with the tears and all.

So instead I said, 'I don't know, love. But I tell you what, why don't I go and get us both a couple of glasses of something to cheer us up.' And I was going to add, 'And a box of tissues while I'm at it, seeing as you don't seem to have a handkerchief on you.' Only I should have moved a bit more quickly, because blow me if that hand of hers didn't shoot out again and this time actually grab hold of mine. 'Larry,' she says, but she didn't get an answer. All I could think of was how I was going to get my own hand back again. The fact is, there's no words to describe how unpleasant it feels to have a clammy paw clutching at yours, and no idea of what it was she had in mind.

And then it came to me. She was all set to tell me something. There was a look in her eye and it set the alarm bells ringing. What's more I knew, as sure as I was standing there, that whatever that something was, I didn't want to hear it. Because depend upon it, once I did hear it, it would rebound on me. It's what people do all the time. They go for the sympathy vote, and the next thing you know, they've got you just where they want you, regardless of what you might have in mind.

There was only one way left to me. Prepare to take back my hand and say to her, firmly, 'All right Mandy, love, get a grip. I can see you're upset, but you've got to remember it doesn't always do to go burdening other folk with every little problem. Some things you have to learn to face up to by yourself.'

As it turned out though, I was spared having to say a word. Suddenly from below comes the voice we know and love so well.

'Amanda, telephone for you.'

Saved by the bell.

For a moment the silly girl just stands there, mouth

open. Thankfully, the grip on my hand lessens. Even so I have to say, 'Don't you think you should go and answer that, love?'

She nods, pulls back her hand and starts rubbing at all the mess of tears and hair. A good wash and a brush-up is what it needs, but there's no time. The next second she's off and away downstairs, leaving yours truly to breathe one big sigh of relief.

Of course you know who was on the phone. And sure as anything you know what the news will be. Mr Adultery himself will be here to ruin the last weekend before Christmas.

But at least it will mean fewer tears and funny turns. And what's more, this time Larry isn't going to be downhearted. First there's still a world of shopping to be done before the big day, and second, much more important, there's this thought to buoy me up:

A few minutes ago that kid was half out of her mind with gloom about something. And who was the first person she turned to for cheering up? Who else but Larry. Now you tell me if that doesn't mean something.

Makes you feel all warm inside.

Chapter Eighteen

Now, you know how I feel about Mandy. I wouldn't hear a word against her and that's final. But there comes a time when you have to be honest, and say what's in your mind. Which in this case is – if things go wrong from now on, then we know who to blame. A certain young lady who need not be named.

Nothing is quite the way it was before yesterday. Until then everything was going swimmingly. Then Mandy comes up here, acting up, and everything else starts doing the same.

What's outside, for instance.

Look out of the window, and it's staring you in the face: that brilliant weather that seemed set fair to continue for the next week has taken a turn for the worse. Makes you shiver just thinking about it. You can actually see the wind, see the shape of it in the dust, kicking up the crisp packets like some great big lout in the street. What's worse is that it's waiting for you, for the moment you step out of the house so it can rush up from behind the hedge and throw you straight into the road, spitting gobbets of freezing rain at you as you go. Struggle as far as the bus stop and you're wishing you were home again. I tell you, practically the only people on the streets early this morning were the tramps and the dossers and that's because they're used to it. The rest of the old folk were at home, toasting themselves beside their gas fires.

Do you see the way things seem to be drifting? One day everything seems just wonderful, and the next it's all going awry, as if one thing is simply leading to another, starting with Mandy. With the Holloway Road acting like a great wind tunnel, the only thing to do was escape to the West End and let the old spirits get a lift from the lights and the better class of crowd, but it wasn't possible. Thanks to Joey gone to meet his maker untimely there had been a slight change of plan, and I had business in this part of the world to get over with first. Well even then the day might still have turned out right – if I hadn't decided at the last minute to slip into Woolworths on the way. Silly me, there wasn't a thing there that I hadn't already got, yet all the same I found myself queuing in the pick 'n' mix for half a pound of coconut mushrooms. And that's when it happened. I must have put my shopping bag down to reach for the scoop, and the next I knew the bag was gone. I could hardly believe it. Someone had stolen it right from in between my legs.

Fortunately it was only a plastic bag from Tesco and my wallet was sitting safely in my back pocket, but the point is, little Joey was still wrapped up in the bottom of it, so now the poor old blighter is not only dead but stolen property to boot. And what it does is leave a nasty taste in your mouth to think that, even at Christmastime, there isn't a soul you can trust.

Well, that just did for me. Knocked me right out of the ring. No way could I find it in me to battle with the buses and crowds all across town. So I traipsed back home, thinking that none of this might have happened if Mandy had never put her foot into what I can only call *the right flow of things*. Added to which there was always the thought that this might not be the end of it. That things might even get worse.

With the best will in the world on my part, then, Mandy was hardly going to get the sort of welcome she was used to. She was up here early enough this evening, I'll say that for her. But then I was half expecting that. If we were going to have our usual time together *plus* an apology, she was going to need to allow for a few extra minutes. What I hadn't expected was to feel so lacklustre about her visit. I suppose I was dwelling on it all – first the manner in which she spoke to me yesterday and then the way everything seemed to have gone wrong after. In other words, I couldn't see why I should put myself out to make her feel so comfortable that she might decide to do it again. After half an hour, then, of me being polite but distant, and of her struggling to make some kind of conversation (hard for her at the best of times I reckon), she tried another tack.

'I'm looking forward to the weekend, Larry. Are you?'

'You got that friend of yours coming?' I said by way of a reply, and when she nodded, I told her. Oh yes, I told her. 'Then I don't suppose I shall be looking forward to the weekend very much. I'm a man who likes his peace, and if you'll excuse me, I think I'd like a little peace now.'

In point of fact, I didn't say it nastily, even if I was surprised to hear myself say it at all. But you should have seen her face. Shocked is hardly the word. Mind you, it's only what I should have said to her months ago. Trouble was, I didn't know how she'd have taken it then. But it's different now of course. If someone is a close enough friend, you can say practically anything you like. Besides, she couldn't afford to be too offended, because who else has she got? 'Where are they all, Larry?' Her own words.

All the same, I felt the teeniest bit sorry when I saw the colour drain from her face. And she even looked a touch shaky when she got up. It was almost enough to make me want to shout, 'April Fool Mandy, love.' But I didn't. For one thing, it's the wrong time of year. And for another, I couldn't see any harm in it. Let her think she's in Larry's bad books for a while. On the big day she'll see there's not a soul who can forgive and forget like he can.

But oh, Larry, you can be stupid when you like. There you were, telling yourself you knew it all, thinking that the first thing she'd do was run down those stairs and start sobbing into her pillow the way she does when *he* goes and upsets her. Thinking you'd be kept up all night with it.

Well, I was wrong, wasn't I. About half an hour later, I start to notice this racket coming from downstairs. So I took a little walk to the smallest room hoping to find out what it was all about. It was her, Mandy, in the bathroom, splashing about and – singing again. Christmas carols this time. Christmas carols at the top of her voice at nine o'clock in the night.

She's still there, and what's more that's the second time she's sung 'Away in a Manger'. She sounds as happy as a lark. How can that be? I told her off. I sent her packing. She's my sensitive Mandy. She should be sobbing her heart out at least. I'm all she's got.

But of course I'm not. That's why Stupid is my middle name. *He's* coming to stay, which means she's thinking on different lines altogether. She's got her company after all. So she doesn't need Larry. Why should she?

And there was I, giving her the idea I don't need her. Thinking I could let things slide, we were that settled. Even thinking I'd got Christmas sorted out. But I haven't. Nothing's sorted.

And I still haven't found the one thing that could put her straight. Her present.

Next morning, it's no better. I tried to catch her on the stairs on her way out, but she mutters something about a bus, and with just a quick glance at the hall table, off she goes. Leaving me like a lemon, staring after her.

After an encounter like that, the only thing to do was to get out and get going. Remind myself that this is Thursday and with eight shopping days to go, I should be there with the best of them, buying our Christmas.

But it's an unforgiving world. No exaggeration, half of London was out today, cramming up the streets, filling up the buses, causing the sort of queues you only ever expected to find in Russia. Normally there's nothing Larry likes better than holding his own in the riot for the 104, but not today. Believe me, it was no place for an OAP.

Still, queues or no queues, you know where I was headed, even if it meant finally stepping off in the middle of the Brompton Road and walking. That bus was going nowhere, trapped in all the traffic like one of those flies in amber. Even Larry had never seen it that bad.

It's only then, half a mile further on, that I see the reason. Blue lights flashing and police ribbon everywhere. Walkie-talkies clicking and people standing around waiting for something to happen. Bomb scare. They've closed the entire block. Go home Larry, if you can.

All of which must have taken me the best part of three hours.

I know how men must feel coming home with the battle behind them lost. Walking up the garden path, the only note of comfort was the thought of a basin of steaming water for my feet, and the hope that Mandy would have come home in time to read what I'd left for her on the kitchen table. 'Dear Mandy, was ever so out of sorts last night. Please do not take offence or do not know what I shall do. Love, Larry.'

A short note, but heartfelt. Then there was the little

box of presentation nuts that I'd bought this morning and been carrying around with me all day. They were for her as well. She could have them the moment I got back.

Then it happens, the event to cap it all. The front door opens and there *he* is. Francis. A whole day early.

'Ah, Mr Mann,' he says. 'The second person I've surprised today.'

As he speaks, Mandy comes and pushes her way between us, actually brushes my arm, yet she never gives me a look. It's as if I wasn't there. She goes and stands by the gate, waiting for him. You'd have thought he would have joined her, but he doesn't. He stays where he is, suddenly all charm and smarm, wearing one of those long posh overcoats you only find in gentlemen's catalogues. 'Been doing a spot of Christmas shopping, I see.' And so saying he points to that little bag of speciality nuts. After all this long exhausting day, the one thing I've brought home with me. And he smiles.

For a second, I don't get it. That smile is about something, but I don't know what. And then it clicks. He's smiling because he's thinking he's just seen the full sum of Larry Mann's Christmas. A bag of nuts and the Queen's speech.

Now, the good Lord knows I've been tempted before this, tempted to blow the gaff and ruin it all, spill the beans and let the cat out of the bag entirely. But those times were nothing, nothing compared to this. That umbrella hanging off my other arm, I wanted to take it by the handle and thrust it, pointed end into his stomach, turn him round and march him up those stairs, past Mandy's rooms, and up again into my kitchen. And while I held him there at bay, empty out the cupboards before his lizard eyes and show him what Larry's Christmas was all about.

A bag of speciality nuts.

Only in the nick of time does the voice of reason come to my rescue, whispering in my ear. 'He's not worth it, Larry boy. Think what you've got to lose. Just get yourself up those stairs and you'll be all right.'

And I was – just about. But it meant getting everything out of its place to prove it, pulling out the crackers and the chocs and the drink and the nuts and the paper and the baubles, and the rest, to make myself remember it's the future that counts and not the here and now. That the Mandy we know and love is waiting, sitting there in the middle of next week, feasting her eyes on a World of Christmas created and brought to her by her own Larry. Other parties will be significant only for their absence.

And the night helps.

Yes, it does, really. Staying awake, listening to the silence in the room below, knowing that she's there, sleeping like a baby, alone, herself again.

See, she might only be doing it in her sleep, but so long as she stays that way, asleep, alone, innocent, she's fighting the good fight for both of us.

Chapter Nineteen

And so we come to today.

Haul myself out of bed. There's no rest, even if I had the time for it. It only takes the sound of a laugh to drag you out of what little sleep you've had.

No-one saw me set off – not even Ethel. Today was her day for Christmas Cheer, when she rounds up the house and gathers them into her kitchen. She does it every year, treats us all to cheesy snacks and Cyprus sherry and a lot of talk about us all being one happy family. So that's where they all were now – her, Gilbert, Mandy, *him*. The whole household, except one, who preferred to leave quietly.

Naturally I was invited. When was there ever a Christmas when I wasn't? Not turning up this year was my idea of giving them something to think about. If I wasn't there, who was going to pass round the cheese straws?

It wasn't a question that needed answering – I thought. Then just as I was walking out, it came to me. If I wasn't there to do the honours, and Gilbert was incapable, then guess who would step in to fill the breach. All of a sudden I could see Ethel smirking and nodding at the plate. *'Oh Francis, would you be so kind? I wouldn't ask, only seeing as Mr Mann has let us down . . .'*

Mr Mann? Who's he? The last person on anybody's mind.

I almost turned around to go back. But it was too late, of course. I'd already said I wasn't going, so what would they all think if I showed up now? I for one knew exactly, and I wasn't going to give them the satisfaction.

So there you have it. Here was a day that should have started off with so much promise, and already it had gone sour on me.

But there's something called the Dunkirk spirit, which is another way of saying that even when all the world has turned its face against you, you keep up the good fight no matter what.

So what did I do? I gave myself a good talking-to — right there on the doorstep. Said to myself, 'Larry, my boy, this is no time to go weak at the knees. No, lad, this is the time to stiffen the sinews, show them what you're made of. They may be in there enjoying themselves at your expense, but there's only one among them worth the heartache. And it's for her you're doing this.'

And then I added something else — the clincher, the ideal strengthener. 'Yes, my boy. Today is the day when you walk back with the goods under your arm. Because today is the day you find her present. The one that says it all.'

And that's when I felt it. The thrill of anticipation chasing up and down my spine. I was a man with a mission again. Suddenly it was almost as if I was there already, returned from the fray, holding her present under my arm, hugging it close, feeling what it was going to say to her. The best feeling ever.

In five short seconds I had become a man renewed. It didn't matter if it was raining, it didn't even matter that it was cold enough to freeze your heart. I took off my cap and let the weather wet my forehead — good London weather giving me its blessing. Then I put my cap back on and marched off, into the day.

And what a day it was. At first it seemed as if all the world was keeping up the conspiracy. I tried the Tube

211

this time. But that was no better, sitting there for hours in the dark like something undigested. Back up amongst the living, it was almost worse. The pavements had disappeared under a heaving swell, as likely to wash you up in the nearest door of Harvey Nichols as let you come safely to where you wanted to be. But I kept my head, never lost my cool, not even when the hands on my watch kept showing that more and more of the day was escaping just in the travelling. I felt that all these things were sent to try me. A test, if you like, of whether I was worthy.

And then, a few steps more and I was there. The police ribbons had gone and there was nothing to stop me walking through the swing doors, feeling the wafts of warm air blowing a welcome on my face. Not that the old ticker knew the difference, not at once. For the first two minutes all I could do was stay there, between the inner and the outer doors, waiting for the steam hammer pounding away inside to rest up. When I took off my cap for the second time that day the inside rim was wringing wet, a sure sign I'd been overdoing it. Elderly folk aren't meant to sweat, after all. They're meant to take things easy. But today it was all part of the test. Mandy love, I told myself as the breath came back, if only you knew.

Then it was time to go inside, properly.

And all I can say is: thank the good Lord I knew what to expect. Namely that the moment I stepped through that door there really would be an explosion. A deafening blast of colours and shapes of Things, all different, all wonderful – all impossible to tell apart. And wouldn't you know, I was right.

For a second I thought maybe I was going to panic after all, but that little voice of reason that's been standing me in such good stead recently, said, 'Hold hard there, Larry. Get a grip. What you want to do now is relax. Take an interest. Look around you, and enjoy.'

And gradually, very gradually, that's what I began to do. And just as gradually, I started to notice not the shop so much as the people. Hardly surprising in a way, seeing as how we were kindred spirits, all here while the rest of the world was somewhere else, in search of inferior goods at inferior prices which they would carry away with them in bags that bore an inferior name on the front. We were different from them – a different class of shopper. And these folk, who were the same as me, I began to see in glorious detail, from the headscarves on the women to the gold caps on the tips of their shoes. Most of them had a man in tow – someone has to pay the bills after all – but still it was mainly the women I watched. Watched them circling displays, watched while they stopped for no obvious reason that I could see. What made one cabinet of gloves which they ignored less interesting than another which they examined with the attention of a nuclear scientist? I didn't know, but I wanted to find out. And pretty soon, simply from watching the women, I thought I'd discovered a way of seeing things, of making objects come into focus out of the blur. What they looked at, I looked at too, just as closely, and ignored the rest, as they did. You could say that it was like finding a pair of spectacles that made you able to see everything that was worth seeing.

Of course, that's not to say I always agreed with their choice. Take the case of the woman buying that hat. I'd got that close, the shop assistant, mistaking me for a husband, turned and asked me what I thought. Now I could have stopped and been a bit more helpful than I was, in other words told the truth, namely that you could pay a quarter of the price for a sou'wester and not look any different, but seeing the way the other woman was staring at me I thought – why bother? Let her waste her money. And off I went.

Money. I can almost hear what you're saying at this

point. Larry, Larry, what's it all for? Are you really going to shell out an arm and a leg just to impress some little bit of a thing *who might not even appreciate it*? And the answer is – yes. As much as it takes. Because the simple truth is, she *will* appreciate it.

It all boils down to the kind of girl she is. You only had to look around you to see the difference. At first sight you might think it would be no bad thing to be a man dragged along in the shadow of some of the women here. Attractive, they were, most of them, well-dressed, every hair in place, as much at ease in this place as they would be in their own front rooms. A far cry from Doreen you might say. But no, not really. In one way they're no different. These are the women who have seen it all, done it all. The same as women the world over. It shows in their faces, in the way they walk. Worldly, that's how you could describe them. And what was Doreen if not that? And what's the betting that *his* wife isn't exactly the same? I'd wager anything that she tows him up and down the posh shops of Edinburgh with exactly the same expression on her face – the one that tells the world, 'He may be paying, but I'm the boss.'

There's not a farthing of difference between them. And I bet there's not a man here not praying for release.

And that's the secret, isn't it. I mean it has to be. The reason he's messing around with a girl like our Mandy. Because she *is* different. Because she's young, and innocent as the day. She'll hang on to every word, never argue, never laugh. When they go out together, it's him that people will talk to, not her, because he's the one with the clout. In short, she's everything a woman should be – and everything that women aren't.

Bingo.

Young and innocent as a child, that's what I said, wasn't it. Naughty even, when she's got a mind to be.

But she sleeps by herself and has all the experience of a baby. My Mandy. My old kid. Who will never let you down.

And all at once I knew exactly where to look.

Where I needed to be is right at the top of the shop, as far away as possible from where I had been searching all this time. No wonder nothing had appealed, down here amongst the perfumes and petticoats. All that stuff is for the likes of Doreen and June, not her, my sweet Mandy.

I'd been in the right shop, looking in the wrong place. Until now. But when I stepped out of the lift, I knew. I'd come to the end of the rainbow.

The Toy Department.

Like a rush of blood to the head it rises up to greet me – Christmas, the very essence of. They've got it all here, enough to make what you have at home seem like a poor imitation. So better not to compare. Just take a look and be satisfied.

You see, it's a different world. It's as if every possible object and surface has been touched by a magic wand – glittering, frosted, reflected and trembling in the baubles weighing down the branches of Christmas trees greener than the real thing. It's a shop turned into fairyland. Those aren't walls any more, dividing one display from another, but banks of holly, or is it ivy? You could be in a garden, a garage sale in paradise.

Then there were the toys. You wouldn't believe them. Toy cars buzzing underfoot, toy trains chugging through papier-mâché mountains, lights winking at you, tiny silver wheels moving, and from elsewhere, the gleam from the polished sides of robots. Everywhere you look, something seems alive. You have to stand back a moment, with the solid wall behind you, and remind yourself it's all clockwork.

Did I say it was paradise? Not quite. You see, there were the kids, hundreds of them it seems like, screaming and bawling, running riot as you'd expect when parents turn their back on their responsibilities and let the rest of the world take the brunt. They'll bring the place down, these kids, treating it like a council playground, and no-one, not even the shop assistants, raising a finger to stop them. If I weren't in such a hurry, if I didn't have a good idea of what I'd get in return, I'd be tempted to say something, really I would . . .

Well, no matter. At least I was here, and the thing to do now was find and take the best of it home with me.

Only once again, and how often had it happened now? I had to get my bearings, think about why I was here. Young and innocent as a child she may be, but that didn't mean I had come in search of a nurse's outfit or a box of Lego. That would have been daft. I wasn't here to buy a toy, so much as something that was going to reflect back at her the very essence of what she was, something to remind her of her own true nature. And it certainly wasn't going to be here, amongst the remote-control toys. So what I had to do, having somehow stepped right into the middle of them, was get away. But even a simple move like that turned out not to be so easy. The blasted things followed you around. I hadn't gone five steps before a chieftain tank crashes into my ankles, nearly tripping me up. And don't try telling me that was an accident. Not when there was some bright spark not six feet away with a joystick laughing his head off. He knew what he was up to all right.

The worst thing about wall-to-wall kids, though, was you couldn't navigate. It was no good trying to walk in a straight line when they were there, every few feet, crowded round some toy or other, blocking the way. Which probably explains why after getting out of the robot displays, and passing through the computer section (computers for kids – no comment) and travelling past the board games, and taking in other bits and pieces on the way – I ended up right back among the remote controls, where I'd started. There was even the same kid there waiting for me, pushing his joystick in the direction of my feet.

Suffice it to say, my one thought was to get out of there as fast as I could. I didn't stop to choose a direction this time, half expecting a certain small thug to be following me whichever way I went. But he didn't, which was one thing to be grateful for. On the other hand it hardly looked more encouraging here. Now I found myself walking between walls of babies' toys, or rather one hundred different species of rattle for the nipper who has everything. All the same, the further along the rows you went, the more the rattles and tops started to give way to things that had faces and hands. And with that, an idea began to dawn. In other words, something deep down began to sit up and take notice.

You see, I was coming to the place where they kept the dolls. A few more steps, and they were all around, and that vague inkling hardened, turned into something you could almost describe as hope.

Now, don't laugh, you don't have a clue of what I had in mind. Neither did I for that matter. All I knew was underneath my vest there was a faint pitapat that told me I was getting warm. Something was out there, out of sight, maybe, but waiting for me. All I had to do was find it. So I slowed down, and started to use my eyes.

If asked to explain what I was looking for, I think I might have said this. Years ago, Harry and Molly went on holiday to Majorca, the only time they ever went abroad. But they always said they'd never forget it because they had the flamenco dancer to remind them. Near enough two feet high she must have been, all scarlet and black, right down to the red of her lips and the little curl on either side of her cheek. She used to stand on the piano and June loved her. Not that she ever so much as touched her. She just liked to look, tell everyone that *she* was going to be a flamenco dancer when she grew up. So though it was a doll, you could hardly say it was a toy – more an ornament, a thing of beauty, to keep and admire, a souvenir of the past, and in June's case, you could even say, of the future. Well, maybe that's what I had in mind – a doll that could do the same for Mandy as it did for June.

The trouble is, they don't make dolls like that any more. I know because I looked. I walked up and down those shelves, and then did the same all over again, but I didn't see anything remotely similar. I didn't even see the other kind, the big fat baby dolls with eyes that rattled in their head and who went 'Mama' when you held them upside down. That's not to say they didn't have baby dolls. They had them all right – the sort I'd never seen before and, frankly, hope never to see again. Too real to breathe, they were, in their little boxes, faces pinched and ugly, like the newborn, curled up under polythene. Don't ask me what they made me think of. June wouldn't have liked them.

Of course there were other dolls of a different kind altogether. Only, believe me when I say that these were the worst of the lot. These were the dolls I didn't even want to be seen looking at. Grown-up they were, and when I say grown-up, I mean just that – all bumps and curves, and not even dressed some of them. There's a word for what they represented, no doubt about that. Otherwise, why make them that way? It was almost too much, looking at them and thinking about the damage that must be going on in innocent young minds.

Yet though I'd walked the same shelves three or four times over, I couldn't quite believe it, that what I was looking for was not there. That pitapat had turned into a racing trot and even the backs of my hands were tingling. It was as if I'd got caught up in a game of hide and seek, and Mandy's present was there, almost within reach, just waiting to be found. Calling to me.

But not from amongst these dolls, not from the latex babies and the good-time girls, or from the rag dolls with blown-out moons for faces and spots for eyes or the half-size children in frilly clothes who could walk and talk and probably go to school without anybody noticing. There was nothing here for Mandy. And not for me either.

And as finally the pitapat started to fade and the hairs flattened on the backs of my hands, I could feel all the strength ebbing out of me. Like a bad dream it was. Suddenly I wasn't excited any more. Just tired, and with the tiredness comes the thought, out of the blue, impossible to ignore: I might as well have bought a dozen heated rollers and saved myself all this. Because, forget about the damage to young minds, what was it doing to mine? Here I was, stranded four floors up above a city gone mad, suddenly too tired to move, and with nothing to show for it. Better if I'd stayed at home. Better if I'd never dreamed up the idea of Christmas. Maybe even better if I'd never ever met her . . .

And then it happened. Almost the worst sound I'd heard in my entire life. A scream, slicing through all the rest of the racket, piercing to that very place behind your eyes where the headaches start, sparking one off right now. And if that wasn't bad enough it was followed by another and another. Of their own accord, the eyes swivelled round in my head, pulling the rest of me with them.

And there they were, a mother and her child, no more than a few yards away, beyond the dolls. The girl, who must have been three or thereabouts, was staring straight ahead of her and pointing, getting ready for another scream. Her other arm was being pulled high above her head, one small fist clenched above another, that gripped it by the wrist. Because all the time the mother was tugging at the kid, trying to drag her away from whatever she was pointing at. But she wasn't going to budge, not willingly. You should have seen the mother's face, though: white-cheeked, mouth set like a boxer's. You could hear her, pleading with the child, telling her that they had to go, that she was tired, that they were both tired. That she couldn't take much more, not today.

Do you know, I could almost sympathize.

'But I want it. I want IT!' The kid had finally found the words to go with the screams. They didn't do her a bit of good. You could see it happening, how the screams were bad enough, but this was the last straw. I watched the mother drop the girl's hand suddenly, so that she could raise her own, high above her head, saw her bring it down, fast, so it met the kid's cheek with one good hard resounding slap. Then without another word she turned and marched away, leaving the little girl standing there exactly where she was.

If you could have seen the look on the child's face. It was almost comical. What with the shock of that slap and then her mother just walking off, she could hardly believe it was happening. Only that wasn't all. Though she had one hand free to rub her eyes in disbelief, the other continued to point, even though there was no-one left to see – except me. The look on her face now was pure terror – a child's fear of being left alone and abandoned for ever. So why didn't she run, as fast as possible, after the mother who already had disappeared? In another second, you could see her child's brain telling her, it was going to be too late. *So why didn't she run?*

Because whatever had started the tantrum in the first

place was still continuing to hold her now, though by this time almost against her will, against her own small good sense. For a few brief seconds more a miniature war was going on, and all you could do was watch as she stayed there rooted, wanting to run, yet unable to leave. Then, out of the blue, one side won. She opened her mouth and shouted (not screamed) 'Mum!' and sprinted off in the direction she had seen her mother last.

Which left only me. There was no-one else about, not here. Probably her screams had cleared this area of the store as efficiently as a fire alarm. And I was about to leave as well, as best I could, with exhaustion creeping through my legs, and the sap all gone from me. But one thing kept me. I couldn't leave before I'd seen with my own eyes what it was that could keep a child fixed to the spot even despite the nightmare of having her mother walk out on her. I'd hardly have been human otherwise.

So I walked those few extra yards, left behind the dolls which had promised so much, and turned out to be worse than useless. And found I was standing in a menagerie of stuffed animals. The cuddly sort.

And there it was: the cause of all the trouble.

It was a great big brown bear, way too large for any shelf, so that it was sitting on the ground propped up against a partition. He had the blunt bear's face of any normal teddy, only ten times bigger, and with a body so large his eyes must have been at the exact level of the little girl's. And that I reckon was half the reason for all the fuss. Because when I bent down to tie the lace on my shoe, I found myself gazing straight into those same brown eyes myself, and it came almost as a shock. For there we were, the two of us, suddenly staring at each other for all the world like we were real people who had just met. And when I looked closer still, there was me, mirrored in his eyes, two perfect little Larries, in cloth cap and polyester tie, out for the day.

And it was then I knew that I had found what I'd been looking for.

Now for it. *Why, Larry? What on earth makes you think that a great stuffed bear is going to be the present of your dreams?* You may as well ask why women like babies and some men like dogs. The fact is I don't know. But show me a girl who never had a bear. And not just little girls. They're all over the place, girls and their bears. From the covers of children's comics to the pin-ups in the dirty magazines. Especially the dirty magazines. Girls clutching them, covering their modesty, hoping you'll think they're good girls really; or the game-show girls almost weeping because they want to be the ones to lift them off the conveyor belt and take them home. Even Doreen went 'ah' once over one she picked up in a shop to show me, before we were married, nearly letting me hand over the little bit of money I had just to please her. See what I mean? Women. They all like teddy bears. I reckon it's in their nature.

But give a bear to the right person, and not only is the same just as true, but ten times as true. Give it to someone who's young and sensitive, and you've done more than given her a present. You've given her a friend. That's not putting it too strongly. What else do you call someone you share your bedroom with, cuddle up to even, in the middle of the night, whisper all your secrets to, and turn to when no-one else is there? The one who understands that underneath it all, she's nothing more than a kid in a nasty world? A friend. No other word will do. Other people can give her bottles of perfume, and they'll just stay on the dressing table and not mean a thing. But give her a great big brown cuddly bear and the only thing she'll like more will be the giver.

Seek and ye shall find. That's what the good book says, isn't it. And here was the living proof.

Yet even now, at the very end, it wasn't over. Not quite. You could say the biggest test was still to come. Because hanging off his ear, not half so decorative as the scarlet ribbon round his neck, was the price tag, and when I turned it towards me I found I was looking at triple figures. I'm not joking. Buying that bear meant I'd be paying over what I'd spent for Christmas so far and then some.

I'd like to say that that didn't stop me for a minute, that I just reached out my arms and picked him up regardless, but it wouldn't be honest. For a bit I was just like that little girl, torn between what was sensible and what was not, with one voice plain in my head saying, 'Don't do it, Larry. Buy a smaller one. It's the thought that counts,' while another part of me simply didn't listen, stayed with the adding and subtractions, working out how I could swing it.

Then I caught his eye. And once again, it was like looking into another person's. Far from being glassy, they had a look in them that spoke volumes. And what's more they were speaking to me now.

'It's no good, Larry boy,' they were saying. 'You've seen the rest, now take the best. You know there's not another bear to touch me. I'm the one and that's all there is to it.'

And do you know – he was right.

(Only, just for the record, let me say that he wasn't being pushy or cocky. All he was doing was stating a fact.)

So that was that. The bear was coming home with me. For a second, then, I thought I could just stand there, letting the relief wash over us both. Then another thought hit me. What if that woman had caved in? What if the screams had become too much for her, and she was on her way back this very minute? She

223

could march up here and snatch him right out of my arms. I've seen it done, hundreds of times, in the sales. She only needed to appear and Mandy would never see her bear.

Straightaway I started to look for her. But it was no good, she could have been anywhere. She could even be at the cash desk as I was standing there, handing over the notes while someone else was on his way to wrap him up.

I never grabbed anything so fast in my life. Believe me, if there's an Olympic medal for picking up giant bears and fighting your way through a crowded store, I'd have won it. And it was rather like one of those hurdle races, with kids getting under my feet and near enough sending me flying a couple of times. It didn't seem to occur to anyone, least of all their parents, that an elderly man in a hurry weighed down by a bear nearly half his size could have done with a bit of helpful space. But in the end it didn't matter. Despite them all I made it to the cash desk and not a sign of the woman anywhere.

'I want this bear,' I said. 'And if anybody says a word, tell her I saw it first.'

I'd shouted because of all the din, but even so, I'll admit I surprised myself a bit. They must have been able to hear me down in men's tailoring. But to be honest, I was past caring. Still, you don't expect people to stare at you like that. Not that it made any difference: the girl at the counter could spend all day squinting at the light through my twenty-pound notes, the money I handed over was as good as the next man's, and half a minute later the bear was mine.

Actually, he was too big to wrap. Silly of me to have thought otherwise. Still, what better way could there be of laying claim to something than walking out with it for all the world to see? I even thought I should keep a look-out for the mother and daughter, smile at them as we passed just to show there were no hard feelings. And sure enough there they were, not far from the way out. The only trouble was, I couldn't seem to get them to look in my direction. The little girl was trying her best to shake off her mother's arm while pointing at a display of rainbow-coloured ponies. And from the look on her mum's face, you could see what was coming next.

Chapter Twenty

Back down in the street, it occurred to me that I was the only one who had come out today and got what he wanted. Otherwise how to explain why I was walking towards the bus stop with a grin spread like butter over my face while everybody else looked as if all they had got for themselves was a cold? Not that I could see much, not with a big furry brown head two inches from my face, but I knew for certain there wasn't a soul down there walking with the same spring in his step.

It had finally hit me – I'd got everything I set out for in the first place. It didn't matter what happened now; Mandy and me were ready for Christmas. I'd done it all, and the best bit of it was sitting in my arms. And what had it cost me? Only money. It wasn't even an effort carrying him. He might have been as heavy as a small child and twice as bulky, but nothing would have made me put him down, not once I'd picked him up. He even had a way of making you comfortable as you walked along, with your nose pressed into the fur at the top of his head. He had his own smell too, warm and nylony, like a man's shirt that's just been taken off. Not like a toy.

The funny thing was the way other folk reacted. You'd have thought there'd be titters at the sight of an OAP strolling through the West End with a giant stuffed toy in his arms, but that's not how it was at all. On the contrary, getting on the bus, and wonder of wonders, actually finding a seat, you could see people falling under his gaze and actually smiling. As for me,

I just sat there, with him on my lap and a smile of my own, and drifted, not even thinking, into the future.

'Someone's going to love their grandad this Christmas. Who's it for – girl or boy?'

Nearly jumped out of my skin, I did. The voice seemed to have come from nowhere. Then, craning my neck around the bear, I saw a woman – another senior citizen – sitting next to me. She must have got on while I was off with the fairies. Being caught by surprise like that, it didn't give me time to think. Still, I wanted to reply, seeing as she was only being pleasant. So I opened my mouth and said the first thing that came into my head.

'Girl. A little girl.'

'Lovely,' she said. 'Just right.' And she smiled at me all the way home.

Coming in after a day like today should have been a let-down. But it wasn't. In point of fact, as I let myself into a house that was wonderfully quiet, it occurred to me that it was even a good thing that *he* was here after all. It meant that Mandy was unlikely to be around to see me as I carried her surprise up the stairs, while Ethel, having spent the morning imbibing in the company of what she would term The Upper Classes, was probably lying motionless somewhere in a sherry coma. Result – we got ourselves up to the safety of my kitchen without a murmur of interference, which is saying something for this house.

What I wanted then was a cup of tea – for celebration *and* refreshment, but first things first. That's what I said to myself as I looked around for somewhere to put Master Bear. It was no good leaving him in the kitchen or the lounge because as sure as eggs, Mandy would break the habit of a lifetime and decide to visit while His Lordship was still here. Not that it was any great problem: there was ample space for him in the spare bedroom even with all the goodies that were already there. So, the spare room it was. Mind you, I made sure he was comfortable. The Christmas tree, the stand and back-up TV came off the bed so that he could lie there in state with nothing but Joey's old cage to make him have to share.

And only then did I get that cup of tea I'd been promising myself. Yet, considering how I'd been looking forward to it all day, it didn't come up to scratch. Not that there was anything wrong with it. It was me. I couldn't seem to relax. Despite it all turning out the way it had, and it now being a case of full steam ahead to a blissful future for the three of us, something, somewhere was weighing on me, yet for the life of me I couldn't think what it was. It was the same when I started to get supper ready. Pretty near famished, I was, yet not even the thought of steak pie and peas could excite me.

And then it came to me.

It was cold in the spare room, and dark. And lonely to boot. A far cry from what he must have been expecting, what with me nearly busting a gut to claim him and then carrying him home like royalty. Well that was it. Think of me what you like, there was no way I was going to leave him there to languish by himself. I dropped everything and made straight for the spare room. And in the first seconds after switching on the light I could have sworn that his eyes brightened at the sight of me.

'Look here,' I said to him, not making any bones about it. 'You've got me acting like a big girl, fussing round you like this. Bloody good thing Doreen can't see me now. Splitting her sides she would be.' I was going to add 'and so would June', but I didn't. You see, to tell the truth, I reckon June might have understood, long ago, in her younger days.

The upshot was, I found myself carrying him into

my bedroom and settling him down on the chair at the end of my bed. And that's where he stayed, looking as if this was where he'd banked on being all the time. He'd be expecting me to say good night next. One thing was for sure, though: come bedtime, neither of us was going to keep the other one awake with our snoring.

After that, everything was fine. More than fine. I finished off peeling the potatoes, put the pie in the oven and went to watch a bit of TV and all as happy as a sandboy. And it didn't matter what I turned my hand to for the next hour, it always came out right; the gravy was perfection, the pie was cooked to a tee. And me, I just kept smiling. And do you know why? Because sitting in the next room, my own bedroom, was a certain big brown bear, making himself comfortable in my chair, keeping a watchful eye on my bed.

I wondered what sort of name she was going to think up for him. There was always the obvious – the name of the giver. Larry One and Larry Two we could be then. But there could only be one Mandy.

So what do you do to round off a perfect evening? Go to bed. Well yes, but what if the night is still young, and you're in a mood to keep going? To which thought could be added the reminder that elsewhere, certain other people were out and about making the evening last, indulging in all sorts of excess – probably – while you sat here, wondering whether to have a cup of cocoa before turning in.

In other words, why bring a perfect day to an end before you have to? Why not go mad and stay up a while, live a little?

If I was going to stay up, though, it wasn't just so I could drink more tea and watch more television. You can see the sort of mood I was in. What I really wanted to do was celebrate. So while breaking open a box of luxury biscuits might be a thrill at any other time, it wasn't enough, not tonight. Opening a cupboard in the kitchen, however, gave me the idea. One clanking mass of bottles it was in there. Bottles of this and bottles of that, and I'm not talking about lemonade, or even whisky for the matter. I'm talking about another world, a veritable treasure-house of novelty tipple. I'll explain: not knowing what Mandy likes – only that sherry doesn't seem to do a thing for her – I'd tried to buy one of everything that looked interesting. Bottles I'd never set eyes on before then. Expensive – yes, though not compared to what I'd shelled out today. The laughable thing was, however, I didn't even know what half of them contained. Of course, I'd read the labels, but they didn't tell you much, not with names like Ocean Paradise and Irish Milk. Most of them I'd only bought for their labels, or the funny colours shimmering unexpectedly through the glass. Yet what if Mandy wanted to know before she partook? A right Charlie I'd look, lining up all these sophisticated drinks, then having to show my ignorance.

And that's when I thought – why not kill two birds with one stone, give each of them a go, and have that little celebration while I was at it? Then it would be off to bed, a nod to my old pal the bear, and a good night's sleep.

Just bringing them all into the lounge took a time. Honestly, there were that many. Lined up side by side they took up practically the length of the coffee table. Then there were the glasses to go with them – an entire boxed set of them. You couldn't call them brand new; I'd had them for years but never even unpacked them till tonight. I suppose I should have given them a wash, but they didn't have a fleck on them. Lovely little things they were. I could see now why I'd bought from that catalogue. Not one of them could have held more than a thimbleful, and each with a miniature old-fashioned motor car painted on the side. In other words you could fill all six to the brim, but with the amount any one of them contained, not even a tee-totaller could have objected.

For a minute or so, though, half the joy was just in sitting there, reading label after fancy label, admiring the detail on the little tiny cars, and thinking – this time next week, there'll be two of us here. Or three, if you count a certain large bear.

Then it was down to business. Lucky for me, most of them had lids that twist off. I never was much of a one for a corkscrew. It was just a question of which to choose first. In the end I plumped for Jamaican Orange Cream – for the simple reason that it was a name you would trust yourself with in a box of chocolates. It looked like cream, too, when you poured it out, thick and faintly orange, but you could smell the liqueur.

Want to know what it tasted like? Heaven, that's what. You'd hardly know you were downing something alcoholic. I'd have had another glass straight off, but I had a duty to keep on and give them all a go. I needn't have worried, though. Waiting for me were peppermint, coffee and coconut, not to mention peach, cherry and almond, each one nicer than the last. Halfway down the line I began to laugh, suddenly thinking I was like Goldilocks, having a little taste of this and a little taste of that. Then I thought of Mandy doing the same and instead of laughing I almost felt like crying, only with sheer joy.

And it's when I think of Mandy that I feel happiest of all. By the time I get to the end of the line it's somehow as if she's sitting there beside me, matching me, glass for glass. In fact I've decided that her favourite tipple is the very first, the orange cream, and that's the one I ended up drinking in her honour, meaning it to be my last.

Not that having a small celebratory drink was the

only thing I had in mind for the evening. Far from it. I'd got it all planned. A little sip of this and a little sip of that, and then it was over to the organ for a medley of the old favourites. I'd sort of neglected it of late. The trouble was, Mandy and I have that much to talk about as a rule, there never seems to be the time, And then, when she's gone, there's the problem of trying to catch up with what's on the box. There aren't enough hours in a day. At least, there haven't been since a certain young lady chose to come and live here.

What I hadn't banked on though was how, in the end, all the exertions of the day were bound to take their toll. At one stage I did get up off the settee, meaning to make my way over to the organ, but I'm not joking, the room actually started to spin. Exhaustion of course, the direct result of all that running around, with hardly a thought for what it might be doing to a man of my age. So discretion told me to stop where I was, stick to something relaxing – like enjoying myself here, having what you could almost call a rehearsal for next week. And that's just what I did, until, round about ten, I started to notice that the light had got a mite strange. Everything in the room seemed to be turning in on itself somehow – like the table in front of you, solid enough, you'd think, yet not promising to be there if you touched it. Definitely a new light bulb was called for, before the light went altogether. Trouble was, standing on a chair and screwing was the last thing I felt like doing after a day like today. Either I sat there in what might soon be pitch dark, or took myself off to bed like a sensible chap. So that's what I did. Left it all as it was and headed for the land of nod.

It wasn't until I was walking through the bedroom door that the memory hit me: Francis was here.

How to ruin a perfect evening. At the thought of him, I had to throw out a hand to catch the wall, otherwise I might have fallen over. That's how the man can undermine a person, just by popping into his head like that. Up till then I'd been lost in a happy dream, one where there was only the three of us – Mandy and me and the bear – enjoying everything friendship has to offer. But what the thought of His Lordship does, of course, is remind me that it's just that, a dream, and that we were still here, stuck in the middle of the present. Mandy hadn't been with me at all. She'd been with him, was still with him, a different girl altogether.

Not surprisingly, given that I was close to being grief-stricken, it took me a whole minute to find the light switch in the bedroom. But then, when the light came on at last, brighter than in the lounge, what a glorious sight. There was our very own old brown bear, sitting just where I'd left him, looking as if all he'd been doing this long time was waiting for me to come to bed. And you can tell me I was imagining it, but I could have sworn he was even wagging a paw at me for not turning in earlier.

Well that was it. Suddenly I could feel myself coming out all smiles again, just because he was there, waiting for me. And as for being told off for being late . . .

'Get stuffed,' I said, just like that. 'It's not that late. And Larry's a big boy now.'

Get stuffed. Get it? A little joke. The sort you can make with a friend, someone you know will laugh and not take offence. Get stuffed. Good that.

And that's where today ended. In two shakes I was undressed and climbing into bed, still laughing to myself. And I wouldn't be surprised if I was still grinning a minute later, as I lay there flat out. You see, I wouldn't know; I was asleep the moment my head hit the pillow.

Chapter Twenty-One

I don't know what woke me.

Maybe it was a noise. The sort that's been and gone before you wake up, leaving nothing more than a ripple in the darkness. It could even have been a lorry, one of the specially noisy ones, a juggernaut heading north, its driver trying to fit in one extra trip before the holiday begins. It could very well have been a lorry.

Go back to sleep, Larry. That's what I said to myself. It's half-past two in the morning, lad. This was no time to be awake, not when for once I'd managed to go to sleep without the waiting, and the listening, and everything that usually goes with a visit from His Lordship. I'd managed without all that and known only peaceful slumber as a result.

And peaceful slumber being all I wanted again, I closed my eyes that had opened for no reason that I could see, and tried to sleep. And couldn't. And couldn't. In fact the more I tried, the more awake I became. Until finally I had to face it. It wasn't going to happen, not for the time being.

Something was nagging me, pecking away at the back of my head like a woman's voice. Now that I was awake, I wanted to know why. And until I knew, I wasn't going to sleep.

So what was it? A noise? A dream? That's a good one, because there's nothing like dreams to wake you up, specially the sort I have. And come to think of it, there had been something happening over there, on the other side of sleep. But it wasn't the kind I normally have, I can say that now, because it suddenly struck me that half the reason I really wanted to be asleep again was to get back to that dream, whatever it was. Something told me I'd actually been enjoying myself. And now I felt cheated.

So it must have been a dream, not your normal kind certainly, but the sort that can wake you all the same. Not the smell of gas, or a light burning up money, or a sound from down below that never should be there . . .

Tell that to my hands, though. Do you think they could stop fretting? They hovered about like a pair of restless souls until finally, I got a grip and clasped them above the covers just below my waist, told them to lie there and keep still.

And that was when I discovered what it was really that had woken me.

Underneath the covers, underneath my hand, something was alive. Something I'd thought had died long ago. Still there, still alive, still hard. Not my imagination.

Don't. Don't say anything. Larry's not that kind of man. Doreen could have told you that. I mean, she told everybody else didn't she, as if there was something wrong with being clean-living. As if it mattered, as if we didn't have June already. It wasn't my fault then, *and it's not my fault now,* when it's all turned round. So don't.

Just make it go away. And let me sleep the sleep of the just.

Light. Light is what I need. Light to drive away the evils that creep under the darkness to play tricks on a decent man. Only it can't be the usual kind of light, not when you might end up seeing things you don't want to see. It's got to be another kind altogether, spiritual even. In other words, Lighten my darkness, oh Lord. Relieve me of this.

But the answer comes as nothing but a continuation

of the same, and down below, still there, is the hard thing that could kill a man with shame. So it's got to be light, any light. In this case the lamp beside the bed. The important thing is not to look, not down the bed, not in the mirror, just straight ahead where it's safe. And so it is that the first thing I see is the bear, staring straight back at me.

And, oh God, don't tell me I'm going to blush in front of a flipping stuffed toy. But I do. I can't help it. He's looking at me, and has been all this time, never mind the dark. Those eyes of his, yellow in this light, can see everything, and as much as on me, they are fixed on the stranger halfway down the bed.

So I lie and I blush and I lie and I stare until . . . until the impossible happens, and out of the blue, out of the impossible, he winks at me.

So help me God, he winked at me.

'What?' Despite myself, I've jumped out of bed. Because what else do you do when a toy bear winks at you, then seems to sit back, smug and knowing as any joker in a pub? Yellow eyes laughing at you and accusing you of all sorts of nastiness. What you really want to do at that moment isn't just jump out of bed, of course it isn't. You want to lunge forward and yank him from the chair, give him the hiding he deserves. But you don't, because the fear is you will feel a small animal heart beating under the nylon of his fur.

So when you can't do what's normal, you do the next best thing instead. In this case, sink down on the bed, and let the conversation run. Because those eyes of his, they're speaking volumes.

Or a few words, anyway. And those words are, 'Who've you been dreaming of, Larry?'

Then it all comes flooding back – the whole bloody dream, washing over me. I could see her face and everything; what's down below explodes, killing itself. And it's all over.

At the end of my bed, slumped in the chair is a stuffed toy like any other, nothing in its eyes but the glint of glass. The only living thing in the room is Larry, sitting bolt upright in his bed shivering with fright and – something else.

Relief, probably.

All the same, it's a good few minutes before the voice of reason strikes up and, without a word of apology for its absence, tells me to pull myself together. It was the dream that did it. And you can't blame yourself for your dreams. It's other people who force their way in. At least there was nothing Doreen could say about it, because for once it wasn't Doreen I'd been dreaming about. Meanwhile there were still hours of peaceful sleep ahead of me.

But not tonight. No way was Larry going to sleep again, not right away, and certainly not when somebody else was sitting there, watching. The bear – be he ever so blameless – would have to go. So I went to pick him up, meaning to carry him into another room where he could be just as comfortable. Imagine my surprise then when the very next second I find myself standing outside the bedroom door in pitch dark. The bear has stayed exactly where he is and it's me who's ended up going.

After the initial shock though it occurs to me that it's come to the same thing: I've got that bit of privacy I needed and now that I was up, and sleep being the last thing I wanted, I might as well just go with the flow, carry on into the kitchen and make myself a cup of something comforting.

So that's what I did. I put on the kettle and made myself a pot of tea. Laid it all out nicely on a tray, almost as if I was expecting company. But when it was brewed I just stood there, staring at it, didn't even pick up the cup.

You see, something else had happened. For the first

time in all the years of living here, I'd noticed the smell. It crept up on me as I was waiting for the kettle, getting stronger and stronger, until when everything else was ready my nostrils were full of it. I knew then, before I'd even worked out what it was, there was no way I'd be drinking anything. If I swallowed so much as a drop now, I'd be taking that smell right down with it, and I could tell you what would happen next. There'd be one great heave as I threw up over the kitchen floor – no better than Mandy, down there in the loo after one fig roll too many.

Old gravy. Stale. Coming out of the walls, hanging in pockets below the ceiling, the smell of every dinner cooked here in the last ten years and from long before that. All this time I must have lived with it and never known it was there. Until now, when suddenly it didn't agree with me. What's more, you could open windows, pull doors off their hinges, take off the whole blooming roof even, and it would still be there, hanging on in cupboards, seeping out from under the linoleum. Inescapable, part of the very fabric of the place. My place.

And it's no better in the lounge. If anything it's worse. It's in the wood of the cocktail cabinet, smeared along the spaces between the shelves, clinging to the flock of the wallpaper, part of the pattern of the rugs. It's everywhere. There's too much stuff to hold it in, there's furniture where there should be air. I haven't left myself room to breathe.

Come the morning, I won't believe I said that. In fact, come the morning, I'll be able to point to the row of bottles on the coffee table, and say, Larry, you poor old bugger. You just got yourself drunk and never knew it. Now all this, the bad dreams, a tiny bit of incontinence in the early hours, it's the price you pay. The sting inside the sweetness. It's the reason some men keep drinking, simply so as to stave off the after-effects.

Makes you wonder what their wives would have to say about it though. I suppose it would depend on what sort of wife you had. If you were married to the right sort of woman, then drink or no drink, she'd be up this minute, wanting to know why her husband was sitting in the dead of night, trying not to breathe the very air around him. Come to think about it, even if you were married to a Doreen she'd be here, pestering to know what the matter was. Someone to talk to.

I know what you're thinking. You're saying to yourself: poor old Larry, he's lonely. He's almost wishing Doreen was here to hold his hand. Well, you're wrong. Larry Mann hasn't been lonely since a certain party stepped through the front door. With a friend like that how can you be lonely? Even when she's somewhere else it doesn't matter, because she'll be here in spirit. Last night I could practically have reached out and touched her. My problem is that just for once, having her in spirit isn't enough. It's not Doreen I miss, or anyone. It's her, Mandy. I wish Mandy was here now. There'd be nothing wrong then.

Want to know the way I see it?

It wasn't an accident, the two of us ending up in the same house. We were put here for a purpose, Mandy and me. I mean, think about it. She could have lived anywhere – Crouch End, Finsbury Park, anywhere, but she didn't. She came here, to the very place where she was guaranteed a friend from day one. Then there's Ethel, dedicated to having only Indian girls in these rooms, taking one look at my girl and changing her mind. Don't tell me that's coincidence. It's destiny, part of some Great Plan. After all these years, after all the insults and the griefs, Larry's getting what he deserves. You could read my story in the Bible. I am the righteous man.

And what about Mandy? Where would she be without her Larry, befriending her, protecting her from a world that's working to make her ordinary? He's been doing what her parents should have done, guarding that spark of goodness that makes her so unique, keeping her the way she is. A girl in a million.

She may be my reward, then, but I'm her salvation. Together we make a team. And that's why we should never be apart. Anything else is unnatural.

Do you know, I never saw things so clearly until this minute. It's almost enough to make a man glad he woke up – despite everything – just for that glimpse of the truth, and the wonder of it all. Except that in another way it makes it so much worse, knowing that she's down there with him, and he's down there with her, upsetting the natural order of things.

You see, nothing will be right until he goes. He's keeping us apart, keeping us from Christmas.

Go to bed, Larry.

It's not all doom and gloom, though. Because back in the bedroom, a certain bear is waiting, and you only have to look at him to know – he's on the level. It almost makes you want to apologize. Then again, you only have to look deep into his eyes to see there'd be no need anyway. He understands everything I'm going through. Having him stare back at you is like a quiet hand upon your shoulder, telling you everything's all right.

And very soon, he'll be doing just that for Mandy. He's every kid's dream.

'But why wait?'

The words made me jump. I was lying on my side, about to put off the light, and there they were in the very centre of my head, clear as a bell. It wasn't me that spoke them, and as sure as anything it wasn't him, the bear. What's more, I knew the voice. It was the one that spoke the day she arrived, the same voice that marked her out as different. The sort of voice you listen to.

240

And this time it was saying: why wait?

Now that might make you ponder, but not me, not for a second. I knew what it meant all right. There's a great gulf between Mandy and me, and there will be all the time that *he's* here. But it doesn't have to be like that. Not if I forgot about waiting for Christmas. In other words, give the bear to Mandy tonight. This very minute. Make Christmas come early, bring the future forward. Bridge the gap. Let him be the very first thing she looks at in the morning, sitting there at the end of her little bed like her oldest friend in the world, bar one. Nothing will be the same after that. She'll be up here, clutching him in her arms to see her old Larry. And the other one? He won't get a look-in. Because what has he got to give her in comparison to that?

Of course it means a radical change of plan, but answer me this one question: with a bear like him on my side, how can I go wrong?

First I needed to work out the risks involved. As far as I could see, there were hardly any. I was somebody's dad once, remember. I'd done all this before, crept into a kid's room, and out again, pretending to be Father Christmas, and I've never been caught yet. How to tell if she was asleep though? Even that was no problem. If she had been awake, tossing and turning the way you do, that old bed of hers would have given her away long ago. But there hadn't been a sound.

No, there was only one real risk that I could see. *He* was down there too, in the lounge as usual. If he caught me creeping past the door then that would be it. The game would be up. But there you are – nothing ventured, nothing gained. So I picked up the bear and made for the door.

And the first thing I notice is that the smell is gone. Or to be more exact, it was still there – I'd always notice it now – but it was a welcoming familiar smell,

241

part of the atmosphere. And that was a sign in itself that I was doing the right thing.

Coming down those stairs, I don't suppose a mouse could have made less noise, yet it wasn't as if it was easy. Naturally I could have found my way down blindfold, but you try it when there's a bundle of fur bumping up against you on every step. Still, I didn't put a foot wrong. The result was, I felt that cocky, passing the lounge, that I did a silly thing. I pressed my head against the door and thumbed my nose at the nasty piece of work there, snoring away in his adulterous dreams on the other side.

And then it was to the hard part. Clicking open Mandy's door, tiptoeing inside, keeping all my fingers crossed that I wouldn't bump into anything. You see, I'd expected the difficulty to be that it would be darker here than anywhere else. But it didn't turn out that way. I stepped into Mandy's room to find it was lighter here than on the stairs. The curtains were open, drawing in the moonlight, making the whole room seem nearly bright in comparison. And that's how I could see straightaway that there was no-one there. The bed was empty. Hadn't even been slept in. After all this, they were still out, painting the town red somewhere when she should have been home, getting her sleep. All that tiptoeing, all that effort, for nothing. I couldn't even leave the bear now, not when *he* might be the one to see it first.

Yet I didn't have the heart to be angry, not looking around this little room of hers. I couldn't imagine what she'd been up to since I was in here last. For a start, though I'd seen it done in the daytime, I never dreamt that she would be leaving her window open even now, in the middle of the night, in the dead of winter. It was as if she was trying to get rid of every scrap of air that belonged to the house. But that wasn't all, though it took me a moment or two to realize it. The room was strangely bare, unnaturally tidy. All the funny rugs had gone from her bed, and off the walls as well. If there hadn't been the jumble of bottles and boxes still on her dressing table I might have been tempted to think the worst, that she had done a midnight flit. But there were her shoes, lined up under her bed, neat as anything.

But oh, it was sad. Seen like this, the room was so cold, so unwelcoming. This was what she would be coming home to tonight – or the small hours to be exact. And there wasn't even a pillow on her bed. What had she done with her pillow?

One thing was for sure. I wasn't going to leave the room like that, not for Mandy, not even when Francis was around. I put the bear down for a second and closed the window. It was all I could do for her, and yet I doubted if it would so much as take the chill off the room. Then I picked up the bear, gave him a quick hug because I reckoned we both needed cheering up, and made my way out again. At least on the landing I didn't have to creep, not when the only people I could be disturbing were Gilbert and Ethel. And passing the lounge door, I began to smile. Because just then another thought popped into my head: I could do more than simply thumb my nose at someone who turned out not even to be there. I could actually manage a tiny piece of mischief. Harmless, of course, but satisfying enough. I could run in quickly and open all the windows, making sure to draw the curtains after me. That way, when he got back, it would be like an ice-box, and with any luck he'd never realize that the windows were wide open behind the drapes. He might just end up freezing to death and serve him right.

One thing, though – you get into the habit of moving quietly in this house, even when there's no need for it. So when I opened the door, it was as silently as if it was a draught that was doing the work. That's why no-one heard me.

That's why I saw them before either of them saw me.

You see, they were there after all, together. On Doreen's aunty's settee, the one with horse's hair falling out, the one that makes up into a beautifully comfortable double bed. Only I'd forgotten all about that. Until now.

At first, it's only the bed that makes any sense. That and the light which is no more than the glow from the gas fire. It's enough to see the two of them on the bed, a slow tangle of naked arms and legs with Mandy's funny covers caught here and there between them. And still it takes a minute to understand. He's on top of her, his back and buttocks like the heel of a hand pinning her to the bed, pushing to and fro, head buried in the pillow beside hers. But it's her face that brings it home, unmistakably Mandy's, turned away from him, and the fire, towards the door. And me.

You never saw a face more peaceful. Eyes closed, cheeks as rosy as a child, not thinking of anything but the here and now. The face of someone making music, listening to herself. And it was her face that kept me standing there, watching, long after I had begun to believe.

Then, of course, it was too late. Something made her stir, open her eyes, and there we both were, the two of us, and nobody else in the world. Mandy and me. That's how it was, then slowly, like someone turning on a tap, the tears began to roll, ever so quietly, down her face.

I was gone before he saw me.

All I could think of was that I had to get up those stairs, that if I could get to the top before anything else happened, then somehow we would all be all right. But it was no good. There were only two more steps to go when his voice broke, smashing the little bit of silence that was left.

'What the . . . ?'

And somehow that did for me. The legs gave way from under me and I couldn't take another step. I ended up half falling, half sitting on the stairs as far away from the top as I was from the bottom. At the same time, downstairs, a light goes on. But after that, nothing. There was no more sound from anywhere. Then the minutes began to pass, until little by little I must have forgotten even to listen. The bulb was burning in the kitchen behind me, lighting up the walls on the stairs, and for some reason that started me off thinking on another tack altogether. Every now and then perhaps, I would look again and wonder what I was doing here four steps from the top, staring down at a big brown bear that someone had left lying at the bottom. But then I'd forget about that and get back to what I was thinking. The fact is, I used to sit here all the time, years ago when June was little. She would sit on the top step, legs dangling, while I stopped here, telling her I was checking her laces were done up properly before we went out. It was a trick I thought up for her when she was a nipper, to make sure she didn't just run helter skelter down the stairs and out into the street. This way, she always had to wait for me first.

So I started reckoning up the years since then and found the effort was more than I could manage. There was too much fog in my brain. Something else was beginning to bother me. For the first time ever, I was wondering why it was I'd never got round to re-decorating these stairs. I'd done all the rest within a month of Doreen leaving, but not here. As it is, the paper is still the same as what Doreen chose, the summer before the Christmas before she left – all big gaudy flowers, roses or something, hardly what you'd call tasteful. Only I remember her saying that there had to be something bright here or else you'd never see it, and I realize now that she was right for once. Normally the light on these stairs is so bad you'd practically need a spotlight before you noticed what was on the walls. Added to which, there's the brown mark that goes all the way up at elbow level where my coat must have brushed every time I'd come in or out. But the paper itself is still there, and you can see it if you look hard enough, like I'm looking now. And what that means is, even after all these years and all my hard work, Doreen has still managed to leave traces here to remember her by.

It's enough to make you weep really. I mean you go to all that trouble, toil and labour to scrub out every last speck of something rotten, and what happens? It pops up to meet you when you're least expecting it. And the result? I'm sitting here with Doreen all around me.

And then the shouting starts.

'That's it, Amanda. That's bloody it. I've had it up to here with this place. This is the last time, do you hear me?'

A small voice interrupts – too small to make any difference.

'It's no good, Amanda. You pester me to come down here, all this way, to this shit-hole of a house, just so that every Tom, Dick and Harry . . .'

Larry. My name is Larry.

'. . . Can come and gawp at us just at the very moment I'm . . .'

She's trying to interrupt again, but nothing's going to work, you can see it straightaway.

'No, Amanda. You've got to look at it from my point of view. I could raise the dead with the lengths I go to make sure Sheila doesn't get to hear about this. Then what happens? I find you might as well be selling ring-side seats.'

Why is it such a surprise to discover that he is married after all? Maybe because he never did act as if he was. Not really. Not when you sit here in Doreen's place and look back.

Downstairs, it's gone quiet. He's thinking about what he's going to say next. But me, I know what's coming.

'Listen to me.' He's not shouting now. The idea is to sound considerate. 'It's got to end you know. We can't go on like this. I've got too much to lose. I don't have to tell you.' Then his real feelings get the better of him and it's back to the shouting, loud enough to wake the dead. 'Damn it all, you little idiot. I can do a lot better than help you provide live sex shows for an old pervert.'

'Oh no, Francis.' That little voice again. Then: 'Francis, don't go.' And this time, finally, her voice rings out. Does more than that. It echoes, high enough to set the glass trembling in the mirrors, making all the windows hum. It spills out and fills the landings and passages of the house. That's all she says, but the words have a life of their own. They follow him as he tramps along the landing, past her kitchen and down the stairs, must still be ringing in his ears as he thuds along the hall. They only stop, at last, when the front door opens and slams closed again.

There's a moment's pause before a smaller door opens, this time belonging to the Ducks, with Gilbert's voice escaping briefly into the hallway, before it, too, closes in its turn.

After that, nothing.

And now here we all sit, each in our own little bit of house, for once in our lives staying out of each others' business. Yet I can see us all perfectly, the way we would look to anyone else who could see us. Ethel and Gilbert in the dark, mumbling across the pillow about what will have to happen tomorrow. Mandy sitting on the edge of Doreen's aunty's bed, shivering because she's naked and too thin and won't keep down what she eats, not daring to cry, because who is there left now to hold her hand?

And then of course there's me, still sat here on the stairs, still trying to get my bearings. But even I can't stay here all night. I've got things to do.

It took me a while though, getting off those stairs. First I had to wait for the shaking to stop and for the old knees to get a bit of strength back in them. But there was more. Call it the influence of Doreen coming at me from all sides, stopping me thinking straight just the same way she ever did, call it what you like, but all the time I was there I couldn't have told you if I was coming or going. If anybody had bothered to ask, more than likely I'd have said I was still waiting for June to dangle her legs over the top of the stairs for me to check those shoes of hers.

Then all of a sudden, the fog clears and I'm thinking straight again. Larry's not waiting for anyone, least of all June who went the way of her mother long ago. There's not one ounce of her here, or Doreen come to that. Never mind the flowers on the wall, this is Larry's place. And Larry's in charge. When I get to my feet I'm light as a feather and fairly float up those stairs, back to the kitchen, and civilization.

And I'll tell you what, having that funny turn just now has gone and improved my memory no end. Because the trouble is, a busy chap like Larry is bound to forget all sorts, until something comes along to jog his mind. Take my fireplace for instance. I can look at it for months and never remember what's there. Yet it was me that built it, brick upon brick, twelve years ago now, straight after she left. Took my time about it too, making sure I got it right. But the last brick I left loose, and that's the one I keep forgetting, until just now on the stairs.

Well, everyone's got a secret place haven't they, where things can get tucked away, without having the whole world in on it? In my case, it's not so much a secret as wanting to keep the rest of the place nice, and not spilling over with odds and ends that frankly you'd rather not have around, not on a daily basis. All the same, I can't help shaking just that little bit when I take the brick away, because in the back of my mind is the fear that someone else might have come along and stolen what's inside, as if there was another soul who knew.

But I didn't need to worry. It's still there. Doreen's scarf. Or to be more exact, Doreen's scarf and a few other bits and bobs besides.

Well, I said I had all sorts tucked away, didn't I? What's more I know what else I said – about me throwing out every whipstitch belonging to her, Doreen. I keep meaning to get rid of this scarf and all, but it's like the brick in the fireplace, I keep forgetting about it. Then something like tonight crops up, and not only do I remember it, I'm actually glad it's there, that scarf of hers. You see, believe it or not, it's come in handy a couple of times over the years, as I daresay it will again tonight.

Anyway, there's the scarf, but what appears next is a bit of a surprise even for me. It's a present, wrapped up with gift tag and everything. And just for a second it's got me wondering if there's not someone else coming back and forth here after all. Then I remember the reason for that too. Read the message. *'To Larry, with all the love in the world, Mandy.'* I'm going to open it, of course. Well, we've had Christmas come early this year so why wait? You'll never guess what's inside. Or maybe you would, seeing as you could smell it even before taking off the wrapper. Mediterranean waves washing over broken columns. What do you know, after that larking around in gentlemen's perfumery, Larry's got a whole bottle to himself.

All right, I'll own up. I bought it. And wrapped it up myself. And wrote the message. You can laugh, but with all this present-buying, what was wrong with a little something for me? Only, unselfish to the last, I went and bought something she liked, didn't I. I mean, we know what that scent does for her.

Funny, the effect of smells. Here's me, only just back to normal after noticing the smell of this place after all these years, half a century of dinners that refused to lie down and die. Then there's Mandy's smell, telling its lies, making her out to be some kind of kid and not a sprinkle of malice in her. Doreen with gin on her breath, laughing in my face. And now this, the one to take the biscuit. Not that I'll ever get the knack of wearing it. It's begun to drip all down my neck again, just like in the shop, only worse this time because now it's gone and soaked the waistband of my pyjamas. Still, I'll be putting a coat over that. And I'm not washing it off. Because this is the smell that does things to Mandy, isn't it? The more you put on then, the more you'll do.

Which means I'm nearly all set. Except for the lipstick. Orange, naturally. Doreen's colour. Doreen's lipstick. They've got to be wearing it at the time, otherwise it's not the same.

You don't know what I'm talking about, do you?

Then it's off down the stairs again. You wouldn't believe how lively I feel. It's what comes from knowing it's all about to slip into place. Take that scarf of Doreen's for instance. You'd be surprised at how natural it felt. Yet when was it I used it last? Six, seven years ago? Christmas, seven years ago. After June's visit. I don't know what they make them from, but hold a bit of scarf like that normally, and it causes no end of problems. It's the fake satin effect, meaning that the darned thing will slide in between your fingers like a piece of wet fish. But show a bit of nous, hold it properly, with one end wrapped round one wrist and the other end round the other, and Bob's your uncle. You've got a good few inches in the middle with which to do exactly what you like.

I know which room she's in, of course. She slipped into her bedroom half an hour ago, probably hoping no-one heard her, and there hasn't been a sound out of her since. But she won't be asleep. She might even be waiting. But what for? For someone to come back to her wearing that good old familiar smell she knows and loves? Maybe.

There's no light under her door. And none out here on the middle landing. I even made sure to switch off the kitchen light before I came down. No point in burning money. Talk about dark then. Right now, I can't even see my hand. But there, I was forgetting, there's the scarf wrapped around it anyway. After that it's a case of just walking in. Don't ask if I knocked. You have to earn your privacy in this house.

She doesn't know I'm here, though. Not yet. She's pulled the curtains at last, is lying here in the dark because she can't face the Light of Truth. You can just about make her out, curled up on the bed. She hasn't even heard me. Too wrapped up in herself, and how she's going to face a world that's seeing her with new eyes. Blind and deaf she may be, but it makes no odds. All I have to do is stand here in the dark, and pretty soon she'll know. And sure enough you can begin to feel it happening as the air around her changes. Over on the bed, something stirs. Two quick breaths, and then her voice, sharp and high and unbelieving: 'Francis?'

And at that I close in.

I left her as I found her. No, really. And if that surprises you, you want to hear what happened. Truth is, I don't even like thinking about it. I took it slow, sat down on the bed beside her, didn't say a word. Pitch dark it was. But you could practically hear those waves breaking in Mediterranean fashion. And that's when I feel these arms going up around my neck. Slowly to begin with, as if she can hardly believe there's anyone there. And that was bad enough, not least because the suspicion was that she still hadn't bothered to put her clothes back on. But what's worse is her face, trying to find mine in the dark, like a baby looking for its mother, and what does that show except that she's up to her old tricks even now. Still making out she's nothing but a big kid with none of the drawbacks.

Enough is enough. 'Give over, Mandy,' I say to her. 'It's not nice you know.'

It's my voice that does it to her. At the back of my neck her hands seem to go into spasm, and lock. Then let go and fall to the bed with a thud like two dead birds. Since she seems incapable, I lean across and switch on the light beside her.

'Oh Mandy girl, you should see yourself.'

It's all I can do not to laugh. She hasn't got a stitch on, but that hardly counts, not with a face like hers at the moment. Eyes like two pork pies, all swelled up and pink, nose the same, lips too big and fat to close properly. Just for a second there I thought he must have clouted her, and no bad thing, but then I realized it was because she'd been crying after all. It must have been the silent variety because I haven't heard a thing upstairs. Anyway, there's Mandy – no oil painting at the best of times, and certainly not now, kneeling on the bed facing me, with an expression that is just plain stupid. I mean, there are idiots in institutions who can manage to look a bit more with it than her right now. Given all that, then, you can see why the rest of her is hardly going to appeal. Least of all to Larry.

'You know what, Mandy,' I say. 'You need a bit of colour.' She doesn't say anything. She's begun to rock back and forth slowly like some big doll in motion. 'Try this,' I say. 'It was Doreen's, but it would suit you. You're the kind of person that it would.' Again she doesn't say a word, doesn't even look at me and the rocking, it just gets worse. So the only thing to do is help her out. I take the lid off the lipstick and the next time she rocks in my direction, I catch hold and smear the stuff on. Not exactly what you could call neat. You're not meant to wear it halfway across your face like some kid who's been in its mum's handbag. But it's still an improvement. And at least it's stopped her rocking.

'There,' I tell her. 'Just right.' And pick up the scarf again, this time with both hands. Hold it up for her to see, a bit miffed maybe because those eyes of hers, they don't seem to be taking in a thing. But I needn't have worried, she understands all right. You only had to watch the sheet. There's a stain the shape of Australia there, spreading out and darkening, and for an instant you can catch it, the tang of pee. Little girl's pee, like June's.

But then, would you believe it, a couple of seconds later she starts rocking again. Lifts up her head in the process, looking not at me but at the wall behind. Not what you would expect in the circumstances. You could almost think she was trying to make it easier. Then suddenly it hits me: that's exactly what she was up to.

All I was doing was saving her the trouble.

Well, you can imagine, that stops me, dead in my tracks. Turned me right off. Next thing, I was unwrapping the scarf and putting it away. *Let her do her own dirty work.* Blowed if Larry's going to smooth her path.

And what's more, if she does, and they come round, asking what happened on the middle landing, I'll tell them exactly. That should put a few cats among the pigeons up in Edinburgh. Ethel will back me up, she'll be feeling that vicious. Tenants doing themselves in on her furniture. It's only a pity Mandy was still hollering when he went.

I switched off the light for her though.

So now Larry's got to go out after all. Well, deep down, I knew it was a bit too close to home. Me sitting up here and her down there, and any number of people to point to the fact that I was the only one who knew her, I mean really knew her. You never would have caught me making that mistake with Doreen, or June come to that. Besides, can you imagine trying to collar a woman like Doreen? The strength in that woman's arm, you wouldn't believe. It wouldn't have been a fair fight. What it boils down to is, women like her have a wall of wickedness around them, and there's no getting over it. It's just that Mandy got me that angry, I've never quite known anything like it. Not even Doreen let me down the way she did.

But there are plenty of others, aren't there? Out there, looking for victims, telling their lies. Women wanting to injure and maim. Women with men in their sights. For every Doreen, or Mandy come to that, there are a thousand more raring to do the same thing to some other poor bugger. Catch one at it, and you've caught them all. So when it comes to getting a bit of your own back, it makes no difference who you choose in the end. Pick any one you like, you'll still be doing society a favour and saving some other poor bloke from the inevitable. In an ideal world there'd be men queuing up to shake your hand.

But I'll tell you the real problem this time, it's all the weather we've been having. Why do they always have to choose Christmas? Don't laugh, but I'm beginning to think the only female ever to pay any attention to it being the Season of Goodwill was the bloody Virgin

Mary. First Doreen, then June. And now Mandy. And that being the case, you know exactly what it's going to be like, the minute you step out the door. Shocking that wind is, coming right at you in the dark, straight across the road from Finsbury Park. What's more, it's worse this time. Twelve years ago, even seven years ago Larry still had the constitution for it, but that's hardly the case now. No-one in his right mind would expect an elderly man to go out, risking his health in this climate just so he can do his bit for the rest of mankind. But, as I've always said: someone's got to do it.

This will be the last girl, though. Then I reckon I'll deserve a rest. The one comfort is, she'll be easy to find, like the last time and the time before that. It even helps having this wind. She'll be huddled in some doorway, trying to keep warm regardless, waiting, just asking for it. I might not have to go very far. The one thing you don't do is ask her name. And if she tells you anyway, remember it's only a ploy, her trying to make out she's different. Forewarned is forearmed. In this case, a bit of lipstick to remind you who you're dealing with, and that scarf of Doreen's, shutting off the lies, all that loose talk, before the words even have a chance to get out. To be honest, I don't think anything else would do the trick.

And after that, back to the warm. Tomorrow I'm going to clean out my cupboards, and think about a bit of paper-stripping.

Merry Christmas Larry.

THE END

Joanna Carr awakens in a hospital after six months in a catatonic state, only to be told that her beloved husband, David, has been brutally murdered, and police are still searching for the killer. Grief-stricken and confused, she flees to the safety of the country home they once shared to try to piece together the crime—and her life. But Joanna knows that something is dreadfully wrong—and that the nightmare is just beginning...

MEG O'BRIEN

I'LL LOVE YOU TILL I DIE

A WOMAN'S DESPERATE SEARCH FOR THE TRUTH PLUNGES HER INTO A WEB OF DECEPTION, DESIRE, AND DANGEROUS OBSESSION.

I'LL LOVE YOU TILL I DIE
Meg O'Brien
_____95586-3 $5.99 U.S./$6.99 Can.